TOUCH
OF
LIGHTNING

SUSAN McKENZIE

ReamStories subscription:
https://reamstories.com/susanmckenzie
Amazon author page:
https://www.amazon.com/author/susancarter
Visit Sue's website:
http://susanmckenzieauthor.com
Follow Sue on Facebook:
https://www.facebook.com/SueMcKenzieAuthor

YOUR FREE BOOK IS WAITING

The novelette

THE ALIEN

is free for a limited time. You just need to tell me where
to send it

When Lilliana crash-lands her spaceship on a Primitive
planet, she'll have to rely on help from an attractive
local to survive.

**Use the QR Code to follow the link, then enter your name and
email address to get your free book delivered to your inbox**

Or type this link into your browser: https://

www.sub-scribepage.com/thealien

WHAT READERS LIKE YOU ARE SAYING...

"Emotions can be dangerous. This kind of reminded me of Star Trek. I did like how it just seemed to flow from one page to the next. Love and jealously with wild emotions is a blend that can be very gripping."
– **S. Lipman (Amazon review)**

"Touch of Lightning absolutely captivated me from start to finish. The characters are fabulously crafted and the story was exciting and the author has done a fantastic job with the world building. This is one of those books that will sweep you away to another world and take you on a journey that will leave you wanting more."
– **Annie555 (Amazon review)**

"It had me sitting in angst on the edge of my seat, to up in the clouds and everywhere in between. It is very different from her last books which I think is good. I can't wait to read the next one to see where she goes with it."
– **Kimberly Rose (Amazon review)**

To my awesome father, John McKenzie.

You will always be my daddy, my rock, my anchor in a wild sea. You are so brave facing the world without Mum, and I love you.

CHAPTER 1
(Not) Good Vibrations

The screen on the Navigational Computer flashed red in the top right corner and my heart stuttered. It would've taken a fraction of a second to bring up the following warning message, but to me, it felt like minutes.

No...

This was the part of my job that I hated.

There was ground movement predicted in the area. *Strong* ground movement. They estimated a 4.5 on the meter, complete with after-shocks.

"Javolo?" My heart was pounding in my throat and I could hardly push the word out.

"Yeah?" His voice sounded extra scratchy over the Com system today.

I could feel a cold sweat forming on my forehead. "You need to hang on to something. You're about to get a four point five."

"Okay, Cal. Will do."

Another thing I couldn't stand was the wait. I couldn't breathe properly. I tried to sit still in my seat and calm down. It didn't work. It *never* worked. If they knew how badly the quakes affected me, I'd lose my job instantly.

Breathe... Just breathe. In. Out. In. Out.

My hands were shaking so badly that I shoved them under my thighs to stop them.

"Are you somewhere relatively safe?" I could hear the tremor in my voice and hoped the distortion through the Com would hide it.

"Yep."

I resisted the urge to ask Javolo if he felt anything yet. I couldn't ask any questions that could give away how I was really feeling. I had to appear calm. They recorded *all* conversations.

In. Out. Relax...

I wasn't scared for me. I was safe and sound in my little cubicle up on the space station while Javolo was underground down on the planet, Kronos, mining the universe's most sort-after mineral, Amakio, and putting his life on the line. I was scared for *him*, and all of the other Diggers down there.

Most of the quakes on the planet were minor, and there had only been one partial collapse of one of the tunnels since I'd started working for Katoa Intergalactic Mining and Exploration five months before, but that knowledge didn't help to ease my panic every time it happened.

"Okay, here it comes..."

My heart stopped, I was sure of it. Then galloped ahead full speed as I waited.

Breathe. In. Out. In. Out. Relax... Let go of the desk... Relax... Start with your fingers and toes...

I kept trying to relax, one part of me at a time. Maybe it helped. I couldn't tell.

Why did I even apply for this job in the first place? Yeah, I know. I gotta start somewhere and work my way up... But I don't think I can handle this. Panicking every time I see those words on the screen... I couldn't cope if something happened to Javolo... He's my friend... My best friend.

Sure, there were the girls I knew from work — the other Nav Operators and admin staff — but it was different with them. They were friends, but not *real* friends. I couldn't really talk to them. Not about the important stuff.

Then there was Malvolio. We'd been seeing each other for about four weeks, but that was a totally different kind of relationship.

"Cal?"

Javolo's voice brought my thoughts back to the present. "Uh, yeah?"

Only Javolo would think to shorten my surname from Callista to Cal, as if it was my first name.

He reported exactly what the Nav Computer had told me as it happened. Three smaller tremors... Then...

"Whoah!"

I put my hand over my mouth so I wouldn't cry out. Then I started my relaxation techniques again. I had to pull myself together, and quickly. I had to wipe the image of being surrounded by dirt and tree roots from my mind.

"Okay. It's gone."

I remembered to remove my hand. I took a deep breath and opened my mouth to talk, but Javolo beat me to it.

"That was a big one. Nearly knocked me on my butt."

A picture of him falling onto his butt in his cumbersome Mech-suit popped into my mind. Now *that* would be funny to see. And it would be even funnier once he tried to get back up. I'd seen footage of just how difficult that task was in a training video.

Mech-suits were big mechanical suits that the Diggers could climb into that supplied oxygen and boosted their strength so they could dig up the Amakio and bring it back to the waiting shuttles. They had arms and legs powered by hydraulics that were extensions of the Diggers limbs, allowing them to dig and lift heavy weights while mining.

"I *told* you to hang on to something."

There really wasn't anything he could hold on to down there, but I had to say something to try to lighten the situation.

I forced myself to breathe slower and waited for my heartbeat to return to normal. My hands still shook so I clasped them together in my lap. I hated feeling like this. It was overwhelming, but I was thankful he was okay.

"Yeah, that you did..." he said.

I braced myself and waited for more aftershocks. They were only minor. I had to keep telling myself everything was okay and to relax.

I pulled my thoughts from the images in my mind that I wish I could forget and I tried to keep my voice even. "Okay, report."

"No damage. No more ground movement. The suit's reporting that all systems are functioning normally. Anyway, guess what?"

I smiled. Javolo didn't miss a beat. It was straight back to our conversation. "What?"

I busied myself with the Nav Computer terminal, collating all the information that Javolo's Mech-suit had reported before the quake so it could correlate with the sixteen orbiting navigational satellites and make the necessary corrections to his position on the screen. Now I had his exact location.

"Last night I saw the most beautiful woman I've ever seen!" he exclaimed through the static over the Com.

Where did that come from? I wondered.

The last thing we were talking about that wasn't work-related was a HoloMovie I'd seen recently about a droid that thought it was human. But I couldn't pass up an opportunity to tease him.

"Ah-huh. Like the redhead you saw last month?" I laughed. "Or the brunette in the grav shaft last week?"

"No," he said quickly, "this is different. Cut me some slack, huh?"

"Nah. Can't do that." I giggled. I couldn't help myself. I didn't care that I was sitting in my dull little cubicle all by myself with a wide grin plastered on my face.

This was the part of the job I loved the most. I could dig at him like that and he knew I was kidding. He may have been my work partner, but it wasn't all business. We could joke around and be ourselves, even though it was frowned upon by 'The Company' as we called it.

"She looked amazing," he continued.

I rolled my eyes and stopped myself from laughing out loud. "*Suuure* she did."

I couldn't *agree* with him. What would be the fun in that?

"I'm serious."

The Nav Computer was taking its sweet time. We couldn't do anything until I had all of the information. There could be warnings in the last few segments of data.

My mind wandered while we waited. Rogan, the partner I'd had before Javolo, was all business and no interesting conversation. Once he'd been replaced by Javolo, my job had become a lot more interesting. A lot more fun.

I looked back at the data on the screen. Still not finished. Talk about slow. It was frustrating. Everything was so out-dated and archaic here. They needed to update the whole system and I knew exactly which one would be able to handle the workload. Computers were something I knew well. Something I'd excelled in throughout my schooling.

I'd majored in Polymer Science and Engineering and wanted to work for Katoa's research department on things like improving the materials for the Mech-suits and oxygen masks, but I'd quickly realised once I'd started working here that they weren't interested in keeping their technology up-to-date. It seemed they didn't like to spend money, even if it would improve efficiency and safety. I only had to look at the ridiculously archaic equipment we were forced to work with to see that. Typical. Were all large companies like this?

I seriously hoped not.

This low-end job was supposed to be my start so I could move up to Research and Development, but I'd decided on a different strategy. I'd already started to research other companies. There was no way I was going to stay here once my two-year contract was up. It had turned out to be a dead-end job, even if it was with one of the biggest companies in the Known Universe.

"Where to now, Boss?"

I tried to suppress a giggle, and failed. "Ah, I like that."

"Like what?"

I sat up straighter. "You admitting I'm the boss."

"Well, you order me around all day and I have to obey your every command. It's almost like we're married."

CHAPTER 2
Why Do I Feel Like This?

I stopped what I was doing. Why did my stomach do a little fluttery dance when he said that?

I tried to concentrate on what I was supposed to do next. "Umm, still waiting on the computer to give me everything."

Then the last of the information finally hit the screen. I read through all the relevant stuff. No warnings. No problems.

Good.

"No probs with the report. Time to get back to work."

"Yes, Ma'am."

I checked the blurb on the side of the screen telling me where the next vein started. "Head down the tunnel to your right."

"On it."

I remembered what we were talking about. "Come on then, tell me about her."

"She has long dark hair and bright blue eyes that seem to flash at you when she smiles," he began.

Oh, wow... What a description! I thought, a smile tugging at my lips. Javolo was such a romantic.

"Turn left at that intersection and go down about twenty metres," I said. I could hear the suit's hydraulics as he walked the distance. That was unusual. The connection was clearer than normal for a few seconds.

"And she has the most perfect bod..."

Typical male, I laughed to myself. So much for being a romantic. "Yeah, I believe you..." I told him. "Stop there."

"It's true," he protested. "Okay, it's true *this* time... Well, ya know, last time the girl wasn't perfect like I'd said, but still really pretty. And a really nice person... and married."

And not even human. Not that he would've had a problem with that — but it was funny that Javolo had thought she was. I guess her tail would've been hidden under her dress. I giggled. "Now go forward. Bit more... Bit more. Stop. Turn to your right. You should be facing a wall with a visible vein through it."

"Yep."

"Okay, start. Middle of the road."

"Yes, Ma'am."

He immediately started up his rock-breaker, which was attached to the left arm of his Mech-suit. The other arm sported a four-pronged mechanical hand for picking up samples, with a shovel-like scoop on the back of its "wrist" for scooping the debris away. The mechanical hand and other parts of the suit contained sensors that detected traces of Amakio and transmitted the locations to the Nav Computer. This information was triangulated with data from the other Diggers and the sixteen satellites to pinpoint the mineral deposits under the ground.

While Javolo worked, it was too noisy for us to talk, so I twirled a piece of my long hair around my finger as I watched the screen to check for any new data or warnings, and was left to my thoughts. More and more often lately, my thoughts came back to the end of our partnership — our Rotation — together and I couldn't help feeling anxious about it.

The contract with Katoa was for two years. They divided the time up into four Rotations of six months each. We worked with one partner for six months, then, so we didn't get too attached, we were assigned a different one for each Rotation. This was my first Rotation, and after a short stint with Rogan, I'd been paired with Javolo. Javolo and I only had about a month left before we were assigned new partners. Maybe we *were* too close according to the company's guidelines, but we were just friends. Really good friends. I felt a sense of loss at the thought of never being able to talk to him every day, and I hadn't even experienced the loss yet. It was weird. And really awful.

Why do I feel like this? I thought as my fingernails tapped the grey desk. I had no answer. *Why do we have to part ways? And why is this cubicle so drab and grey? It's enough to make anyone depressed.*

I thought about who I might end up working with. What if it was someone I didn't like, or someone like Rogan that didn't share my sense of humour? The chances of being partnered with someone with the same sense of humour and/or the same interests were pretty slim. That wasn't a very encouraging thought.

Who would I be working with after next month? If we didn't get along, I'd be stuck with him — or her — for *six months*. That would make my job difficult. It would make my life miserable. Of course, it was my job and I'd suck it up and do it, but I wished I could keep things the way they were.

I pushed all that aside for now.

I thought about what I might do on my next rostered day off. Maybe go swimming. It was always refreshing and it helped me to clear my mind so I could think and reflect. Something about water had always made me feel calm and relaxed. Or I could take a long walk in the park near my apartment. That was always good for my soul. I loved to lie on the grass and watch the birds flitting amongst the trees.

Those pleasant images were replaced by images of Malvolio's angry face the night before at dinner when the waitress brought him a "slightly cold" meal. I couldn't believe how angry he'd been over something so trivial...

CHAPTER 3
Nothing But the Best for My Girl

I couldn't think about Malvolio now. I had to concentrate on work. I tucked those thoughts away for later and thought about the park again.

After a few more minutes of noisy rock-breaking, Javolo began scooping out the rubble from the hole he'd created. "I can see the rest of the vein. It goes off to the right. Just need to collect this lot first."

"Okay."

I felt myself relax a little. I needed to concentrate on the job at hand.

I encouraged him to tell me what he could remember of the 'perfect' woman and it turned out that he'd only seen her for a brief moment as the door to the grav shaft slid shut near the entrance to the Golden Palace restaurant.

I gasped when I heard the name. The restaurant stood on the border between the Diggers' Section and the rest of Perseus Station and was divided into two separate establishments. One for the Diggers and one for the rest of the space station. I'd been there the night before with Malvolio in the main section where he'd had his little tantrum. Javolo had obviously been in the Diggers' Section.

A strange feeling crept over my skin as I thought about the fact that we'd been within fifty metres of each other and neither of us knew it. The sad part was that even if we'd come face-to-face, we wouldn't have recognised each other. Diggers and Navs lived in separate sections of the space station and were never allowed to meet. That way they couldn't get personally involved and it couldn't affect their job performance. I had no idea what Javolo looked like.

I tried to shrug off the feeling.

I was amazed that Javolo could give me so many details about the girl after such a quick glance, and I suspected his mind had filled in some of the blanks. If he saw her again, it would be a different story. Maybe her eyes weren't even blue, but I loved his poetic description of them.

It took Javolo the rest of the morning to extract the Amakio from that location, having to make more than one trip with his floating tub in tow. I was always amused when imagining the floating rectangular tub harnessed to the Mech-suit, hovering along behind him at mid-thigh level wherever he went. I'd seen them on the training videos. It was a strange sight.

My mind wandered again. It was almost time for lunch and I had to force myself to stop thinking about food and focus.

"Hey, Cal, how's What's-his-name goin'?" Javolo asked.

A weird sensation flowed through me at the question, like all the air had left my lungs, but I responded automatically. "It's not *What's-his-name* — it's Malvolio."

I heard him snicker. "What kind of name is Malvolio anyway?" he jeered. "Do you call him Mal for short, or just Vol?"

Of course, Javolo couldn't pass up an opportunity to tease me about him.

"No," I answered flatly. "Neither. He wouldn't appreciate his name shortened like that." I tried to imagine Malvolio's reaction if I called him either of those names. A cringe. Or maybe an eye roll. But I didn't want to be thinking about him right now.

"Oh, too good for the good ol' nickname, 'ey?"

"Lay off him," I warned. "He's a nice guy."

I grimaced inwardly and frowned. He was far from nice last night. That poor waitress.

How did things change so much? He was such a gentleman when we'd met. He'd somehow managed to make me break my promise to myself that I wouldn't get involved with anyone while I was working here.

I wasn't sure what to do or what I'd say when I saw him. I would have to deal with that later. Right now, we had work to do.

The Nav Computer spewed out our next location. "Okay, we have our next place..."

——— ⋆·☆·⋆ ———

I'd just sat down at an empty table with my lunch when I heard a familiar voice.

"Lennina, darling. How are you?"

My stomach dropped and I looked up to see Malvolio smiling at me. I forced a smile onto my face. "Oh, hi."

That's not the reaction I should have felt. I should be happy to see him. What was wrong with me?

He sat across from me and grabbed one of my hands in both of his. I felt something small and rectangular against my palm and turned my hand over to find a small gift box.

"Oh! Um, thank you!"

I didn't know what to say. He never listened when I told him not to buy me gifts all the time. It was nice to receive them, but I didn't feel comfortable when he spent so much money on me.

"Well, aren't you going to open it?"

I sucked in a breath. Why was I just staring at it? I pulled the tiny ribbon and opened the box to find a sparkling pair of diamond earrings sitting neatly inside. "Oh, wow... They're beautiful..."

I was lost for words. They *were* beautiful. And expensive. Something I could never afford. I had to keep reminding myself that he had a high-credit position as the MIC of a company called Galaxy Mech, the company that made the Mech-suits for Katoa, and he probably didn't consider them to be expensive.

I didn't think I'd ever get used to receiving such expensive things.

I looked up at him again. He was smiling and his grey eyes were so intense. He was good looking in a sophisticated sort of way and I knew all the women drooled over him. It felt good knowing he was mine and that they were jealous.

"Nothing but the best for my girl," he said. When I didn't respond, he said, "Aren't you going to put them on?"

"Um. I thought it would be better if I waited till I got home."

He frowned. "Why? Don't you like them?"

"Yes, of course I do. It's just..."

"Just what?"

"I'm at work."

"And?"

"I don't want anything to happen to them. They're too expensive. I don't want to lose them."

"You'll be sitting in an office in front of a computer. How could anything happen to them?"

I squirmed in my seat. How could I explain? I wasn't even sure I understood what I was thinking. "Uh, I just don't think I should—"

"You don't want them, is that it?"

"No! I didn't say that."

"You didn't have to. Actions speak louder than words." He rubbed his jaw for a few seconds. "Who is he?"

CHAPTER 4

How Long Has This Been Going On?

"I'm sorry, what?"

"You seem distant lately. And then last night you acted like you were so disgusted with me."

Yeah, because I was. "Was that outburst really necessary?"

"That was *not* an outburst," he said, matter-of-factly. "I was trying to tell you the rules and regulations of the company you work for as you seemed to have forgotten."

I'd been referring to the outburst with the waitress. How could I have forgotten the outburst over the way I talk to Javolo too much?

The heat was creeping into my face. Sometimes, he could be so... so *arrogant.* I managed to keep my voice level. "I know the rules. You don't need to point them out. You were—"

"Don't make this about me."

"*What?* But it *is* about you. You didn't just lecture me in front of everyone; you insulted that poor waitress too. I was—"

"She deserved a dressing down. My meal was slightly cold."

I rolled my eyes at him and he scowled. "That's no reason to—"

"A Nav Operator is not permitted to become emotionally involved with her Digger as it can put lives at risk in an emergency situation. The Digger's job is dangerous and—"

"I *know*. You don't have to keep telling me."

"Don't interrupt me. It's rude."

"But you keep doing it to—"

"I am *trying* to get a point across to you and you're not listening."

"What?" I sat there staring at him with my mouth hanging open. My stomach churned as it tied itself in knots.

He leaned closer. "You never were a good listener."

And you don't listen at all...

I sighed again. "I *know* the rules. I've worked here long enough. I'm not 'involved' with my Digger. I'm not breaking any rules. You were being stupid and ridiculous." His eyes darkened. "You weren't listening to me and you were putting Javolo down by calling him a Neanderthal and—"

"Oh, it's always about *him!*" he scoffed. "You never shut up about him. Why do you even *talk* to him?"

I couldn't believe he'd said that. "It's part of my job, for a *start!*" I snapped. "If I *don't* talk to him, he could *die* down there on the planet!"

My chest felt tight and I seemed to only be able to take small breaths. I could feel the beginnings of a headache too.

"That is *not* what I meant," he snapped back. "I mean, why do you talk to him any more than you have to — like, about social things?"

I felt the heat flood through my body as I watched the anger building in his eyes. "Well, for one, it would get pretty boring if we didn't talk. Two, it's common courtesy. And three, he's my *friend!*"

I was getting worked up and I knew it, but I couldn't help it. I was fed up. Javolo didn't deserve his crap.

"Oh, I see." His narrowed eyes were cold steel. "It is all crystal clear now. You talk about him all the time." He counted it off on his fingers. "You talk to him too much while you should be working. You've been warned about talking to him too much and it hasn't stopped you. You and this... Javolo are getting it on together, eh? *Eh?* It all makes sense now..."

I felt my eyes go wide. "*What?*"

Where was this coming from? How could he even *think* that? It was the most ridiculous thing I'd ever heard. Javolo may have been my friend, but we could never meet, so it was impossible for us to be 'getting it on together.'

Was Malvolio serious? Surely he wasn't serious.

He snorted. "You heard me." There was no humour in his dark eyes.

I gasped. My heart pounded against my ribcage. "How could we be— How could I— I've never met him. I can *never* meet him. You know that."

"No. I *don't* know that." The wild look in his eyes was unnerving.

My eyes widened again. "What, you mean it's possible for a Digger to get into the Navs' Section?"

"It has happened in the past."

"Oh..." I was speechless for a few moments. "But even if Javolo could do that, he doesn't know what I look like. I don't even know if he knows my full name."

"What do you mean? Is he really that much of a simpleton? You've been working with him for months."

I gritted my teeth. "No. He's not stupid. We only call each other by our surnames at work. It's the same with all the Navs and Diggers. Javolo is his last name."

I wasn't about to tell Malvolio I'd actually forgotten Javolo's first name.

He looked down his nose at me. "How primitive. You lot can't even be civilised."

Primitive? Seriously? I let out a growl of frustration.

"Really, Lennina. That's not very ladylike."

"I don't care."

"You should care. Why do you think I've been trying so hard to help you? You need to set aside your upbringing and learn to act like a lady."

I ignored that. I didn't want to get into a bigger argument right now.

He sniffed. "So. How long has this been going on?"

I balled my hands into fists. "We are *not* 'getting it on' together!" I said, using air quotes as I spoke. "We're just—"

"You know it's against Katoa's policies." His eyes were cutting into me, like he was trying to see right into my soul.

I know! I sighed. "We're just fr—"

"You could lose your job over this!" He moved closer to me again.

My breaths came out in short gasps and it was hard stay in my seat. "Just *stop* being such a—"

"It is my duty to report you to the HR Unit at Katoa."

Shut up and let me talk! "I said we're just *friends!*"

I remembered that we were in the cafeteria and looked around. Most people had finished their lunch and had gone back to work. The few that were left looked decidedly uncomfortable and were suddenly fascinated with their food.

Malvolio leaned back in his seat and sighed like I hadn't said anything at all. I didn't want to be near him right now. In fact, I wanted him to leave. I sat still and stared down at my uneaten food. My stomach felt like I'd swallowed a brick. I couldn't eat anything.

It felt like being in an out-of-control hovercar and I found it harder to breathe. I was full of nervous energy and fidgeted with the gift box.

I should tell him it's over right now, I thought to myself.

I stopped fidgeting. Was that what I wanted? To stop seeing him? Was I overreacting?

I needed to think. I didn't want a relationship when I'd first arrived here. Wasn't planning on finding love. I was here to work. But somehow, Malvolio managed to get into my heart. He'd made me so happy. I'd tried to forget all my misgivings about love and enjoy feeling wanted.

Was this ridiculous accusation enough for me end our relationship?

I didn't want to give up so easily. So quickly. I couldn't make a hasty decision. I really needed to wait till things had calmed down. Think things through on my own. Maybe tonight when I got home I'd be able to think straight.

"Yes, well, you *would* say that," he continued. "It's a weak defence at best. You'll have to think of something better than that..."

I frowned at him. I really couldn't believe he was serious about this. He seemed to really believe what he was saying.

"What I don't understand is, why are you seeing him when you're my girl?" he asked in a strained voice.

Oh, my stars! "I'm not see—"

"What do you see in him?" he asked me. "He's just a *Digger*. He doesn't have any of the wealth and standing that I have."

Get over yourself! I thought.

Then his face changed as he turned to face me again. It kind of twitched and contorted into a weird kind of frown. A cold feeling inched its way down my spine.

He grabbed my arm. Hard. His voice was low and deadly. "Are you fucking him?"

CHAPTER 5

We Are Through, Missy!

My breath caught. "*What?* No!" My mind reeled. I couldn't believe what he'd just said. And I'd never heard him swear before.

"You're lying. Don't lie to me, Lennina. Tell me the truth; are you fucking your Digger? Is that why you won't fuck me?"

Was he *serious?*

I felt the blood drain from my face. I hadn't taken things that far with Malvolio yet, so because I'd said no, he thought I was sleeping with someone else?

"No! I'm not sleeping with anyone and I've already told you the reason I didn't—"

"Lies!" He had a wild look in his eyes. "Fucking bitch! How could you drag my reputation through the mud like this?"

Is that all you're worried about? Your reputation?

I sure as hell didn't care about his wealth or his reputation. And then there was the fact that I wasn't doing anything to ruin it anyway.

He tapped his fingers impatiently on the table. "Never mind... I will tell them you were too young. To immature..."

What?

"Yes. That's a plausible scenario... I can do that... No one needs to be concerned..." He kept up the tapping.

I shook my head. Now he was talking to himself. I gave up trying to reason with him and sat there looking at the patterns in the tiles on the floor of the cafeteria while he kept ranting.

I realised I was clenching my fists so hard that I was digging my fingernails into my palms, so I made a conscious effort to stop.

Why is he doing this? Why am I putting up with this? I asked myself.

I looked around us. Everyone had left the room. At least there was no one here to hear his accusations.

"Just go, Malvolio. I need to go back to work and I don't want to speak to you right now."

"Don't fucking tell me what to do!" he shouted. The veins in his neck stood out and his face was red. "You have no right! I don't have to put up with this rubbish! We are through, Missy! Do you hear me?"

I blinked.

Through? I thought. *As in, over?* I stared at him. Then I thought, *Missy? Seriously? Who even talks like that? How old are you, really?*

Through.

It was so unexpected. I didn't know how to react. I think I stopped breathing. I made myself take a deep breath.

Four weeks wasn't much time to get to know someone, but with the number of times I'd seen him and the number of Vid calls and text messages we'd shared, it seemed like six months had gone by. I thought I knew him fairly well. I was wrong.

He glared at me, waiting for a reaction. He was being so dramatic about it and probably expected me to cry and beg his forgiveness or something. I did nothing. In fact, I felt nothing. It surprised me, but I didn't feel like crying. Didn't even feel sad. There was an empty void where my heart should've been. Was that normal? Surely I should feel *something*. Was there something wrong with me?

Why did I feel numb? I hadn't been prepared for him to break up with me, so shouldn't I be upset? Shouldn't I feel something? The last time someone dumped me, I'd been devastated. I'd thought Jace and I had a long future together and he'd thrown it all away. He'd thrown *me* away.

I shouldn't have let Malvolio in. I should have known it would end badly.

Malvolio's brows were drawn together. He seemed to be more confused than I was. Could it be that he didn't know what to do? This wouldn't be the reaction he was expecting and definitely not the one he would've been used to. He probably had visions of comforting me as I cried helplessly and begged him to take me back. And of him telling me he forgives me and then him giving me 'another chance.' Or something like that.

I folded my arms across my chest and leaned back in my seat. I was *not* going to play the role he wanted me to.

I should never have fallen for him. I should have stuck to my plan and stayed single. Relationships always led to heartbreak.

He stared for a while longer, sort of stuttered, then regained his composure. "Well, I can see that this news has devastated you so much that you're speechless..."

I narrowed my eyes at him.

"Maybe I was a bit harsh..." he continued, not reading my body language at all. "After all, you weren't brought up in the right sort of environment and I need to take that into consideration... Yes... I must be more careful... more understanding..."

My eyes widened. I couldn't believe what I was hearing. Was he serious? Was that what he really thought of me?

I sucked in a breath. I didn't want him to change his mind and give me another chance. "No. It's okay. I understand. Let's just part on good terms..."

That felt false. We weren't parting on good terms, but I thought saying it would keep things calm and maybe I could get him to leave. I really wanted him to go, but if he thought it was his idea, he would be more likely to do it.

The way he could go from calm to furious in an instant was scary. I didn't want to do anything to make it worse.

If we broke it off, he could find someone else quite easily, I was sure. Someone who was more like him. Someone who would fit in with his friends.

And I could go back to being on my own. I could do that. It was the best way to keep focused on my career goals.

He stood and paced up and down and my eyes followed him, waiting to see what he'd do next.

Then he turned to me, his expression unreadable. "Maybe you could convince me to have you back again if you swear to me you will end it with your Digger this afternoon."

CHAPTER 6

My Best Friend

I felt myself tense up. "What?"

I wanted to scream. I wanted to punch something. *You really are serious, aren't you?*

He stepped forward, arms outstretched. "Just promise me you will tell him it's over, and I won't inform Katoa of this... this... *scandalous* behaviour... This... breach of company policy."

Crud. He was totally serious about this. *He's lost it...*

I wasn't even going to justify that with an answer. My stomach twisted. I was still finding it hard to breathe. He couldn't really believe I was cheating, could he?

I thought about what he was actually saying. He was threatening me. Blackmailing me, really. If I stopped having an affair with Javolo, he wouldn't turn me in — wouldn't tell The Company I was in a relationship with my Digger. If I stayed with Malvolio, I wouldn't be fired... It was straight-out blackmail. Made worse by the fact that I wasn't guilty of having an affair with Javolo in the first place.

I could see the disgust on Malvolio's face, but I was way past trying to tell him he had it all wrong. He wouldn't even let me finish a sentence, anyway.

He looked directly into my eyes and leaned forward. "So, do I have your word?"

I looked at him in disbelief, trying to calm my erratic heartbeat and my breathing.

No, you don't.

After staring at me a few seconds longer, he clapped his hands and rubbed them together. "Right. Okay. It's settled then. You may break

What's-his-name's heart, but your heart belongs to me. It will always belong to me."

Will *always* belong to him? I shivered inside at the thought.

Without warning, Malvolio pulled me from my seat, took me in his arms, and kissed me on the lips, which didn't stir any of the emotions it should have, then left the cafeteria with a dramatic turn and swish of his hand over the sensor to open the door.

What just happened?

The door swished shut behind him and I stood there for a few seconds with my mouth hanging open. I breathed a sigh of relief when it finally hit me that he was gone, then my heart clenched in my chest. *What if he comes back?*

My breath caught. I needed to get out of here. As I walked toward the door, I glanced at the time on the digital display on the wall.

Dammit!

I was ten minutes late. I hurried back to my cubicle and apologised to Javolo as I ran the necessary checks for him to start work. How much trouble would I be in for being this late?

There was nothing I could do about it now. I'd have to deal with it later.

I tried to understand what had happened. Why didn't Malvolio listen? Why did he dump me just like that? Why did he think he should be giving me another chance? I didn't even want him to! Why was he so convinced that I was cheating on him?

I ran my hands over my face.

Focus.

I had to get my mind in the right place so I could do my job.

Why didn't he just leave after breaking it off? That would have been easier. I would have preferred that it stay that way. So why didn't I say more? I should have told him I didn't want a second chance. So why didn't I tell him?

And why did I feel nothing?

Get back to work!

"Cal?"

"Uh, yeah?"

"Am I set to go?"

I checked my screen again. "Um, yes. Head back to where you were before lunch."

"Yes, Boss."

I couldn't help giggling at that.

Then my thoughts returned to Malvolio and I wanted to cry.

How could he treat me like that? Why wouldn't he let me explain, or even talk? Had I even finished a sentence at the end? He hadn't listened to a word I'd said — or tried to say. He didn't even need any input from me at all.

"So, I turn right here, right?"

Shit. I looked at the screen for confirmation. "Yes."

I pushed Malvolio out of my mind and managed to get Javolo to the site safely. I had to concentrate on the job. I still had a few hours ahead of me.

But I couldn't help the words that kept circling through my mind when I thought of him breaking up with me.

Everyone leaves.

———— ⋆·☆·⋆ ————

"Hey, umm, Callista, you're kinda quiet this arvo. Is everything okay?"

I felt a twist in my stomach and sighed. *You know me too well.*

Javolo had just finished with the last load of Amakio from the vein he'd been working on since lunch. We were waiting for data to be sent through to the Nav Computer to pinpoint the next one.

I'd been trying to sound cheery, or at least normal, but it wasn't working. Javolo had noticed my mood, and as hard as I tried, I couldn't bring myself to tell him what was wrong. So much for me being able to talk to him about anything. I felt guilty. Why couldn't I tell him? Every time I told myself to go ahead and tell him about it, I'd clam up. Nothing would come out of my mouth. It actually felt like my throat was closing up and preventing me from speaking.

"Cal?"

I jumped. I'd gotten lost in my thoughts and had forgotten that Javolo had even said anything.

"Yeah, I'm okay," I lied. "Just a bit tired, that's all."

That was lame, I scolded myself. *Just tell him. Who cares who's listening!*

But that was the thing. People were listening. I didn't want them to know something so personal. I really didn't have anyone to talk to about this.

Just a bit tired? Was that all I could come up with? I'd never been any good at lying, and I was kind of proud of that fact. I'd always figured that that made me a better person. Someone who didn't have a problem with lying couldn't possibly be a good person deep down.

"Oh yeah?" Javolo dragged the words out. "Late night with What's-his-name, hey? Where did you guys go after dinner this time? The Big Screen? Out dancing?"

There was something in his voice. Something I couldn't quite put my finger on. There was an emotion there I couldn't place. Or maybe I was imagining it...

Malvolio didn't dance anyway. That was something that had always bothered me because I absolutely loved dancing.

"No. We didn't go anywhere after dinner. Just home..." I couldn't think of anything else to add. I didn't even have anything to say about Javolo calling him What's-his-name for the millionth time. That was bound to raise some suspicion, but I couldn't bring myself to defend him. Not after everything he'd said to me.

He's such a jerk.

Why didn't I tell Malvolio he needn't bother with giving me a second chance? I didn't want a second chance. I wanted out.

I turned my attention back to the computer, but my mind wandered. And I felt like there was a question hanging in the air. I could almost reach out and touch it. Javolo hadn't said anything, but I couldn't shake the feeling. Was there something he wanted to ask me? I couldn't tell.

The information I'd been waiting for came through on the Nav Computer. I sighed again. Now I had something else to focus on.

"Cal?" Javolo asked tentatively.

"Got our instructions." I knew I'd interrupted whatever he was about to ask me, but I didn't want to have to answer any more questions — especially if they involved Malvolio. "Move forward from your current position about twenty metres, then turn to your left, then go another five metres."

"Okie dokie." I could hear the unspoken question still there in his voice. And... disappointment?

Why didn't I wait and listen to his question?

It was becoming harder to keep focused on working when my world was falling apart. I just needed to get through the rest of today. And I didn't like lying to my best friend. Lying by omission was still lying.

My best friend. That's what Javolo was. The full reality of it hit me and I gasped. He really was my best friend — the best friend I'd ever had. Better than any I'd had in my childhood and throughout my schooling. And at this point in time, my only real friend.

I desperately wished that I could talk to him in person. In private. Although we chatted freely on almost any subject every day, we didn't really have any privacy and that sucked. He may not have any answers to my problems, but that didn't matter. I just needed an ear.

"Now what?" Javolo's voice invaded my thoughts.

"What? Oh, sorry." I sat up straighter and cleared my throat. "Can you see a small entrance to your left? I can't make it out clearly on here, but I don't think it's big enough for the Mech-suit to walk through."

"Yes, and no, it's not big enough... yet."

I knew he would be smiling as he started to dig to make the entrance big enough. I found myself smiling too, despite how bad I felt. Javolo enjoyed his work. I guessed it would be like a child playing in the dirt when he got the chance to dig holes under the ground.

While I waited, my thoughts kept returning to Malvolio. I couldn't stop myself. I looked down at the screen and forced myself to think of something else. I closed my eyes and tried to picture Javolo digging and smiling to himself. *I wish I knew what he looked like...*

Then I thought of what Malvolio had said. I was supposedly having an affair with my best friend. What if I did go out on a date with Javolo? I imagined going with him to the Golden Palace. What would he say and do? I knew. We'd talk for ages about anything and everything. We'd tell each other stupid jokes and laugh ourselves silly. He wouldn't be rude to the staff or try to correct me. He had a wicked sense of humour, so it would be a fun night.

I realised I had an idiotic grin on my face, but I didn't care.

Then I imagined being in his arms, safe and happy. It was hard to picture clearly. His face in my mind was a blur. A generic man's face with brown hair and brown eyes. I couldn't imagine kissing him or anything when I couldn't see his face. I knew it could never happen, but I could dream, couldn't I?

I stopped and I gave myself a mental slap. He was my *friend*. A friend I'd never even met. I scolded myself for letting my thoughts run away like that. A lot of people say the best way to ruin a good, strong friendship is to turn it into a relationship. The last thing I wanted to do was ruin what we had.

If we were allowed to see each other, we could still go out together as friends and still have fun like I'd just imagined... purely platonic though...

I needed to focus on reality. *Get back to work*, I told myself.

As soon as I'd given myself that order, my mind started to wander again. I wondered what I'd say to Malvolio that night. I knew he'd come over. I wondered if he'd let me get a word in edgeways...

"All done!" Javolo announced, pulling me from my thoughts.

I looked at my screen again. "Okay, umm, now once you're through, go straight about ten metres, follow it around to your right and head for the wall in front of you."

"No problem, Boss Lady."

I smiled. So now I was Boss Lady.

He sounded better. More cheery. All that digging must've been good therapy for him. Pity I didn't have something to cheer me up.

I checked the readout again to make sure the information was correct. It was so hard to concentrate on anything. I had to force myself to do the most simple and menial tasks. How was I going to last till it was time to go home? Should I tell them I was feeling sick or something and go home? I took a deep breath and waited for him to reach the wall.

"Hey," he said quietly.

"Hey."

"Are you sure you're okay?"

CHAPTER 7
The Forbidden Subject

My chest tightened and I felt the sting of tears. I opened my mouth, but nothing came out. I couldn't answer.

"Cal?" It was almost a whisper over the Com.

"I... umm... yeah. I... I will be..." I was stumbling over my words, but I couldn't say anything about what was really bothering me.

"Okay." It was only one word, but somehow I could tell that he knew it was something I couldn't talk about here. With The Company listening in.

My eyes were full of unshed tears, so I wiped them away and quickly got back to what I was supposed to be doing. I would get a roasting for this conversation. I could feel in my bones. Javolo would too. And there would be extra crap for me for being late.

"Are you at the wall yet?"

"Ah... yes. Been here for a while," he answered sheepishly. It was like he'd forgotten what he was doing, too.

Dammit. How much trouble am I going to be in?

"There should be a vein there in front of you. Or close to you. The computer isn't giving me all the info I need. Maybe one of the sensors is on the blink. I'll have to run diagnostics."

"There is something here, but it is further to the left than where you said," he informed me. "About six metres over."

Six metres? That wasn't good. "Okay, so maybe there *is* a problem..."

Something was malfunctioning, so I needed to pinpoint which piece of equipment, and fast. There were too many safety concerns when one of the satellites or the sensors on the Mech-suit went down.

Javolo went to work and soon had the Amakio ready to take back to the waiting shuttle. Meanwhile, I'd been running diagnostics to try to find the source of the problem.

Malvolio's face kept creeping into my mind. How could he give me an ultimatum like that? There was something cold-hearted about it.

I would be better off with no one. I should've stood my ground and concentrated on work. Now I wanted to be left alone. Was that too much to ask for?

I sighed. Apparently, it was.

"Done," he said.

"Okay, let's get it to the shuttle."

I continued to give him instructions as he walked back through the tunnels. The interference was highest down on the planet, so the GPS systems on the Mech-suits were useless.

Javolo changed the subject once he was on his way. "I'm thinking of what I want to do when my contract is up," he informed me. "I would like to visit Earth, Savanna Five, then travel to Ocanas to see their magnificent sunsets."

What made him think of that?

I sighed. "I heard they're really spectacular."

I'd seen photos of the two suns setting over the horizon on Ocanas, but I'd heard that the images did not do it justice. It was on my list of places I wanted to see one day.

"Maybe I'll go home for a while first... What do you think?"

You're asking me? "I don't know... But I think it might be good for you to catch up with family and friends after being here for so long. I think that that's what I'll do, but my contract has only just started."

Somehow, thinking about working for Katoa for another nineteen months no longer appealed to me — especially since eighteen of those would be with three other Diggers.

My heart sank. The thought of losing Javolo as a friend was too much right now. I would feel so alone out here without him. Tears stung my eyes, but I was determined not to cry. I told myself to get a grip. It was a whole month away.

"Well, I still have another seven months... but only one with you..." he said quietly.

He'd broken our unspoken rule. He'd brought up the forbidden subject. I couldn't stand it. Not on top of what had happened with Malvolio. I couldn't do this. But I held the tears back. I had to concentrate.

I wasn't angry at him for bringing it up, it was just that it made me feel like my world was crashing in on me.

"Yeah..." I couldn't hide the waver in my voice. It was barely above a whisper. Silent tears slid down my cheeks.

"Damn! I wish I could renew my Rotation with you as my Nav Operator."

My chest tightened. I wished with all my heart that we could stay working together. "Me too..."

"Callista, you're a good friend... I'm not happy about the fact that after the six months, we won't get to talk to each other every day."

"Stop it!"

"What?"

"You'll make me cry!" I didn't want him to know I was already crying.

Oops! I shouldn't have said that with them listening... *I'm such an idiot!*

CHAPTER 8
Callista. My Office. Now

"Oh... Sorry..." he said slowly. "I need to take my foot out of my mouth... Don't go all mushy on me now!"

Too late. I couldn't answer. I was busy trying not to make a sound so he wouldn't hear me crying.

"Cal, I'm sorry. Don't cry..."

I'd been holding my breath to keep quiet, but a little sob escaped my lips when he said that.

"Aw, sorry. I messed up..." He sounded upset.

I realised he was standing still in the middle of a tunnel. A rush of adrenalin washed over me and as I thought of how much trouble we'd be in for doing nothing, a tightness spread across my chest. We always made sure we kept going constantly, so they wouldn't have a reason to separate us.

I took a deep breath and let it out slowly, trying to compose myself. How could I keep it together when I felt like I was falling to pieces?

The diagnostics programs had finished and I frowned. "Diagnostics says there are no problems with the hardware or software." I could hear the waver in my voice, but I kept going. "That's weird. Why was it giving me false info?" I shrugged. "I'll run it again later and see if it picks anything up then. Now, I need you to turn to your right and head downhill for about forty metres, then left and keep following the main tunnel."

"Yes, Ma'am." He didn't say it with his usual enthusiasm, and I could tell he was hurting too. His voice crackled over the airwaves. "You okay?"

"Yeah." My voice was strange. Hollow somehow. The tears had

stopped, but my heart was heavy. I had to make myself think about something else. What could I talk about to change the subject?

I was about to ask what he was planning to do on his next day off, but Javolo beat me to it and told me about the storm that was brewing outside on the surface when he was on his lunch break. He wondered if it would still be raging when it was time to return to the station. That could cause delays with take-off and he would be late getting home.

"I'm at the shuttle," he finally announced, "and the storm is starting to get wild."

So he might have trouble getting back to the space station. Besides that problem, I was still relieved. I didn't have to give directions anymore. Directions I might mess up.

My mind wandered to the first day I'd worked with Javolo. It had been like a breath of fresh air when I hadn't been breathing. He charmed his way onto the airwaves and made working as a Nav a thousand times more interesting.

Since then, I'd been much happier in my work. In fact, despite the old equipment and the stresses on me every day, I really liked my work. As soon as that thought had materialised in my mind, I wondered if it was the work, or Javolo's company that made me love my job so much... I knew the answer.

"I'm finished down here," he informed me.

"Head back up the main tunnel." I had to make sure we didn't waste any more time today.

"Yup."

I couldn't stop thinking about everything while he walked.

The thought of having to work without Javolo on the other end of the Com hit me hard again. Why was I reacting like this? I'd known from the start that it was only temporary.

Was it because I was already emotional after Malvolio's crap? It had to be. I wiped my eyes quickly and tried to focus.

"Where to, Boss Lady?" His question startled me.

"Umm, hang on," I stumbled.

I had no idea. I hadn't been paying any attention to where he was walking or where he should be heading next.

"Okay, but you need to focus, girl. You're off with the pixies today. You can't be distracted while I'm out here."

I knew that, but I just couldn't do it. "I know. I'm sorry... Um, go left," I told him.

"Yes, Ma'am!" I could imagine him saluting inside the Mech-suit, the suit's arm moving in time with his.

He walked along for a few moments. "Cal, I can't go through there," he said. "It's a large cavern with a ten-metre drop!"

"Oh, sorry! Let me reconfigure this..."

I wiped away more tears. I needed to get it right, or I would *kill* my only friend. That thought made me feel even worse. How could I face losing him?

I gave myself a mental slap. *Get it together, girl! Focus!*

"Turn around and head back to the turn where I told you to turn left and turn the opposite way instead." I sat up straighter and tried to reign in my thoughts.

"Okay... Hang on... I recognise this place. You know I've been here before, don't you? We've covered this section before and cleaned it out."

My stomach sank. "Oh, crap... I'm really sorry..."

I couldn't do this. I had to get out of here before I really messed up.

"Are you sure you're okay?" he asked me, and I could hear the concern in his voice, even with it being off-frequency.

"I... I'm... not feeling well," I stammered. It was partly true. I didn't feel well at all. The tension was tying my stomach in knots and giving me a killer headache. And I hadn't eaten any lunch. I took a deep breath. "I need to request a replacement Operator. Please stand by."

I was fumbling for the words, but also choking back tears. I didn't want him to know I was crying again.

Why? I asked myself. *Why can't I keep it together?*

Malvolio had really messed up my head. How could he just come in here during my lunch break and drop a bomb on me like that? How could anyone go back to work and pretend nothing's wrong?

Everyone leaves.

I took a deep breath. *I can do this.* "I'll guide you back to the shuttle."

"Alright," he said, "Just make sure you don't give me the wrong directions on the way back. Then go home and rest, but hurry up and get better — I don't know who they'll pair me up with while you're gone."

"Okay. Sorry." *I can do this,* I told myself again.

"Don't be sorry. Just get yourself better."

He started heading back as I put in my request. I managed to guide him back out without messing up again.

"Just kidding about hurrying up. You take all the time you need to get better."

I tried not to think too much about how much his words affected me. I needed to focus.

"Are you sure you're okay?" he asked again once he was back at the shuttle. His voice had an edge to it, and I could feel that he genuinely cared about my well-being, which only made me want to cry more.

After taking a deep breath, I said, "Yeah. I just need to rest, like you said..."

Need to sort my head out. Need to get out of here...

I took in another big breath. *Just need to wait for the replacement... You can do this... Just a bit longer...*

Javolo told me he'd gone to wait inside the shuttle out of the storm. I tried hard to hold it together, but talking was too hard for me to manage. We waited in silence.

After waiting what seemed like an eternity, my substitute Operator arrived. It turned out to be Nadesha Salvani. *She should be okay,* I told myself, *Javolo shouldn't have a problem working with her.*

As I greeted her, Salvani asked me if I was okay.

"Yeah, I'll be alright. I'm just frustrated because the way I'm feeling is affecting my ability to do my job."

It wasn't a lie.

Salvani nodded, causing her dark curls to bob about on her head. "I totally understand," she told me.

I wasted no time getting her up to date with what we'd done during the day. I said goodbye to Javolo, which upset me more than it should have, but I managed to hide it from him and Salvani. Well, at least I thought I did.

I logged off, said goodbye, thanked Salvani, and left the room, then headed straight to the nearest restroom. I felt like I was out of control. I could feel my emotions rising to the surface. I had to get away from everyone.

Once I'd reached the ladies' room and checked that it was empty, I rushed into the nearest cubicle and burst into tears. I put the lid down and sat on the toilet, covering my face. Everything was too much for me and I knew from experience that letting it all out would make me feel better and make it easier to deal with getting out of here and going home. Bottling it all up always made it difficult for me to function. I'd proven that to myself yet again.

This confirmed that I'd been right all along. I shouldn't have started a relationship with Malvolio. I should have known I'd end up getting hurt. Again.

Are all men the same, or is it just the men in my life?

My father left us when I was eight-years-old and my brother, Adamo, was five. I'd watched as our mother fell apart. I'd helped her out as much as a young kid could and kept Adamo company while she cried alone in her room. We were a broken family for a long time, but she'd eventually recovered enough for us to be a family again, and I missed them both right now.

It had been twelve years, but the pain was still raw. My father had found someone new and moved on.

I'd met Jace at uni and we'd been together for two years before he dumped me. Said it wasn't working. Said I was too boyish. Too much like his mates. And I found out later that he'd been seeing someone else while he was still with me. That messed me up for a long time.

Once I felt that I was over Jace, Malvolio came along and made me feel loved. Made me feel special.

Now Malvolio had left me. Sort of. The conditions for his offer of a second chance were ridiculous, so I was sure it was over between us. Especially since I couldn't meet those conditions.

I pushed those thoughts away. They were not making me feel any better. There was no one I could talk to here on the station. I knew I'd have to get through this on my own.

After I'd calmed down, I felt I could tell Malvolio that I didn't want another chance. I forced myself to stop crying so I could get home.

I wasn't sure how I was going to face work tomorrow. I'd deal with that when I came to it. Right now, I had to get out of the restroom and go home. I stepped out of the cubicle and washed my face.

I'd have to hope I wasn't seen by too many people on my way out. I didn't want anyone to see that I'd been crying. There would be too many questions. The very nature of my job required that I be emotionally stable and focused, so I worried they'd send me for some counselling sessions. I did *not* want to sit in some psyche's office and talk to some stranger about my problems.

I debated whether to call in sick in the morning. That would buy me some time to sort my head out. I decided to see how I felt later that night. I didn't want a repeat of today.

As soon as I left the restroom, I heard a familiar voice. "Callista. My office. Now."

CHAPTER 9

Do I want to fix this?

I quickly obeyed, even though my supervisor was the last person I wanted to see right now.

"I need to speak to you about your work," he said.

"Yes, Mr Janga." I resisted the urge to roll my eyes. I knew what was coming. It was always the same lecture. And today there'd be extra because I'd messed up so badly.

He got straight down to business.

"The percentage of private conversations in each of your shifts is, on average, sixty four percent," he told me. "This is unacceptable."

"I've been through all this with Mr Sonrisa. Have you spoken to him? He looked at all the stats. The more we are allowed to talk freely, the higher the Amakio intake. It's all there. Have a look for yourself."

"Don't get smart with me."

"I'm not trying to be smart or whatever. I'm just sayin'. Check it out for yourself."

Janga scowled at me. Maybe he hadn't checked all of the stats. He changed tack.

"You seem to be getting too close to your Digger, which violates Employee Condition eight point one two, paragraph nine, which states—"

"I know what it states."

"Do not interrupt me, Callista. It states that a Nav must not become emotionally attached to her Digger and under no circumstances at all, enter into a relationship with him."

I resisted another strong urge to roll my eyes. Not him too. Had he been talking to Malvolio? How could he and Malvolio seriously think it was possible? Like we could ever meet and start a relationship together.

"Are you emotionally involved with your Digger?"

"He does have a name, you know. And no, we are friends and we enjoy conversing while we work, but it doesn't go beyond that. It can't. We'll never meet each other. You know that. And it would not affect my judgement in an emergency situation."

I added that bit on the end, knowing that that's what this was leading up to.

"Well, that remains to be seen. We are watching you and I personally believe you should be assigned another Digger immediately, before the attachment is strengthened and lives are put at risk."

"No, I—"

"I told you not to interrupt me! You are treading on thin ice, Callista. Don't make me reassign you to desk work."

I opened my mouth, but quickly shut it again. It didn't matter what I said. And the last thing I wanted was to be taken off my Nav Station away from Javolo.

"And then there is your performance today." My stomach dropped. I prepared myself for the worst. "You were ten minutes late back from your lunch break. You let your emotions affect your work. What do you have to say for yourself?"

"It was nothing to do with work," I said. "Nothing to do with Javolo at all." Janga stared at me with narrowed eyes. "I have a personal crisis that I'm dealing with. That's why I was late back from lunch. I won't let it affect my work again. I called for a replacement because I'm feeling sick too."

He didn't look convinced. I wouldn't have believed me either. "That's not good enough. You have to be focused. Your Digger's life depends on it. You need to sort this 'crisis' out and fast. Do *not* bring it to work tomorrow, or you will be suspended immediately. Do you understand?"

I cringed inwardly and looked down at my feet. "Yes. I understand." I was definitely going to call in sick.

He glared at me. "This is an Official Warning, Callista. I am putting forth a formal recommendation to Sonrisa today for you to be assigned another Digger for the remainder of this Rotation, and for you to start sessions with the counsellor asap. We're watching you, and listening."

I sighed and tried not to react.

"And Callista?"

"Yes?"

"Lose the attitude. It will get you into big trouble one day."

"Yes, Sir."

"Now get out of here."

Janga was such a dick.

———— ⋆·☆·⋆ ————

I wandered through the streets on my way home, trying to clear my head.

It was still strange to me that there were streets and apartments and shops on a space station. The park with trees, birds, and a fountain seemed out of place, but I loved the park. They were trying to reduce the stress of living in a tin can by emulating home and bringing some nature to the place. It worked, especially the park.

I needed to think. Malvolio would probably call me after work, as usual, and I could tell him I didn't want to see him anymore. The thought of it made my stomach twist itself into more knots, but I had to do it.

Wait. No. I couldn't tell him on the Vid. I should at least have the decency to tell him to his face. The thought made me cringe inside. But only cowards broke up with someone over the Vid or a text-only message. I took a deep breath and resolved to just do it.

Suddenly, my front door was in view. My heart sank. I didn't want to go home, but I plodded over to the entrance.

I stood in front of the Door-cam and the security system's retina scanner signalled its recognition with a flickering green light. My door swished open. Immediately upon entry to my small apartment, the lights faded on. Everything still swirled around in my mind as the Home Computer greeted me in a dull female voice.

"Good evening, Lennina. You have two new messages."

Of course I did.

I ignored the messages and the sinking feeling they caused and headed straight for the bathroom. The shower was my thinking place. I'd changed my mind. I did want to be home.

If the messages were anything like what Malvolio had said at lunch,

I didn't want to play them back. Everything he said kept playing on a loop in my head.

I had to somehow tell him I didn't want to see him anymore and get him to leave as soon as possible afterward. Yeah. Simple.

I might have felt numb earlier, but it hit me now.

I'd known Malvolio for about seven weeks and been dating him for about four. It had been a whirlwind kind of romance. He was always giving compliments that made me blush, bought me gifts and flowers, and was so sweet. He told me how he felt about me before I could even decide if I liked him enough to say yes to a first date. He was charming and witty and didn't give up. I'd finally said yes and things had been so wonderful.

Tears slid down my cheeks. What had gone wrong? Things were so good before all of this happened. He seemed like such a great guy. He'd changed. I didn't understand. I wanted the old Malvolio back.

The things that had happened at work popped back into my mind. It was hard to think.

I closed my eyes and breathed deeply as I concentrated on relaxing my body.

It wasn't enough. I needed a hot shower.

When I stood in front of the bathroom mirror, I noticed that a long piece of my dark hair had fallen out of the untidy bun I'd put it in that morning. I was looking pretty wild and unkempt. I pulled my hair from the bun and turned to watch it fall down my back. I'd always had long hair and it was long enough now to reach the middle of my back.

Malvolio always told me it looked untidy and dishevelled. He thought it would really suit me to have a short pixie cut that left some of my hair curled around onto my cheeks. I would never wear it like that — but didn't tell him that. Sure, my hair had a mind of its own sometimes, but that wasn't a reason to cut it all off. He didn't understand. There were a lot of things about me he didn't understand.

I tossed my clothes into the laundry chute and stepped into the shower cubicle, the glass door sliding shut behind me.

The shower unit was linked to the Home Computer and at my command, jets of hot water sprayed me from all angles except my face.

I closed my eyes to try to relax. It didn't work. I tried rubbing my face and temples. It helped, a little.

Am I doing the right thing? Shouldn't we be trying to sort things out? Am I giving up over something trivial? I didn't want to give up. Too many people gave up when it got too hard. Like my father.

I squeezed my eyes shut. This wasn't something trivial. He'd accused me of cheating on him. This was too big to ignore. I couldn't wrap my head around how he'd come to the conclusion that I was sleeping with my best friend.

How could I make him see how wrong he was and how impossible it was for me to be seeing Javolo? Malvolio needed to know that I would not betray his trust and cheat on him. Because that's the last thing I'd do. I may not have wanted a relationship to begin with, but I would never cheat on someone. I knew what it was like to have someone cheat on you and it was deeply painful. I would never want to make someone feel like that.

I had to ask myself, *Do I want to fix this?*

My head ached from the stress.

Sighing, I placed my hands on the tiled wall in front of me and tried to picture a tranquil scene. Trees and flowers moving in the breeze. I slowed my breathing. Refocused on the scene. It was where I used to go when I was a kid. A place near my home where I'd always found peace. There were trees and flowers in a large clearing in the bush, with a creek running through the middle of it all.

I still needed something more.

I turned around and leaned my back against the wall, the jets of water tickling my skin. I slowly let myself slide down until I was sitting on the floor of the cubicle, thankful that the water had warmed up the wall and the floor. I pulled my knees up to my chest and wrapped my arms around them.

"Fill," I ordered, and the whole cubicle began flooding with water.

I waited with my eyes closed, wishing I could relax completely and shake the anxiety and frustration that were eating at me.

When the water level reached my neck, I told it to stop filling and sat with my eyes still closed until I could clear my mind and unwind. I couldn't relax completely, but it was close.

When I finally emerged from the bathroom, the Home Computer reminded me that there were two messages on the Vid for me.

"Hello, Lennina, darling."

I jumped back and made a weird squeaking noise at the sight of Malvolio standing in my kitchen. "*Oh, my stars!* You scared the life out of me!"

CHAPTER 10

Money Suits You

My cheeks flushed. I was only wearing a towel.

He hadn't even so much as flinched. "Where have you been? I've been waiting to take you out to dinner. Have you forgotten?"

What? Dinner? Oh. "Uh, yeah. I forgot."

"We're meeting with the top executives at Katoa and Galaxy Mech. I know you're seeking a better position at Katoa, so maybe if you make a good impression, good things will come of tonight."

My mind conjured pictures of me finally getting into Research and Development, which is exactly where I wanted to be. This could be my chance.

Then I remembered. "Wait. I need to talk to you about lunch today."

He raised his eyebrows. "Oh? What about it?"

Was he serious? "All those things you said..."

"Forget about it. I'd had a bad day. I need you to come with me tonight and we can be together. I've been stressed lately but all that is about to change and it can be like it was when we met. I'll order your favourite meal and your favourite drink and help you if you get stuck for something to say to our guests. I'll put in a good word for you so you'll have the best chance possible to get your dream job."

My head was spinning from the turn of events.

He put his hands on my bare arms and looked into my eyes. "Things at work have been so hectic lately. There's been a lot of interference coming from the planet and we've had some setbacks in the latest models with the Mech-suits. I shouldn't have taken it out on you. You're my girl. Will you forgive me?"

"I..." I was lost for words. I didn't know what to say. Was I being too hard on him? Had I made a hasty decision? Should I give him the benefit of the doubt?

"I love you, Lennina. You're my world. You're the moon and the stars to me. I don't know what I'd do if you didn't give me a chance to prove my love for you. It will be good for you to dress up and eat out at a nice restaurant and forget all the stresses of your workday. What do you say?"

My heart melted. Maybe he did care. Maybe we could put all this nonsense behind us and enjoy each other's company tonight.

"I'll get ready." I squeezed past him and hurried to my room to change my clothes.

"Good girl."

Malvolio followed me, but I stopped him at the door. "I won't be long."

I closed the door on him. Was he going to come in and watch me dress? We weren't at a stage where I was comfortable with that. It had only been four weeks. That may be a bit slow by some people's standards, but not for me. It was going to take me a while to commit fully after Jace. I had given him my everything and he'd thrown it away.

I raced around and dressed as fast as I could, with Malvolio trying to have a conversation with me through the door. I caught most of what he said. Something about how important these people were and that I needed to be more aware of these social situations.

I wasn't very good at small talk and all the etiquette required at these dinners, which made me anxious. But Malvolio had told me he would help me with that. I tried to relax.

Malvolio opened the door as I was putting in the earrings he'd given me. Patience wasn't one of his strong points.

"Oh." He looked disappointed. "You're going to wear that?"

I looked down at my black dress with the low-cut neckline with lace around the edges. "What's wrong with it?"

"Nothing. Nothing. Don't worry about it. You look fine. They'll like you. Are you ready?"

"Yep." I let the "p" pop before remembering that he didn't like it when I used any form of slang.

There was a slight flinch at the word and I cringed a little.

But I should be able to say whatever I want.

Then I reminded myself that he was trying to help me by teaching me how to communicate well and how to comport myself in situations like the dinner tonight. He really wanted me to get the job I wanted.

His expression smoothed over as he approached me. "You're wearing my earrings. Good. Money suits you. You know how much I love you, don't you?"

I nodded as he pulled me in for a hug. His arms encircled me and I felt warm. Some of the tension leached out of me.

"You are like the moon and stars to me. You shine. I am lucky to have you. We go well together. Everyone is so envious of you. There are women that are green with it."

I pulled away so I could look into his eyes. "Yeah. It makes me wonder why you picked me, when you could have anyone."

"After all this time, you don't know? Why do you think I picked you?"

I pretended to think. "Mmm. I got nothin'."

"Really, Lennina. Why do you insist on speaking like a heathen?"

I smiled. "Maybe I am one, deep down."

The disgusted look on his face was priceless. He couldn't take a joke.

He quickly recovered. "Because you're special to me. You're precious, like a jewel. We'll be good together, you'll see."

And with that, he pulled away from me and I felt kind of cold where his body had been touching mine. He headed out of the room without another glance and I followed, feeling kind of dazed. He was like a whirlwind.

I felt a weird sensation as we stepped into the Golden Palace again. Javolo was in the other section last night. I wished I could have met him. It would have been really nice to see his face and know what he looked like. Sometimes it really bugged me that he was this faceless person in my mind. Just a voice on the Com.

"Lennina?"

I jumped. I didn't even realise we'd met up with our dinner guests. "What?"

Malvolio looked annoyed. How many times had he called my name? "Blaine asked you how you were."

"Oh. Sorry. I'm fine. H-how are you?"

Blaine smiled faintly. "I'm well, thank you." The smile widened. "How are you finding your job at Katoa?"

Was she being sincere, or was she having a dig at me because I was only a Nav? I brushed those thoughts aside. "It's interesting so far. I love the technical side of things."

I couldn't read her expression. "Oh, yes. Well. I'm sure it's interesting, dear."

She had no idea. I wondered what her job entailed, or if she even had one.

Malvolio introduced me to all of them. "Lennina, darling, this is Blaine Castaneda and Eldon Bezorgan. They are both managers at Katoa. Bianka Abraxas and Mattais Omid both work in Research and Development. Mattais at Katoa and Bianka over at Galaxy Mech. Her husband, Danaz, is a manager at Galaxy Mech."

I clasped my trembling hands together so they couldn't see them shaking. "Pleased to meet you all."

"Lennina has the misfortune of working in a position that is far beneath her. We're working on rectifying that, as she is a talented scientist."

I cringed. That sounded awful. Their expressions didn't fill me with confidence.

Malvolio smiled. "This way, ladies and gentlemen."

He led the way to a corner table and we took our seats.

Malvolio was the perfect dinner host and conversationalist. He talked about a wide variety of subjects, most of them as boring as hell. Did these people honestly care about the intricacies of the stock market? Maybe they did. Maybe that's how they had become so rich in the first place.

I was asked a few questions about the job and I wanted to tell them some of my ideas about a new computer system, some new designs for breather masks and tubes, and even some more efficient digging tools for the Mech-suits that I'd read about, but I knew I'd go too far into details and probably ruin my chances with how enthusiastic I was. They didn't seem like the type of people who would be interested or enthusiastic. So I held back. I could save that kind of thing for my job interview, if I ended up getting that far.

All was fine until my meal came out. I'd asked for the steak to be well-done, but it was far from it. It was oozing red liquid onto the plate and my stomach lurched.

"What's the matter?" Malvolio asked.

"Nothing. Don't worry about it." The last thing I wanted was to cause a fuss.

"It isn't nothing. Tell me."

I fidgeted with my napkin. "My meat is too rare."

"But that's the dish," Bianka said. "It is supposed to be rare. It's a delicacy."

"I know, but I don't like it like that. It makes me ill."

Some of the people at the table looked at me like I'd grown another head. They thought I was uncultured. I didn't care. I could ask for the meat to be cooked however I liked. I needed to ensure I didn't feel sick for the rest of the evening. And it wasn't like they had to eat it.

Malvolio called a waitress over, told her what the problem was and demanded they rectify it immediately. She apologised and took my plate back to the kitchen.

I was relieved when he didn't give her a dressing-down in front of everyone.

It took a while for them to cook another steak, but I didn't mind.

When it was brought out, Malvolio stopped the waitress before she turned away and I cringed.

"This kind of problem is unacceptable," he told her.

"But the dish requires the meat to be rare," she said.

He raised an eyebrow. "That may be so, but you were told when we placed our orders that she wanted the meat well done."

"It's okay," I said. "It's not a big problem. They fixed it."

He turned to me. "It is *not* okay, Lennina. The service here is rated five stars, but has not been five stars lately. Last night's fiasco, and now tonight. It is *not* acceptable and I will *not* be dining here again."

CHAPTER 11
I Can't Do This Anymore

The waitress had gone pale. "I am so sorry, sir. It won't happen again." She waved at another waiter and he hurried over. "Please accept this free bottle of our finest wine as a token of our sincerity."

The waiter presented the bottle to Malvolio and he took it, giving it a once-over. They waited nervously as he took his time. Maybe he was enjoying making them squirm.

"Mmm. Not a bad year. I will accept your apology." He waved them away once they'd popped the cork and poured our drinks.

I was embarrassed and appalled. I could feel the heat that had spread from my hairline right down to my chest. The others at the table resumed their conversation as if the whole thing was nothing. One even asked to see the bottle of wine.

How could they pretend nothing happened? Maybe it was an everyday occurrence to them. Maybe they all acted like that.

But I wasn't okay with it. I was ready to go home, but of course, I had to wait for the dinner to be over. I forced myself to eat my food. Malvolio would probably have a fit if I didn't eat it after all that nonsense.

—— ★·☆·★ ——

"What do you mean, you want to have an early night?" Malvolio asked.

I cringed inwardly as the lights flickered on in my apartment and the door slid shut behind us. I couldn't deal with this right now. My mind was all over the place. He kept changing his whole personality. Everything had been fine until my meal wasn't right. I felt nauseous.

"I'm tired and I have work tomorrow," I said as I walked toward my kitchen. Maybe I would have a cup of tea before heading to bed to try to relax after he'd gone.

He didn't need to know I was planning to call in sick.

My Home Computer greeted me. "Good evening, Lennina. You have two old messages and no new messages."

No, of course I don't. The only person that leaves me messages is standing right behind me.

I expected Malvolio to say something about the messages I hadn't watched.

Malvolio put his hands on my upper arms and for some reason, it made me cringe. "That has never bothered you before." His breath tickled my left ear and it actually felt kinda creepy.

I stood there wondering why his touch was making me feel this way while my pulse raced. I needed time alone to think about what that meant and about everything that had happened.

He turned me around and his grip tightened. "Lennina?" I looked up into his grey eyes. "Answer me." A storm was brewing in those eyes.

"I'm tired," I told him again. "I really want to just go to sleep." I wasn't lying.

His eyebrows drew together and his fingers dug into my skin. "You're not tired. Tell me what it is."

I shrugged out of his grasp. I'd have to check my arms for bruises later. What was his problem?

I sighed. There was no point in trying to avoid it. I knew he'd keep asking me till I told him what was bothering me.

I thought I might as well go for the direct approach and get it over with. "The way you treated that waitress. It's not right. You know she wasn't the one who cooked my steak, don't you?"

"Of course I know that! Do you think I'm stupid? What do you want from me, Lennina? Should I have dragged the chef out and given him a dressing down? Is that it?"

"No!" I ran my hand through my hair. "I didn't want you to do any of that. Why couldn't you accept her apology and leave it at that. The meal was delicious once they fixed it."

"You've missed the point. You can't let these people walk all over you."

"That's not what they were trying to do."

"They must learn their place."

"What? You think you're better than them?"

"Of course I am. I'm the MIC of Galaxy Mech, and they're just boot-lickers."

"Really? That's what you think of them? Well, I'm only a Nav, so I guess I'm a nobody too."

"Don't talk like that, darling. You're not like them. You're just in an unfortunate situation, which I'm sure I can rectify very soon."

"What if I don't want to change jobs now? What if I've changed my mind?"

I wasn't sure where that had come from. Maybe from my strong desire not to lose my best friend.

Malvolio looked stunned. "I'm pulling a lot of strings for you and you don't even appreciate my efforts. I can't believe how ungrateful you are."

"Ungrateful? I didn't ask you to pull strings for me. I'm perfectly capable of working my way up to the position I want on my own merits."

"Yes, well, how long do you think that will take? I could arrange to have you working in Research and Development by the end of your Rotation."

My heart leapt at the thought, but then sunk back down in my chest. If I let him do this for me, I would owe him. He would expect me to stay with him as a way of repaying him and I didn't want to do that.

I thought about his behaviour at lunch and kicked myself for agreeing to go out to dinner with him. He'd managed to talk me into it. I couldn't think straight. I needed to sort out all of this in my head.

"Malvolio. I need to get some rest. I'll see you tomorrow."

"Why are you so keen to get rid of me?"

I managed to not roll my eyes. "I'm not. I'm tired."

"You want me gone because you're going to meet up with *him*."

"What? No! How can I meet up with him if he lives in the Digger's Section?"

He ignored that. "He is nothing but a dim-witted Neanderthal and he is beneath you." He stepped toward me and I clenched my fists so hard my fingernails dug into my palms. "I don't want you to be consorting with him anymore. And I don't want you to be *fucking* him behind my back! Just do your job. Nothing more."

"I'm *not*... sleeping with him!"

"Just do your job."

I opened my mouth, but nothing came out. I started to shake with rage and my breathing was fast and shallow. I could feel the sting of tears and I clenched and unclenched my fists to try to stop them from flowing.

I needed to calm down — Malvolio wasn't worth it.

Breathe...

Then he spoke slowly, as if he was speaking to a young child. "He is a *Digger*, and as such, should not be considered a friend. Or a fuck buddy. You could lose your job if Katoa knew you were fucking him."

Losing my job was the last thing on my mind. "Stop saying that word as if it's a disgusting thing to sleep with someone! It's not true! And I'm allowed to be his friend — we're just not allowed to be in a relationship with each other — which, by the way, is *impossible!* And I don't care if I lose my job!" My eyes were full of unshed tears and I could hardly see.

"Well, you *should* care—"

"I don't! I wish I never took this stupid job! And I wish I never met you!"

I waited for him to blow up about that, but he didn't. He walked further into my home and went on about how I couldn't "have my cake and eat it too," waving his arms around theatrically while he spoke. He told me I needed to consider others' feelings. *His* feelings. I hadn't stopped to think about how *he* felt. And what about that Digger? How did he feel? Did he know I was seeing two men at once? Did he care?

My face was hot, but I bit my tongue and stayed silent. It was pointless to deny everything when he was so adamant that they were true.

"He is probably such a Neanderthal that he doesn't mind sharing his woman—"

"Shut up!"

I surprised myself, but I'd had enough. And it felt like acid was burning my throat.

"How *dare* you? Do *not* tell me to shut up!" He yelled so loudly that I instinctively took a step back.

I cringed inside, but took advantage of the pause and took a deep breath. "I need to tell you something," I said in a quiet, even tone, but my heart hammered madly in my chest. I clasped my hands together in front of me to stop them from shaking.

"Yes?"

"I..." My legs nearly gave way under me and I reached out to hold onto the wall to steady myself. *Here goes...* "I have decided that I don't want to see you anymore."

"*What?*" He stared at me incredulously, his eyes widening.

It had been difficult to decide earlier, but now I was certain I wanted to get out of this relationship.

I felt a little light-headed. "I don't want to be your girlfriend. Things are not the same as they were when we met. It's all changed. *You've* changed. I can't do this anymore. I can't—"

"*What?* No! You don't get to do this!" It was odd seeing his confidence falter.

"Oh, yes I do. I can't deal with this... I just can't."

It was too much for me. I needed to get away from this stress. My heart hammered in my chest.

"No. If anyone is dumping anyone, it's me dumping you! I did give you another chance to redeem yourself. I gave you the opportunity to dump the *caveman* today. And did you do it? Did you dump him?"

I sighed heavily and shakily twirled a piece of my hair around my finger. *I'd have to actually be seeing him for that to happen...*

I lifted my chin. "No, I didn't!"

Malvolio was glaring at me, hands still on his hips. "You promised me! You were going to fix things. You've broken your promise!" he said. "Well, that settles it then, I am letting you go." Relief flooded through my body. Now I just had to get him to leave. "I won't tell anyone about what happened. What you did to me."

That's because it's not true, I thought bitterly. "You're crazy," I told him. I couldn't help it. It just came out. He didn't seem to notice.

"I will tell them I needed to move on. You're a bit too young and immature for me anyway... Too frigid."

"I am *not* frigid! And you *are* crazy."

His face changed as he stepped toward me. "How *dare* you!" he shrieked, his eyes taking on a strange, hollow look.

Then without warning, I felt a blow to the right side of my face that almost knocked me to the floor.

CHAPTER 12

I'd Just Seen the Real Malvolio

Before I even knew what I was doing, I slapped him back.

I froze. *Why did I do that?*

I couldn't believe what I'd done. But it was too late. I couldn't take it back.

While I was standing there questioning why I even hit back, he slammed his fist into the left side of my face before I could raise an arm to defend myself. My head jerked violently as the pain shot through my cheek and into my eye socket. I saw stars before my eyes and a weird numbness crept over me, along with panic.

As my eyesight cleared, I could see a wall in front of me and realised I was lying on the floor. It scared me to think that I didn't even know I'd fallen. Hadn't even felt it.

Oh, no. Why didn't I feel it? What has he done to me?

The panic spread like ice through my veins. What kind of damage had he caused if I couldn't feel myself fall?

I just lay there, stunned, staring at the wall and trying to think. I couldn't stay on the floor. I had to see what Malvolio was doing. But, as much as my brain was screaming at me to look for him, my body wouldn't obey.

I still felt numb all over. I knew he had a volatile temper, but didn't think he would actually hurt me. I couldn't believe he'd knocked me down. *Punched* me... I'd never been slapped or punched in the face before.

The pain returned and radiated from my left cheek, into my eye, and up through my temple. I groaned. It was better when I couldn't feel it.

Malvolio was yelling from somewhere behind me — still swearing about what Javolo and I were supposedly doing behind his back — but I still couldn't seem to move. My mind reeled. How could he do this? How could I have been so stupid? Why did I give him another chance? He could do anything to me now and I would be virtually powerless to stop him. I didn't even have a friend I could go to for help. No one I could stay with to help me feel safe after he'd gone.

But what if he didn't leave? What would I do?

Then from out of nowhere, pain exploded in my right side, causing me to cry out. I knew he'd kicked me, but it felt like a large knife had been shoved into my ribs and twisted around. My midsection tensed as if I'd been punched in the stomach and I had trouble breathing.

The pain was unbearable. I rolled onto my back and wrapped my arms around myself as if that could somehow stop it.

It hurt too much to stay on my back, so I rolled over onto my left side, curling into a ball. I could only manage short breaths. Thoughts raced through my mind of all the things he could possibly do next and the terror built until I couldn't think. I found myself waiting for the next blow, cringing at the thought of it.

Then the sound of my front door swishing open made me jump. I thought I heard footsteps on the doorstep, then the door swished closed again.

A wave of relief flooded through me. I stayed there for a while. I couldn't get up. Couldn't bring myself to move. After a few more minutes — I think — breathing became easier. Still I didn't move, still seeing stars every now and then. Tears came and I just lay there on the floor and cried, which only intensified the pain in my side. Something must have been broken for it to hurt so much.

I couldn't believe what had happened. Couldn't believe he'd done this. I was so stupid to think I was safe. Stupid to argue back. But then, I had no way of knowing he'd do *this*.

My heart was still thundering in my chest and I tried to slow my breathing so I could calm down, without much luck.

I should've been on the Vid to the Enforcers but I couldn't stop the tears. My ribs screamed at me where he'd kicked me and felt worse every time I moved, and that made me cry more.

When I finally stopped and tried to sit up, I cried out as I felt a stabbing pain rip through my right side. I lay back down on the floor.

I could feel the panic rise again, but couldn't give in to it. I needed to focus and call the Enforcers. I told the Home Computer to call them. No response. After getting no response a second time, the only explanation I could think of was that Malvolio had turned off voice commands before he left. That sent a chill down my spine.

Why would he do that?

I would have to somehow get myself over to the console and place the call manually.

My mind went into overdrive, going over everything that had happened and trying to figure out where it all went wrong and wondering why it went so wrong. Then I had to stop myself. I had to focus and get help. I had to get up.

I moved slowly this time until I could get into a position that enabled me to push myself up with my trembling arms.

I took a deep breath before attempting to stand, but that brought more pain. It took a lot of effort to get up, and I wobbled over to the Vid to press the button to reactivate voice commands and call the Enforcers.

—— ⋆·☆·⋆ ——

Waiting for the Enforcers to come to my apartment was torture. I had a strong urge to pace the floor, but was in too much pain. So I sat on a chair in the kitchen facing the door.

Where are they?

Frustration was eating at me.

I sat thinking about everything and the horror of it hit me. I'd been *assaulted*. By my *boyfriend*. Someone I thought I knew and who I thought cared about me. He'd told me he loved me.

I must have been in shock; I was still trembling and felt deathly cold.

None of it made sense. My mind couldn't wrap itself around the truth. I thought I knew him fairly well. I was so wrong.

It horrified me that it had suddenly gone from an argument to him beating me up. Tears ran silently down my cheeks. There was no way I would stay with him now. I shouldn't have fallen for his bullshit before dinner. All the things he said about him loving me. It had to be bullshit.

I'd just seen the real Malvolio.

The musical tune from the door chime made me jump and caused a jolt of pain, which made me make a dismal little whimpering sound, but I managed to push myself up out of the chair and walk carefully to the door.

It's about time, I thought as I waved my hand over the sensor to open the door, but then gasped in horror.

Malvolio was standing there.

CHAPTER 13
What We Have is Special

Oh, hell no!

I waved my hand in front of the sensor again to close the door, but it was too late. He'd stepped forward so that the safety mechanism in the door wouldn't allow it to close. It paused for an instant, then slid open again.

Fear coursed through my veins. *No... This can't be happening!*

"Malvolio! You need to leave. Now!" I told him, as pain sliced through my side. "I've called the Enforcers."

He grabbed me by the arm, pulling me toward the kitchen, and pain nearly forced me to my knees. "You called the Enforcers? *Fuck!* Are you trying to ruin my life?"

"Of course I called them! You... *kicked* me!" I could hardly get the words out as his fingers dug into my flesh and the door closed behind us.

"You. Hit. Me!" he yelled. "*No one* hits me!"

And with that, he punched me in the stomach with his free hand. I screamed out in pain, doubling over. I couldn't breathe. I was going to pass out. I could feel it.

He let go of my arm so suddenly that I fell to my hands and knees on the floor. My stomach was a tight band. My heart hammered in my chest. My vision was clouding, my body threatening to lose consciousness. I took a few slow deep breaths, but of course, that just caused me more pain.

"Get out and leave me alone!" I tried to scream, but it came out as a hoarse kind of whisper. It was a pathetic sound.

I moved so I was sitting on my heels facing him.

"No," he said calmly. "I will *not* leave."

There was a sinking feeling in my chest. His sudden calm demeanour scared me more than anything else. It made me wonder what he was planning. There were so many horrific possibilities running through my mind that I felt like screaming. My heartbeat sped up; I didn't think it could beat any faster. I seriously watched too many HoloMovies. The scenarios wouldn't stop playing through my mind. My stomach roiled and I tried to think of something else, and failed.

I managed to drag myself to my feet, with the intention of eventually getting to the Vid. He watched me carefully. My mind was racing. Was he going to hurt me again? I was shaking all over. My breaths were coming in ragged bursts. And still he watched me.

"So," I managed to say. "Why did you come back?"

That was a dumb thing to say, but it was all I could think of to try to distract him till the Enforcers arrived.

His eyes narrowed. Silence.

How could I keep a conversation going if he wouldn't answer? I tried desperately to think of something else to say. Maybe if I said sorry for slapping him, it would keep him happy while I waited impatiently for help to arrive.

But the room started to spin and I thought I was going to pass out. It took a few seconds to stop. He must've hit me harder than I'd thought. Maybe I had a concussion.

I took a deep breath.

"I... I'm sorry I hit you..." I said, heart thundering in my ears. I still couldn't believe I'd done that. Maybe it was because he'd made me so angry.

More silence.

Great.

I ran a hand through my tangled hair. I was hoping for something more than that.

But then he finally said something that sent a chill down my spine. "You will be..."

I needed to get out of here. But how? I didn't think he'd let me walk out, and I wouldn't get far with the pain I was in.

Where are they? I wondered desperately. *Please hurry up!*

I'd reached the console for the Vid. My stomach muscles had finally returned to normal, but they still felt like they'd had a thirty-minute workout.

"So, what happens now?" I asked. "Do you want the earrings back?"

"What do you mean? Why would I ask you to do that?"

I cringed. "You said..." I swallowed. "You said we were through."

His face smoothed itself out. "It's not over. Don't worry. We can work things out. We've had some good times together. You can't give up on us. What we have is special. It's worth fighting for."

I closed my mouth. It had dropped open while he was speaking. Was he serious? Who was the one who watched too many HoloMovies? Each one of those sentences could be found in a movie, I was sure.

He came closer and smiled at me. He almost looked like the Malvolio I knew so well.

That I *thought* I knew so well...

"You're mine," he told me. "You are *my* girl. Forget him. He is not worth it."

The surprise I'd felt morphed back into fear. I could feel tears forming in my eyes, but I did *not* want to cry now. I didn't want to give him the satisfaction.

Then he did something I didn't expect. He wrapped his arms around me and gave me a hug. I didn't know what to do. Fear of what he might do to me had me putting my arms around him in return.

He held me gently, then bent down and kissed me on the lips. I felt so revolted by him now and pulled away. He simply pulled me closer and kissed me again and I pulled back, wriggling to try to break free of his embrace and grimaced at the pain it caused me. He wouldn't let me go. He kept kissing me and ignoring my attempts to break free.

"Stop it!" I managed to say between kisses, but he wouldn't listen.

He held me so tightly my ribs felt as if they were being crushed; the pain in my side like someone sticking a knife in and twisting it around, but I didn't want to give in. I couldn't kiss him back and pretend there was nothing wrong. I just couldn't.

My legs almost gave way a few times and my vision clouded. It was too much pain to endure.

"You're mine. I'll treat you right. You'll see. You'll forget about him and you'll stop being such a slut. I'll show you how much of a man I am. I'll fuck you till you beg me to stop, then I'll fuck you some more. And you'll like it."

I felt the warmth drain from my face. *No... He wouldn't really do that, would he? Even if I told him no?*

Uh, yes. He would.

He brought his left hand up to hold my jaw so I couldn't pull away from his mouth and pulled my body against his with his right hand. I could feel something hard against my lower stomach. Panic crawled up my spine.

I had to get away from him. *Now.* But how?

I didn't know how much longer I could bear the pain and it was becoming even harder to breathe, if that was even possible.

The blackness was there, beckoning me. Pulling me into unconsciousness. It would be so easy to let it take me, but what would he do to me while I was out?

I couldn't think about that, I had to focus. Had to stay awake...

I jumped when I heard the sound of my door opening and we turned to see two Enforcers standing at the ready, hands hovering above the stunners at their hips. I hadn't even heard the door chime.

"Enforcers!" the taller of the two officers shouted out as they stepped forward into my home. "We're here to help!"

CHAPTER 14
We Had a Bit of a Tiff

You guys need a new greeting. Seriously. That's so lame!

The security system in the door was set to admit any law enforcement officer on command — following an ID check, of course — so I guessed they decided to let themselves in when I didn't answer.

I saw a look of confusion cross their faces once they'd taken in the scene in front of them. They would've seen Malvolio and I locked in an embrace, kissing passionately, when the door opened. The way I had my hands on his upper arms wouldn't have looked like I was pushing him away. His hand holding my jaw had been partially hidden by his face and my hair.

Malvolio turned to greet the Enforcers and I quickly seized the opportunity to break free of his grasp. He let me go this time and I stumbled a little.

The taller officer spoke first. "Good evening, Miss Callista, is it? I am Officer Sarkozy and this is Officer Parker." He waved a hand in his partner's general direction. "You called the Enforcement Agency and asked for assistance? What seems to be the problem?" Both men looked from me to Malvolio and back again.

I couldn't blame them for being confused. They did get a call out for an assault, after all. This wouldn't look good for my case against Malvolio. Maybe he'd planned it that way.

In fact, now that I thought about it, I was sure of it.

I stepped toward them, feeling nauseous. "Malvolio assaulted me."

I could see their expressions and their stance change instantly.

"Okay, can you tell me what happened, please?" Sarkozy asked. "I need to know more about the situation so a proper assessment can be made."

He inclined his head toward Malvolio. It was very subtle, but I still caught it. They knew each other. That didn't surprise me. Just about everyone on the station knew of Malvolio, and a lot of people knew him personally as well. He had a high position within the community aboard the station, not just at Galaxy Mech.

They looked at me expectantly. The scene played over in my mind, and it scared me to think of how bad things were and how much worse it could have been. He'd been so callous and vicious. And as I spoke, the tears started to fall.

I told them what happened between sobs and the pain was like a knife in my side.

"I think my ribs are broken," I added.

"No, I did *not* do those things," Malvolio said, a look of arrogance on his perfectly manicured face. "*She* hit *me* — she slapped me across the face!"

"You *did*—" I yelled, a stab of pain stopping me.

"Now, Miss Callista, let's calm down," Sarkozy told me as he stepped forward, arms outstretched.

"But he's lying," I whimpered. The room was kind of swimming before my eyes.

"Just continue," he said, dropping his arms. "What happened after that?"

I took a deep breath and collected my thoughts. The room started to go back to normal. Kind of.

"He left... I tried to get up and..." I had to stop for a few moments. "And I rang you and when... when the door chime rang I thought it was you and it was him..." I knew I was rambling, but I couldn't help it and I couldn't stop the tears.

Sarkozy listened quietly.

"He punched me in the stomach... and wouldn't let me go... Then he started kissing me and... I told him to stop and... and he wouldn't stop!"

Malvolio strode forward and I instinctively shrunk away from him.

"No, no, no," he said. "That's not right. We had a bit of a tiff and we were kissing and making up when you arrived. That's all. There's no problem."

So he *did* do it on purpose.

"Liar!" I sobbed. "I told you to stop and you wouldn't let go!" I let the tears fall and didn't bother wiping them away.

Sarkozy stepped forward. "Okay, now. I will need to take your statement, Miss Callista." He looked very uncomfortable. "So you're saying he was making advances without your consent?"

"Yes—"

"No, I wasn't," Malvolio countered, stepping forward again. "We are a couple — engaged, in fact — we were kissing and making up, like I said before—"

"Liar!" I shouted. The pain made my knees feel weak. My face felt cold. "And we're *not* engaged! We're not even together anymore!"

CHAPTER 15
Please Don't Leave Him Here with Me

"Now, Miss Callista, please calm down. Mr Dermid, you will have your chance to speak." Sarkozy turned to the other officer. "Parker, can you take Mr Dermid into the other room to speak to him further?"

Relief rushed through me.

"Yes, sir," came the quick reply. I couldn't help thinking Parker's voice didn't match his appearance. He was a short, stocky man and his voice was a strong, deep baritone.

Parker escorted a protesting Malvolio into my bedroom and I watched the door slide closed behind them. The next room wasn't far enough away, as far as I was concerned.

Take him to the nearest moon! I thought angrily.

I wished it wasn't my bedroom they were in. The thought of Malvolio being in my room right now creeped me out. Now that I knew the real Malvolio, it gave me goose bumps to think I'd been intimate with such a monster.

I had to push those thoughts from my head as Sarkozy asked more questions and wrote down the details. I was light-headed and asked him if I could sit down, so we moved to the lounge chairs.

I felt awkward and embarrassed when he asked about when I'd hit Malvolio back, but I answered truthfully, adding that I didn't know why I'd done it and that I'd never hit anyone before in my life.

Which made me ask myself again, why did I do it?

Maybe I'd finally had enough of him yelling at me. Maybe I was fed up with him insulting the best friend I'd ever had. And the accusations he threw at me without any proof.

Even still, that wasn't enough to warrant hitting him. I was so surprised by my actions, but I was also worried. It scared me that I'd even lashed out at him.

As I spoke to Sarkozy, I stressed the fact that everything was not fine between us and that I had fears for my safety if they left him here with me when they left. He said he could see the bruises forming on my face and I told him again about my ribs and that I thought that they were broken.

"Do you want to go to the station's Medical Facility?"

I felt a sinking feeling inside. I couldn't do that. I wasn't sure why I didn't want to go there, but just the thought of it had me wanting to run and hide somewhere. Maybe I didn't want to have to answer the hundreds of questions they would ask me. It was hard enough talking to one person about it. It felt humiliating and seemed to me to be such an invasion of privacy. "No, not right now," I told him, "I will see someone tomorrow. Thank you."

"Are you sure?" he asked, and I could see genuine concern in his eyes. "You look so pale. I could call and arrange it..."

"Yes, I'm sure," I assured him, "I couldn't face it now. I promise I will go there tomorrow. Thanks." I plastered a smile on my face and hoped he would leave it at that.

"I will put that in my report and they will be expecting you," he told me. I could see by his expression that he meant for me to go or he would be coming back to see me. Then he asked me a few questions to see if I was coherent, just in case I had a concussion. I could answer all questions correctly, except when he asked me how old I was. My mind drew a blank. I told him it was probably because I didn't really care about my age. Sarkozy didn't look convinced, but he didn't say anything more, just wrote a note on it on his Palm-pad.

I was relieved when he strode over and knocked briefly on my bedroom door and when it opened, he asked Parker if he had finished with his questioning.

"Yes, sir."

They left Malvolio in my room and spoke in hushed voices near the front door. I tried to eavesdrop, with no success.

They glanced at me a few times, which made me feel awkward and self-conscious. I twirled a lock of my hair around my finger and waited.

I winced when my fingers revealed some swelling around my left eye. *Oh, great...*

I looked back at the two Enforcers. *Please don't leave him here with me...* I begged silently.

If they believed his story and tried to leave without taking him out of here, I would demand that they get him out. If they didn't listen, I'd do something to make them lock me up. I would do anything to avoid being left here with that madman...

Once they'd finished speaking, they approached Malvolio and told him he was under arrest. I sighed heavily and felt some of the tension leave my tightly-wound shoulders as they put cuffs on him, but the pain in my side made me whimper.

The officers looked around.

"I moved too suddenly and hurt my ribs," I said, pointing to my ribs like an idiot.

I saw their concerned expressions, so I assured them again that I was okay. "I *will* go to see a doctor in the morning."

That seemed to satisfy them. They said their goodbyes and turned to leave. It felt good to see Malvolio being led out in handcuffs, even with him giving me a death-glare.

—— ⋆·☆·⋆ ——

After a rough night with virtually no sleep, I finally drifted off, only to be woken by my alarm at 0630.

I groaned when I heard it, but didn't make a move to get up. I lay there for a few moments listening to the music and wishing I could stay in bed because I felt so tired. Why did I feel so tired?

The events of last night flooded my mind and tears stung my eyes. The argument. Malvolio hitting me. And kicking me... I still couldn't believe he'd done it. What a despicable thing to do.

I didn't need the alarm though. There was no way I was going to work. Yesterday was already a disaster and today... today was for recovering. And visiting the doctor.

My heart clenched as I thought of how much I'd messed up yesterday. I'd jeopardised Javolo's safety when I couldn't concentrate. I couldn't deal with that right now.

Then without warning, a feeling of being overwhelmed hit me and tears ran down my cheeks. It was all too much. My life had changed in an instant and everything was turned on its head.

Crying was too painful, so I forced myself to stop. I had to think of something else. The creek near my home on Azaeli. The peaceful sound of running water and the smell of the damp earth after the rain. I took a few slow breaths.

It was too early for me to call work, so I decided I would set my alarm again for 0730 and call them then.

Reaching over to turn off the alarm caused me to yelp as the pain seared through my right side. Taking some careful deep breaths, I managed to kill the alarm. With the press of another button, I was able to switch to voice command mode to set a new alarm time.

Carefully settling myself back down onto the mattress, I thought maybe I should have gone to the Medical Facility the night before, but then had to remind myself that if my ribs were broken — and I was sure now that they were — there was little they could do for me anyway. They would only bandage my ribs and tell me to take it easy.

And give you some stronger painkillers too, you idiot!

The painkillers I'd taken last night were useless. I'd suffered in pain all night, just for the sake of avoiding awkward questions. I'd only treated my eye and the side of my face with some bruise cream and crawled into bed after the Enforcers took Malvolio away. Crying had been painful. And of course I didn't fall asleep once I'd stopped crying. I'd just lain awake.

Sighing, I closed my eyes and tried to go back to sleep.

When the alarm sounded the second time, I didn't want to get up. I hadn't slept at all. I couldn't. I'd stared at the ceiling, thinking. Once I'd made my way to my dresser at a snail's pace, I looked in the mirror.

My eye and cheek looked terrible. I'd put ice on them the night before and used a bruise cream, but because I hadn't done anything immediately after it happened, it was swollen and the colours had already established themselves around my left eye and across my cheek.

My blue eyes made the colours in the bruises stand out more.

Great.

I had to remind myself that I didn't put ice on it right after it happened because I couldn't even get up off the floor.

I stared at my reflection. It looked like I hadn't slept for a week.

I knew the bruises would have been worse without the bruise cream and I wondered how well it would work on my ribs. It wasn't meant for broken bones, but it could probably help reduce the pain and bruising. It was worth a try. I wished I'd thought of it sooner.

I carefully lifted up the dress I was still wearing from the night before and could see dark purple, with some splashes of yellow. I winced.

Taking the dress off was painful, but I had to do it.

As I was putting the bruise cream on and wincing with the pain, I caught sight of my digital photo frame that was perched on my dresser. It was set to show a different picture each day and today's photo was of me with my mother. It was taken at the beach when I was fifteen. We looked so happy. How had my life become so hard and so complicated so quickly?

I sighed and put a hand on the dresser to steady myself. Wishing my life could be as happy and carefree as it had when the picture was taken was a waste of time. The only thing I could do now was to go to the doctor and start myself on the road to recovery.

I dressed — carefully — and headed out to the Vid to make the call to work and to get ready to go out.

With the fast-acting cream, the bruising would clear up within a few days from my face. I would have to be off work 'sick' till then. My ribs were another story, but no one would see them.

Everything kept going around in my mind. I didn't know how long Malvolio would be locked up for, but the thought of him strolling back into my home turned my legs to jelly. "Computer?"

The computer's voice answered instantly. "Yes, Lennina?"

"Remove Malvolio Dermid's entry rights from the security system."

"Yes, Lennina. Command completed."

A flood of relief made me feel warm. Now he couldn't just walk in here without my permission.

The scans had showed that I had three broken ribs and as I thought, they just wrapped a bandage around my ribcage and told me to try not to move too much so I could give it a chance to heal. They had also given me some painkillers that were stronger than the ones I had at home, and they worked well. I kicked myself again for not going the night before.

While I was there, they gave me my monthly blood test, which was mandatory for all personnel to test for any contaminants in our blood due to being on a space station close to The Fringe. The Fringe was what we called the edge of the Explored Universe.

Because of the blow to the head I'd received, the nurse gave me some information on concussions so I knew what kind of symptoms to look out for, and then the questions really started. I told them everything and tried not to leave anything out. I told them that the Enforcers had already been involved and I'd given them a statement. And that Malvolio had been hauled off.

They were able to look up the Enforcers' report on their computer system and added their reports to it. At least there would be a record of me coming in to see the doctor, so Sarkozy wouldn't be paying me a visit later for breaking my promise.

When they'd finally finished with me, I headed out, feeling humiliated and sick. I went straight back home, ate something, and climbed into bed. Thinking about what had happened caused the tears to start. I managed to curb them before I actually started crying. I already knew that crying was not a good idea.

Eventually, I dozed. After a while though, if I moved too much, the pain would flare up again. The painkillers must have been wearing off.

I'd finally given up and made myself something to eat. From there, I tried to watch a HoloMovie to take my mind off things. It didn't work. My brain wouldn't shut down and relax. I couldn't remember any of what I'd just watched.

Stupid brain.

As I stood up to stretch and work out the stiffness in my limbs, the door chime rang. There was a sinking feeling in the pit of my stomach and a coldness spread throughout my body.

Could it be him?

CHAPTER 16
Open This Door! NOW!

They didn't say how long he'd be locked up for. Maybe they meant overnight. I couldn't move. Couldn't even bring myself to call out to ask who it was.

It rang a second time. Still, I couldn't move. What if it was the Enforcers? Maybe they wanted to ask more questions. I needed to see who it was. But I couldn't. The door camera would tell me who was there, but my feet seemed anchored to the floor.

It started ringing continuously. It was definitely Malvolio. No one else was that childish.

"Lennina! Lenninaa!" he bellowed. "I know you're in there! Why am I locked out? Open this door!"

My back stiffened and I felt my eyes go wide. Panic clawed its way into my brain.

What am I going to do?

Tears stung my eyes and my mind was in overdrive.

Get it together... focus... He can't get in... What can I do?

I thought of calling the Enforcers. They would protect me. They could take him away if he wouldn't leave.

That should've been my first thought. I was panicking for nothing.

I took a deep breath to calm my nerves and told the Home Computer to call the Enforcers. They told me they would dispatch someone right away. I thanked them and asked them to hurry. All the while, Malvolio bellowed at me from outside.

The tension in my body was making me feel like a tightly-wound spring. I pressed my fingers to my temples in an attempt to relieve some of the pressure.

I checked the console to make sure the voice commands for the Home Computer were on. Then I realised how stupid that was. I'd just used voice commands to call the Enforcers.

"Lennina! I know you're there! Let me in! Why won't you let me in? It's him, isn't it? He's in there with you, isn't he?"

No! Go away!

I realised I was holding my breath and let it out slowly. *All I have to do is hang tight till they get here…*

"Lenninaaa!"

I started to chew my nails and then stopped myself. And frowned. I hadn't chewed my nails since I was twelve.

"Lenninaaaa!" he bawled.

Leave me alone! There was no way I was going to answer him. *I can't deal with this. Where are they?*

"I know you're in there with him! Now let me in! You're mine! I'll rip his head off!"

What did he think was happening in here? Javolo was at work. I should be at work. If I'd gone to work with broken ribs, would he still be out there yelling for me to let him in? Probably.

I started pacing the floor, only partly aware that I was doing it. Waiting for the Enforcers was utter torture. I kept thinking he would somehow get in before they arrived. I knew it was impossible for a human to be able to break through the door, but that knowledge didn't help. My hand went automatically to my cheek when he started bashing harder on the door. I traced the swollen area with my fingers.

"Let me in!" he demanded. "We still need to talk!"

No, we don't!

I desperately wanted to tell him to go away and leave me alone, but forced myself to keep my mouth shut. I knew answering him would make things worse and the Enforcers had told me to keep quiet and wait. Putting my hand over my mouth helped.

"Lenninaaa! Open this door! NOW!"

I ran my fingers nervously through my hair and wished he would stop calling my name. It was grating on my nerves.

Where are they? I thought desperately.

I made myself stop pacing and stood in the middle of the kitchen.

I heard the Enforcers arrive and breathed a sigh of relief. I padded over to the door and listened, but could only hear muffled voices. Then I remembered I would be able to see what was going on outside on my security screen. I pressed the power button, but it didn't turn on. I tried a few more times.

Great. I'll have to get The Company people to fix it.

The last thing I needed right now was a failure in my security system.

The voices grew louder. I heard them tell him he couldn't come over after what had happened last night. He started swearing and protesting loudly. Big surprise. They threatened to lock him up again if he didn't leave immediately.

"But she's in there with another man. Cheating on me."

"We've scanned the apartment. There is only one life form inside," one of the Enforcers told him.

He finally left and I was able to open the door for the Enforcers. It was the officers from the night before. They took some details about what had happened this time and I made sure I told them I'd been down to the Medical Facility, adding that I had three broken ribs.

"Sorry to hear that, Ma'am. We're here if you need us." Sarkozy said.

"Thank you."

"Call us if he returns," Parker said.

I smiled. "I will. Thanks again."

They started to go, but Sarkozy turned back to me. "I'm glad you went down to get yourself checked out. It's a relief to hear it's only some broken ribs."

Only? I asked myself, but then I thought, *It could've been worse.*

Sarkozy and Parker had probably seen much worse...

I said goodbye to them both again as they walked away.

I was relieved that Malvolio had left without too much trouble, but I knew I hadn't heard the end of it. He wasn't going to leave me alone; that I was sure of.

What was I going to do? Surely I couldn't just sit around and wait for the next time. I decided I would call the Enforcers in the morning and ask them what my options were. I couldn't face doing it tonight; all I wanted to do was curl up in bed. So, after eating something for an early dinner, that's exactly what I did.

———— ⋆·☆·⋆ ————

I sat in my favourite lounge chair staring at nothing. I'd woken up feeling like I hadn't slept for days. It had been another restless night, even with the stronger painkillers. Maybe I could expect to not be able to sleep a full night until the broken bones healed.

How long did the doctor say? I couldn't remember, but I did recall him saying it takes a lot longer than usual because the ribcage moved with each breath, making it almost impossible for the bones to knit back together. Somehow, though, the human body managed it. Nature never ceased to amaze me.

I'd notified work and stayed home again. I tried to rest, but that left room for thinking. I didn't want to think. My mind played everything over and over on a loop. I needed something to do.

I'd tried to sit and play something relaxing on my keyboard, but it was too hard to concentrate or be inspired to make music when my mind was in turmoil.

I wish I had someone to talk to! I thought to myself.

That brought Javolo to mind immediately. He was always good for a laugh and a decent conversation. I really didn't care about the increasing amount of trouble and lectures about company policy. It was worth it just to have some enthusiasm and humour in an otherwise dull job.

The sadness crept in. Javolo was my rock. Malvolio had only been in my life for a short time, but I realised now that he wasn't really someone I could count on for support or good conversation. I'd thought that both men were keeping me sane this far from my home and my family, but it had only been one.

Malvolio was not the man I thought he was. It only proved to me what I'd known all along. Men didn't stick around. They didn't take their responsibilities seriously enough and eventually, they left.

Malvolio was no different than my father. Well, except my father didn't hit my mother. I thought that Malvolio would be different. I thought I could keep our relationship together. I'd failed.

Is this how Mum felt?

I pushed those thoughts away. They were not making me feel any better.

I thought about Javolo and what he'd be doing now. He'd be hard at work, watching the clock and waiting for his lunch break. I wondered how he was getting along with the other Nav Operator. Probably Salvani again.

I felt a twinge of jealousy run through me at the thought of Salvani enjoying his company, while I was stuck at home with no one to talk to and nothing to do but sit and wait around. Then I felt stupid for even feeling that way. But I needed someone to talk to so desperately.

If I could just spend like half an hour on the Com... that would do me for the day — maybe even two days...

That made me sound like an addict. Was I addicted to good conversation, or to Javolo?

The Vid rang out its tune, making me jump and hurt my ribs. My heart sank.

Now he's calling me?

CHAPTER 17

You Need to Come Home!

"Computer. Identify caller."

"Caller: Myesha Callista," it droned in its monotone voice.

Mum!

"Answer." I nearly fell over in my haste to get to the Vid. This was exactly what I needed right now.

My mother's face appeared on the screen and her smile turned to alarm. "Lennina! What happened to your face?"

My breath caught. I'd forgotten about my black eye. "I..." I couldn't lie. "Um. I'm not seeing Malvolio anymore."

I scolded myself for not being able to come out and say what happened.

"What? Did he do that to you?"

"Yes." I looked down at my feet as heat burned my cheeks.

"Oh, my stars!" When I looked back up, tears trailed down her cheeks. "I... What did... You need to... You need to come home!"

"I can't, Mum. I have a two-year contract."

"Forget the contract! You can't stay there."

"Mum. It's okay. I called the Enforcers and they arrested him."

She seemed to calm down at that, but then Adamo stepped in front of the Vid and all the questions started again. I told them what happened and that Malvolio had to keep away from me or risk trouble with the Enforcers.

I was going to tell them about my broken ribs, but they'd already reacted badly, so I kept quiet. Knowing my mother, she'd be on the next flight out here.

They settled down after I'd said he'd be in trouble if he came here, but I could see they weren't happy.

I told them about other stuff that had happened since last time they'd called — which wasn't much — and they even asked how Javolo was going. Neither of them had been enthusiastic about me seeing Malvolio, but they both liked to hear about Javolo and our conversations over the Com.

I told them about him seeing a pretty girl at the restaurant and my mother winced, which was weird. I ignored it and changed the subject.

"You're getting so tall," I told Adamo. He towered over Mum and it looked like he'd grown an inch or two since I'd left. I was glad she wasn't living alone while I was here working.

Her lips pursed together in a straight line. "If you won't come home—"

"Mum. I can't come home."

"—then I want you to get an RO against that monster."

"Mum—"

"Just promise me."

"Okay." A Restriction Order was actually a good idea. "I will do it tomorrow."

Adamo leaned in closer. "You better make sure you do, or I'm coming over there."

I had no doubts that he would.

"It would take you a week to get here."

"I don't care. Anything for my little sister."

"Hey! I'm older than you!"

"You're still my little sister."

I chuckled.

We talked for a while longer, then they had to go. We said our goodbyes and I assured them that I'd apply for the RO in the morning.

———— ⋆·☆·⋆ ————

I'd fallen asleep on one of the lounge chairs and was startled awake by the Vid's call. I yelped as the movement sent a ripping pain through me. The adrenalin rushed through my veins and my heartbeat quickened. It wouldn't be my mother this time.

I couldn't ignore the call, though. It could be the Enforcers or even someone from work, so I commanded the Vid to identify the caller again.

"Caller: Malvolio Dermid," it said.

I almost swore out loud. Then I thought that if I had, the computer might have mistaken that for the command to answer. I'd have to be careful. I didn't give any other commands — I let it ring.

It soon stopped and I sighed with relief.

It was short-lived. And, of course, it was him again. What could I do? How could I get away from him? How could I stop him from calling me?

"Computer. Block all calls from Malvolio Dermid."

"Sorry, Lennina. That command is not authorised."

Of course it wasn't. I guessed I would have to call someone from The Company and put in a formal request for something like that. But that was stupid. Why did I need authorisation for my own privacy?

It rang again.

"Sound off!" I commanded when I couldn't stand to listen to it any-more.

—— ⋆·☆·⋆ ——

The next morning, I called the Enforcers and told them what was happening and that I wanted to apply for a Restriction Order. The woman transferred me to another section that dealt specifically with Restriction Orders.

The operator explained how it would place restrictions on Malvolio so he couldn't call me or come to the apartment. I could extend it further so that he was not allowed within fifty metres of me at any time. I wasted no time in organising it.

My mind was reeling with all the information she'd given me and the implications of having to put legal restrictions on a person that had said he loved me.

It was all so surreal... and so *wrong*. How did this even *happen?*

The next piece of advice was to change the number for my Vid and list it as private. I thanked the woman and ended the call. My next call was to the Vid service.

I was glad I only had one Vid number to worry about changing. Well, technically, that wasn't true. Malvolio had insisted on me getting a personal Com and had bought one for me. I hadn't had a personal Com of my own because they were so expensive. The Company didn't supply us with one — no surprise there — and I didn't want them to be able to contact me day and night anyway, so I was happy to not have one.

Malvolio wouldn't hear of it of course, but after he'd bought it for me, I would deliberately leave it at home so I couldn't be harassed. He wasn't happy about it, but I needed time to myself sometimes.

I didn't get the personal Com's number changed; I didn't plan on ever turning it on again. I'd have to find a way to return it to Malvolio without actually seeing him.

There were only three people back home that had my number here on the station — my mother, my brother, and my friend, Mazuma. I'd send them a text-only message to notify them of my change of number. There was no need inform anyone else. Company records would automatically update, so the next time work needed to contact me, they would get through with no problems.

After writing down my new number and sending the three texts, I sent a request for someone to look at my security screen for the front door, then I finally felt like I could relax. I headed for the shower, feeling numb.

I thought about how pitiful it was that the only people I kept in contact with from home were my family and Mazuma. I didn't have any really close friends there. Mazuma was a friend, but not someone I could completely confide in. I'd always been a bit of a loner and kept some distance between us. I didn't mean to do it, and she understood.

Why? I asked myself as I got undressed and removed the bandage. *Why am I such a loner? Why don't I have any friends I can rely on and pour my heart out to? I need to get out more and meet people, but not Malvolio's snobby friends. I need to find people who are genuine.*

I stepped into the cubicle and let the warm water rinse away some of the stress. It was hard to shower and so hard to relax when the jets of water hurt my ribs so much. I manually closed some of them and stood so no water sprayed directly on that area. That made it a bit more bearable.

I thought again about my loner existence. It had been enough for me to concentrate on my studies and strive for a good career, but since coming to the station and getting to know Javolo, something had changed. I was restless when I was on my own now and I often felt like I needed someone to talk to.

Malvolio didn't really fill that need because I couldn't talk about just anything with him. A lot of the time, he talked about himself, his work and The Company's great accomplishments on the station and on Kronos. And that got very boring very quickly.

I'd changed over the last few months and right now, I felt like I was alone in the universe with no one to talk to, even when I was with Malvolio and his friends, which just felt wrong.

Javolo had changed me. Had made me feel alive. I now craved company — mainly *his* company — but still...

And I no longer wanted to be a loner.

—— ⋆·☆·⋆ ——

The silence was heavenly. The Vid hadn't made a sound since Katoa changed the number.

There'd been no one coming to my door. After a few hours I felt like I should fill the silence.

My keyboard stood in the corner of the lounge room. I'd hardly touched it lately. The stress had taken over and drowned my creativity. I tiptoed over and sat down. I flipped the switch and my hands found their place on the keys.

I started with some slow songs, just getting the emotions flowing through me. The music took me away from this tin can and back to my favourite place back on Azaeli. The movement of the trees. The sound of the running water. The smell of the flowers. I let it overwhelm my senses.

Once I'd finished, I felt relaxed and my heart soared. I should play music every day. Nothing compared when it came to relieving stress and lifting my mood.

I just needed a nice hot cup of tea now and maybe a book to read.

As I put some water on to boil, I realised I couldn't keep pushing my thoughts away and distracting myself. Maybe I needed to face this thing head-on.

Okay, so one thing I did know was that I was never going to fall for

Malvolio's lies again. All that stuff before dinner about loving me had to be lies.

If you love someone, you don't assault them.

I didn't ever want to see him again, but it was probably impossible, even though it was a large space station with thousands of inhabitants. He would make sure I ran into him.

We didn't work at the same place and I knew all the places he frequented, so I could avoid them.

The next thing I needed to do was decide if I was going to stick it out here till my two years were up, or go home. I really wanted to go home, but thoughts of Javolo had me hesitating. I couldn't leave without at least having a way to contact him outside of work.

Just as I resolved to get his details no matter what, the door chime made me jump and I yelped. The Home Computer told me it was Malvolio. I felt all the tension return to my muscles. In five seconds, he'd undone everything I'd achieved.

CHAPTER 18
I Should Just Stay Single

I thought of calling the Enforcers, but decided to wait to see if he gave up and went away. After all, he would know he's not allowed to come here because of the RO.

I decided to give it five minutes. If he wasn't gone, I'd call them.

He gave up after three.

—— ⋆·☆·⋆ ——

Looking in the mirror the next morning, I could see that the bruising on my face was almost gone, but it was still noticeable. That would have to do.

I winced at the memory. I still couldn't believe it. Things like that only happened to other people. You heard about it and shook your head and made a comment about how terrible it was. People never think anything bad will happen to them. Until it does.

I pushed those thoughts from my mind and looked ahead to my day. I'd already decided I was getting out of the apartment. I couldn't stand the thought of staying indoors again by myself today.

I had to chuckle at that. On a space station, everything was indoors. Getting out of the apartment and walking down to the shopping district was as close as I could get to going outside. There were wide open spaces at the park and the trees even had birds living in amongst their branches. I walked past it every day on my way to the shops or to work.

I put my sunglasses on. They wouldn't look out of place as the lighting and temperature on the station were set to simulate Summer.

It was mid-morning and I assumed Malvolio would be working, so there should be no chance of running into him.

I'd played some songs on my keyboard and felt uplifted, so I set out with a determined attitude and felt a sense of freedom.

It was a rostered day off for Javolo and I, so had been no need for me to call in sick today.

While wandering around some of the stores, I remembered something my mother had told me many times about how clothes shopping is the cure for any sort of depression, anxiety, sadness, or when you were just feeling down.

It had never worked for me. Shopping had always been more like a chore than a fun day out. Despite that fact, I slowly browsed through some shops and bought a couple of blouses. I preferred to wear pants than dresses — something Malvolio didn't like — but I never let it stop me. I wore dresses when we went out to dinner, but that was about it.

It still amazed me that when Jace had dumped me, one of the reasons was because I was too boyish. I couldn't understand why that was such a big issue for him.

I'd been devastated because there had been no warning. He hadn't even hinted at the fact that he wasn't happy. And when I found out he was seeing another girl? Well, that was it for me.

I sighed.

Why do I even bother anymore? I should just stay single.

That was exactly what I planned to do. I squared my shoulders. I needed to keep focused. I would quit this dead-end job and put all my efforts into getting a job in Research and Development at a better company. No more distractions. No more getting hurt.

I had to stop shopping after only half an hour as the pain kept increasing, which only made my stress levels rise.

It didn't work this time either, Mum...

Maybe I should have gone to the Observation Deck instead. The sense of calm that always flooded through me as I looked at the planet below us and the surrounding blackness of space made me feel at one with the universe.

I exited the store, shaking my head. As I popped a painkiller into my mouth, I thought I saw someone from the corner of my eye in the shadows, watching me. My heart skipped a beat and when I looked back, a man ducked around a corner. I couldn't see his face or make out who he was.

What if it was Malvolio? What would I do if it was? What would he do? Would he cause a scene in the middle of the street? Or would he take me back home?

My heart was racing. I had to make a conscious effort to slow my breathing.

It could have been anyone. Malvolio should have been at work.

He had no reason to be wandering around women's clothing stores at this hour of the day. I was getting paranoid.

Pull yourself together, Lennina.

I looked around. Everyone was going about their business. They were totally oblivious to my situation and it only made me feel worse. My throat felt tight. I looked back to where I'd seen the man walking away. He had the same colour hair, but that didn't mean it was Malvolio.

It couldn't have been him. The chances of him being in the area were slim to none.

Unless he was stalking me.

I looked at all the faces of the people walking by and the people sitting at the tables in the courtyard before me. I wanted to scream. How did my life get like this? Why couldn't I be normal like everyone else? I wanted my life back the way it was, not having to look over my shoulder every five minutes to see if I was being followed by a stalker.

Listing all the reasons why it couldn't be Malvolio wasn't working and the tight feeling around my throat and chest wasn't going to go away, so I decided the only way I'd feel better would be to go straight home. At least I could hide inside and call the Enforcers if he showed up. Out here in the open, I didn't feel safe anymore, even with the lunch-time crowd. I took a deep breath and let it out slowly and started walking.

As I weaved my way across the courtyard, I had the creepy feeling someone was watching me. I looked over my shoulder, the adrenalin pumping.

Nothing. *Good.*

As I turned back, I tripped on something and fell forward, hitting my left elbow on a table on the way down. Pain shot up my arm and was joined by a ripping pain that tore through my ribs once I hit the hard ground, making me cry out.

CHAPTER 19

What Just Happened?

I turned over quickly onto my butt so I could take the weight off my arm as the pain made its way from my elbow to my shoulder. Could my day get any worse?

I lifted my arm up and cradled it in my right hand, but it didn't help. There was a sharp stabbing sensation in my ribs and elbow, and the pain slowly spread down toward my wrist, followed by a creepy kind of numbness.

Tears streamed down my face. My sunglasses were gone. They'd crashed to the ground somewhere when I fell. So much for hiding the bruises.

I felt panic take hold at the thought that my arm could be broken too, then anger followed. What had I tripped on? Had someone left something out in the walkway? What if my arm *was* broken? It hurt so much that I thought it could be. My breathing was shallow and I felt light-headed.

I blinked away tears to see what had caused me to fall. There was a shopping bag filled with clothing lying on its side next to me, the contents spilling out onto the paved ground. The other bags nearby were mine.

I tried sucking in some deep breaths to stop the panic taking over, but my ribs screamed in protest. It took a lot of effort not to cry out again.

It felt like I was in a vacuum with no air left. I needed air.

I was feeling cold and started to shake. Everything sounded far away and kind of muffled. That wasn't a good sign. Maybe I was going into shock.

I needed to stop all my panicked thoughts. They were making things worse.

I realised someone was asking if I was okay.

I was dazed as I looked at the pair of booted feet in front of me. Definitely male.

Am I okay? I thought. "No, I'm *not* okay."

I blinked away more tears so I could see who it was. I saw his legs bend and he knelt down onto one knee.

My eyes travelled up from his knees to his torso, the well-muscled chest and arms under his shirt and up to his face. "I think you've broken my..." I found myself looking into the most intense green eyes I'd ever seen and I suddenly forgot how to speak. I just stared like a total moron. Then my brain kicked back into gear. "Arm," I finished lamely.

Those eyes were... wow... such a rich shade of green... and he had full lips... high cheekbones...

I was sitting there with my mouth hanging open. I closed it and tried to focus instead on what he was saying.

"... so sorry. I didn't realise my bag was sticking out that far. I am such an idiot!"

Yeah. You are.

He looked down. "Can I have a look at your arm?"

I shrunk away from him, my anger returning. Besides the fact that I'd been ogling him, which made me feel like a dork, I didn't want him anywhere near me. This was his fault.

"What do you think you're doing, leaving stuff out in the walkway for people to trip on?" I blurted out before I could stop myself. "I think my arm is broken!" And on cue, the pain increased.

Those perfect green eyes widened. "I really am sorry. Please let me have a look."

New tears streamed down my cheeks. I looked into his pleading eyes and I could see his genuine concern. My heart softened. I nodded and lifted it up so we both could inspect it. There was no hiding how much I was shaking and it took some effort to keep my arm up while we looked it over. There was a large cut across my elbow that was bleeding slowly, and it had dripped down over my right hand. The pain was becoming unbearable and more tears welled up in my eyes.

It was weird. I wasn't crying, but the tears kept coming.

"Let's get you up onto a seat so I can get a good look at it," he suggested and offered me a hand to help me up.

I looked at the outstretched hand, and back up to his face, but didn't take him up on his offer. I was still too angry to accept his help. Plus, I didn't even know him.

He smiled. "Come on. I don't bite."

I looked at his hand again. There was nothing intimidating about the offer of his help. There was a warmth in his smile and I realised I was being stubborn, so I nodded. I couldn't talk. My brain had forgotten how. Again. He was so... strikingly beautiful.

As soon as that thought entered my head, I scolded myself for thinking about how good looking he was at a time like this.

You could have a broken arm, and you're checking him out? You've lost your mind!

I put out my right hand to take his, but it was covered in blood, so I quickly withdrew it, mortified. He grabbed hold of my right arm at the elbow and wrist instead to help me up.

As soon as he touched me, I felt something like a jolt of electricity run up my arm, which made me jump and sent stabbing pains through my side. I let out a sort of yelp, which made him let go. The sensation itself didn't really hurt, but it was unexpected and felt kind of eerie and... unnatural. I pictured my rib bones slicing into my flesh from the sudden movement. It only served to make me feel nauseous.

Think about something else!

What could have caused the electricity? I'd never felt such an intense static shock before. It was like a mini lightning bolt running up my arm.

"Did you feel that?" I asked as I looked up at him.

Then I felt silly. It was probably static electricity. It had passed from him to me and he probably didn't even feel it.

He leaned closer to me, eyes wide. "Yes."

It was just a whisper.

I looked deep into those green eyes and goose bumps spread across my body. The hairs on the back of my neck stood up.

What just happened?

CHAPTER 20

Green Eyes

I realised I was staring again and looked away.

When I finally looked back, he was looking at the bruises on my face. I could see the concern in his eyes. I winced. I didn't want him to see the bruises. Didn't want him to know how I'd gotten them. I didn't want anyone to know. I didn't want all the attention and the questions. Heat flushed my cheeks.

He opened his mouth, then closed it. "Let's try that again," he suggested, and I nodded.

This time the zap was mild, and a buzzing, tingly feeling spread throughout my body from where he was touching me.

I managed to get to my feet and as we headed toward the nearest seat, I felt light-headed from the pain and my legs started to give way underneath me. The nausea came back with a vengeance.

He quickly changed his grip so I wouldn't hit the ground again. "Hey, I got you..." His breath tickled my ear as he spoke, sending a shiver down my spine. But it was a good kind of shiver.

I'm an idiot.

He put a hand under my left arm and supported me as I walked the last two steps to the seat.

He had no trouble supporting my weight, and I could feel the firm muscles in his arms as he guided me to the seat and sat me down. Then he picked up my bags and placed them on the seat next to mine.

What was happening to me? Why was I feeling these weird electric and tingling sensations and why did I feel so terrible? Why couldn't I manage to walk a few steps?

Just too much pain... I answered myself as my head started to spin. I was never really good when it came to pain. I'd fainted a couple of times in the past when I'd hurt myself.

It didn't explain the weird lightning thing though... I couldn't think of a reason for that. Static electricity caused a momentary jolt, not the buzzing and tingling I felt while he was touching me.

I took some slow deep breaths to try to ward off the possibility of fainting. Or throwing up.

As I sat, I scanned the ground for my sunglasses, but couldn't see them anywhere. I wanted to put them back on to hide my bruises and wondered if they were broken. They were probably scratched so much that they would be useless now anyway.

The guy moved his empty plate and cup aside, pulled some serviettes from the dispenser on the table and used them to wipe up the blood on my arm. Then he gave me a few more to wipe my hand. After another inspection of my arm and asking me to move it around, he decided it wasn't broken.

I had a closer look. The table had hit the bony part of my elbow and split the skin, but I didn't think it needed stitches, just those little butterfly strips to hold it together. My wrist and elbow weren't swollen. It was only puffy-looking around the cut. Knowing it probably wasn't broken didn't dull the pain at all, but did make me feel a whole lot better. I took some more deep breaths.

I couldn't help looking at him while he looked down at my arm. His dark lashes hid his green eyes and his strong jaw was clean-shaven. He had a straight nose and kind of full lips for a guy, but it didn't make him look girly. His short black hair was curly and parts of his fringe hung down over his forehead.

Damn. I was staring at him again. I pulled my gaze away, hoping he didn't notice.

"Is everything okay here?" I gave a start and looked up to see a young woman dressed in a uniform and apron and realised she was one of the waitresses from the restaurant we were sitting outside of.

"Yes... umm... thank you," I stammered. "I tripped over and hit my arm on the edge of the table."

"Is it okay?" I nodded as she leaned in to take a closer look. "Well, if there's anything you need, just give me a call. My name is Lani." She straightened up and smiled sweetly.

"Okay, I will. Thanks again." I said. I couldn't help smiling back, even though it was the last thing I felt like doing at that moment.

"Yes, thank you, Lani," Green Eyes said as she took his plate and cup and turned away.

I looked up at him as he gave the waitress a genuine smile. His eyes shone as he turned his gaze back to me and I looked down at my arm to avoid his gaze. I'd already stared at him way too much.

Green Eyes grabbed another serviette and dabbed at the wound as more blood had started oozing out. "Hold this in place and put some pressure on it," he instructed. I nodded and pressed on the spot he'd indicated.

I didn't know where to look; I didn't want to stare at him, but my gaze kept coming back to his face.

My emotions were overwhelming me, engulfing me, and I felt like I was drowning.

Why did this happen? I can't even go for a walk to the shops without something going wrong... Nothing is going right...

With everything that had happened to me with Malvolio, and now this, I felt I was sinking with no way to keep my head above water.

I looked up at the stranger and he was still looking at my arm. He asked me to lift both arms and hold them up so he could compare their sizes. I lifted them slowly and as he looked at them, tears started rolling down my cheeks again. I couldn't help it. I tried to stop myself, not wanting to be crying in front of him, but failed miserably. He didn't notice while he was inspecting my arms. "There's no swelling... That's good."

He suddenly bent down toward the ground and came back up with my sunglasses in his hand. "Uh, you dropped these..."

I took them from his hand and opened my mouth to thank him, but the words wouldn't come out.

His eyebrows went up when he noticed the tears. "Hey, it's not that bad," he said as I put the glasses back on. I knew it was too late, of course — he'd already seen the bruising on my face — but I still wanted to cover it up. "It's just a bump and bruise, really. You'll be right as rain in a day or two..."

"Yes... I know." I remembered to put pressure on my elbow again. "But it's not just the arm. It's just..." Tears kept streaming down my face.

"Oh." He nodded. "I'm sorry. Guess I've just made a bad day worse... I should of been more careful... I'm such a bonehead... I am truly sorry..."

I could see he meant every word. His eyes were sincere, which made me think of Malvolio. Had I ever seen real sincerity in his eyes?

That thought brought more tears.

"Hey..." Green Eyes said as he reached out a hand to me across the table, but stopped himself. Was it because of the electric feeling we'd felt when he'd touched me before? Or was it that he realised he was being a bit too forward?

He looked into my eyes, searching for something. Was it forgiveness, or a sign that I was alright? Or maybe both?

"I know we've just met," he told me, "but if you'd like to talk about it, I'm all ears." He leaned forward in his seat and his eyes darted briefly to the bruises that would be peeking out from under the sunglasses. "Sometimes there are things you can't talk to friends or family about, and it can help to talk to a complete stranger."

My initial thought was that he was joking, but when I blinked away my tears and looked at him, not sure what to think of what he'd said, I could see he was quite serious. But I wasn't ready to pour out my soul to him — or anyone else for that matter.

I fidgeted with the edges of the serviette and a thought came to me. "You're right about the stranger part — I don't even know your name."

His cheeks flushed pink. "Oh, I'm sorry. My name is Daniel. I work for Galaxy Mech. They supply Katoa with their Mech-suits."

"Yes, I know... Uh, I'm Lennina." I stopped there, thinking if I told him I worked for The Company as a lowly Nav, maybe he would think less of me and maybe not want to talk to me anymore. "I work here on the station," I told him, and left it at that.

Now why would I want to socialise with him? I asked myself. *He nearly broke my arm! What am I thinking?*

Then I thought, *A 'lowly Nav'? Man, there is something seriously wrong with me!*

Now I knew the things Malvolio always told me were starting to affect me. Why was I even thinking like that? Everyone on the station were equals as far as I was concerned. Malvolio and the other managers and executives were no better than the Navs or the Diggers. I really needed to straighten my head out.

Another thought occurred to me. If he didn't want to socialise with me once he'd found out I was a Nav, then he would be no better than Malvolio!

Even so, I wasn't about to turn around now and say I'd lied, so I left it.

I sighed. Despite everything, my anger had subsided. It was clear to me that what had happened was purely an accident and there was no point being mad at Daniel, especially since he was nice enough to help me and that he was genuinely concerned about my welfare. I apologised for snapping at him.

"That's quite alright," he said. "Totally understandable."

"Yes, but *not* okay," I grumbled.

Daniel changed the subject by asking me some questions about how I liked life on the station and if I missed home. For reasons that escaped me, I found myself telling him I missed home more than ever and even that I'd broken up with my boyfriend only a few days before, which brought the tears flooding back. I left out the assault, but he'd already seen my face. I didn't mention Malvolio's name either, as he was too well-known, especially at Galaxy Mech. I didn't want the questions.

Daniel looked into my eyes as if to say he could feel my pain. As he spoke, I studied his face. I liked the way his smile always reached his eyes. It was never fake. There wasn't even a hint of the arrogance that seemed to be permanently painted on Malvolio's face the last few times I'd seen him.

I realised I'd zoned out while he was talking. *Focus, girl!*

I had to concentrate on what he was talking about, so I didn't appear to be a total idiot.

"I'm sorry you've had such a bad time of it," he told me. "You did the right thing in getting out. Your safety is the most important thing. You need to look after yourself and not feel guilty for leaving him."

CHAPTER 21
But I Don't Want to Go Home

My chest tightened. I knew he was referring to the black eye, but didn't say anything. It was hard enough talking about it as it was. I was glad he didn't ask a tonne of questions like they did at the Medical Facility. He didn't really need to ask more about it. Anyone with half a brain could see what was going on. I nodded silently, feeling a mix of humiliation, embarrassment and stupidity.

Daniel looked directly into my eyes. "I can't believe someone could treat you so badly. He doesn't know what he had and doesn't deserve you."

Oh... my... stars... My heart swelled and a tear slid down my cheek.

Daniel smiled gently and I thought I would melt into a puddle on the ground. I couldn't speak. If I did, I wouldn't be able to hold back the tears.

He told me he'd actually seen me around the station recently in one of the restaurants. I was with a man that he presumed was my boyfriend. I couldn't recall ever seeing Daniel before. I was sure I would never forget those eyes or his handsome face.

He didn't mention Malvolio, so maybe he didn't know what Malvolio looked like.

Good.

I didn't want him to recognise Malvolio or ask questions about him.

Daniel told me he was basically here till his contract ran out. After that he wanted to go back to his home planet of Taon and continue working there.

I smiled. He was from the same planet as Javolo and Javolo was heading home soon too. My chest felt heavy as I thought about that, but I had to quickly pull myself out of that place. I was feeling bad enough without thinking about working with some other Digger and losing Javolo.

Daniel reminded me of Javolo. Something about the way he spoke. It was probably because he was from the same planet with the same culture. It could also have been because he was so easy to talk to. I felt at ease around him, and we were talking to each other as if we'd been friends for years. It was relaxing.

"Are you on your lunch break?" I asked, hoping he wasn't.

He smiled and his face seemed to light up. "No. Day off."

I smiled. "Me too."

I kept thinking of Malvolio and what he'd say if he knew I was talking to another man. Not just talking to him over the Com, but actually sitting across from him at a restaurant. It was painful to think of him and what happened, but I looked up into Daniel's eyes and the pain melted away. He was looking straight back at me, and normally I would have looked away, but I kept looking into his eyes. They were like wells of green, taking me far away from reality. Which was a good place to be right now.

We sat there in silence, looking into each other's eyes like young teenagers in love. There was something about being in his presence that made me feel relaxed and free. I couldn't explain it. I'd known him for what, ten minutes?

Young teenagers in love?

I needed to get my head on straight.

My thoughts were interrupted by a man at the next table calling to his wife to join him for lunch. We both turned to see what the commotion was about, and when I looked back, Daniel asked, "Where're you from?"

"I'm from Azaeli. It's in the same System as Taon, so we're neighbours."

Daniel's eyebrows drew together in confusion for a second, so quickly I thought maybe I'd imagined it. Then he smiled. "Yes, we are."

It was funny; I'd said the same thing to Javolo when he'd asked me where I was from. *Maybe I should think of something more original to say.*

I needed to work on my social skills. I'd been trying whenever I went out with Malvolio, and he'd been helping me out, but I always seemed to say the wrong things. I'd never felt like I fit in or belonged with his upper-class friends or business associates.

I'd been a loner for too long growing up. Since my dad left, I'd stayed at home more to be there for Mum.

I often wondered how she was coping now that I'd left home to work on a space station. Of course, my mother always told me she was doing fine, and she seemed okay on the Vid call, but I wasn't completely sure.

I looked across at Daniel again.

He frowned. "Oh, I'm so rude. I haven't offered you a drink or anything! Would you like something? Have you had lunch?"

"I haven't eaten yet, but a drink would be nice. Thank you." I smiled and he tapped the button in the centre of our table to open a panel that revealed the small order screen. "Just a Tova juice, thanks."

"With the shock of the fall, maybe you should have a tea instead," he suggested, "with some extra sugar. They say a sweet tea really helps."

"Okay. If you think it would help."

"White or black?"

"White, please."

Daniel used the touchscreen to order two teas for us. I watched him intently while he was looking down at the panel, following the lines of his face. I couldn't help it. He caught me staring as he looked up again and the corner of his mouth turned up. I'd been busted again.

I wanted to look away, but I made myself keep eye contact. There was something about the way he made me feel that was... intoxicating... and familiar somehow. Like we'd met before.

I had to give myself a mental shake. That was silly. There was no way I'd forget meeting him.

He looked away to place his thumb on the scanner to pay for the drinks, then quickly pulled his hand away.

"Thank you for your custom," the computer droned.

He looked back up at me and our eyes met. "How's your arm?"

The pain in my elbow had faded to a dull ache. I looked down and pulled the serviette away, but stopped halfway when I realised it had stuck to the wound in places and peeling it off had caused it to start bleeding again.

Great.

It had started to swell a little more around the cut.

"I'll order an ice pack too," Daniel suggested as I covered it over again.

He tapped in the order. The ice pack was free.

"Thank you," I said.

He looked back up at me. "Any time. How does it feel?"

Those green eyes... wow... "It's just a dull ache now. Thanks."

Stop staring!

I shifted nervously in my seat while we waited for our teas. "So tell me, what brings you over to this area? Galaxy Mech people don't usually hang here."

Why did I ask such a lame question? Couldn't I think of anything better? No. I couldn't. My brain wasn't working right now.

His face flushed a little. "I wanted to see what the rest of the station looked like before I leave. You know, where the Diggers and Navs live mainly. I've already seen the Diggers' Section."

I leaned forward a little. "How did you manage that?"

"I know someone there. They let me in for a quick tour," he informed me as he ran his fingers through his hair. It somehow still looked good, even though he'd just messed it up.

"And is this section any different from the Diggers' Section?" I'd always wondered what it was like.

"Well, in appearance, there isn't much difference between the two besides the size — it's much bigger over here — and there are a lot more females of all races here."

I had to chuckle at that. Of course a guy would notice that. But it was true. Not many females signed up as Diggers. Not many males signed up as Navs either. I wasn't sure if it was company policy, or if the males just preferred the digging to computing and the females the reverse.

Daniel also told me that because the Navs' Section was integrated with the rest of the station, it wasn't as restricted as it was for the Diggers.

We were interrupted when Lani placed our drinks and an ice pack on the table and we both thanked her at the same time. In perfect sync.

I put the ice pack on the table and laid my arm on it. When I stretched it out, I almost touched Daniel's arm. I wondered if we'd get the same jolt if I did.

The cold caused me more pain, but I needed to put up with it if I wanted to reduce the swelling.

The smell of the tea made me feel a little more relaxed. I picked up my cup with my good hand and took a sip. The hot liquid felt good as it slid down my throat and after a few more mouthfuls, the sweetness of the extra sugar seemed to give me an energy boost. Or was it all in my head?

As we talked, I felt more relaxed, like a heavy weight had been lifted from my soul. I had no idea why I felt like that, but it was such a nice feeling. And I needed it right now.

"You're looking a lot better now." Daniel told me when I was about halfway through my tea. "A lot more colour in your cheeks... but are you okay?"

I gazed into those intense eyes and nodded. "Yes, I feel a lot better now. Thank you. The tea was a good idea."

We talked for a while longer. I glanced at the time display on the front of the building behind him. Just after fifteen hundred. How had so much time passed?

Malvolio would be finishing early today. I needed to get out of here. I needed to go back home. And I really needed to lie down. Only, I didn't want to go home. Didn't want to be alone again with only my thoughts for company. Because that had worked out so well so far...

I finished off my tea before it went cold.

I opened my mouth to tell Daniel I had to go and no words came out.

What is wrong with you? I asked myself again. *You need to rest. You have to go. You have to go...*

I sucked in a breath. "I better get moving. I need to get home."

His eyes widened slightly, but he nodded.

But I don't want to go home, I thought. How could I face going home?

I was sure Malvolio would try something else after he finished work. Maybe he would break the RO and turn up at the door again. The RO hadn't stopped him the day before.

"Oh... Yeah... Okay then." Daniel seemed disappointed.

I didn't want to leave, but I had to rest. I started to say goodbye as I stood up, but the pain in my side was so overpowering it made me cry out.

Chapter 22

Please Let Me Help You

Daniel immediately jumped up and rushed to my side and I wondered how he could've moved so fast. His arms were outstretched, ready to catch me if I fell.

"Are you alright?"

He was willing to help in any way he could; Malvolio wouldn't have left his seat.

"Yes..." What could I tell him? I just *couldn't* tell him I had broken ribs. I'd said too much already. I didn't even know him. "I — ah — twisted my ankle as I stood up."

Another lie, but it was bad enough that he'd seen the black eye. And he was just some guy I'd just met that worked here on the station.

As soon as that thought entered my brain, I knew I needed a mental slap in the face. He was more than just a guy that worked here.

I had to be more careful so I wouldn't have to keep lying.

"Let me see." He bent down toward my feet.

I had to quickly choose an ankle so he could look at it. I picked the right one. The same side as the ribs. That way, if I favoured that side, he would just think it was my ankle.

This was getting ridiculous. I never lied.

"Looks normal size..." He crouched down next to me to examine it more closely. "You'll live. But I'd feel better if you'd let me help you to your door."

I stared down at him. I wasn't about to tell him where I lived. He put his hand on the outside of my ankle to feel for any swelling and the lightning raced up my leg. I gasped and he let go, but I managed to stop myself from moving this time.

I felt the tingling all over for a few seconds, then it dispersed. It wasn't a bad feeling. It actually felt kind of thrilling. It was only scary because I didn't know what it was. Where was it coming from? I couldn't think of an explanation.

There was a long pause. He must have felt it again too.

"Did I hurt your ankle when I touched it?"

"No." *Wait. I just told him I'd twisted it, and now it's not hurting?* "Not really."

He looked up at me. "Okay. That's good. But, don't get me wrong. I'm not being creepy. I'm worried about you, that's all."

"It's just my ankle—"

He looked into my eyes. "But it's not just your ankle... You're not well. You're so pale. If you fell on your way home..." He was right. And he didn't even know about my ribs.

A wave of dizziness swept over me and I had to put a hand on his shoulder to steady myself. The electricity ran through me, though it was less potent.

I could see it in his eyes. He could feel it as much as I did. But I was too flustered and in too much pain to think clearly. Trying to work out what was going on was too hard right now. My brain refused to process anything except the way he was looking at me. I could see the emotions swirling in his eyes.

Focus...

I was aware I still had my hand on his shoulder, but I didn't want to remove it. My body was tingling and a warm sensation ran through me. Calming me. I wanted to close my eyes and keep feeling this way, but I knew I had to let him go.

Daniel hadn't made a move to get up off the ground, either. Did he enjoy the strange sensations too?

Slowly, reluctantly, I lifted my hand. The tingling swirled around and dissipated. I tried to hang on to the feeling, but it was gone.

Damn.

Then I remembered what he'd been saying about walking me home. Daniel was concerned about me and the dizzy spell I'd just had made me wonder again if I had a concussion from being punched so hard. Had

I lost consciousness? That would explain finding myself on the floor and not remembering the fall. I should've told the doctor.

I needed to get home to my bed and lie down, but there was no way I wanted to go back to my apartment. Whatever Malvolio was planning to do tonight was something I didn't even want to think about. I pushed it out of my mind.

I had to make a decision. Daniel's intentions seemed genuine and I needed help getting home, but I still felt uneasy. I'd just met him and it was his fault I'd fallen. What if it was all an act? He could have planted the bag so that I tripped over it so he could walk me home and... I didn't even want to go where those thoughts took me.

"Please let me help you," he asked, almost pleaded.

I couldn't just stand here, but it was hard for me to ask for help. I was too independent. I was used to being the one helping Mum and Adamo. The dizziness returned on cue and I had to put my hand back on his shoulder. Falling over wasn't an option. There'd be too much pain involved.

"Are you okay?" He stood slowly, ready to catch me if needed, which was still a possibility.

I nodded, which was a bad idea while feeling dizzy.

I'd be stupid to refuse his help. There was a chance I could collapse on the way home. I was sure no one would help me if I did. They'd probably leave me lying there in the street. And I was sure someone would be upset that I was messing up the street and making the place look like a ghetto.

"Okay," I finally said, hoping I wouldn't regret it.

He looked relieved. "Great." He made sure I was steady on my feet and grabbed our bags. "Ready? Or do you need to sit for a while first?"

"No, I'm ready." I started toward the middle of the courtyard. At the last second I remembered I was supposed to be limping. *Right ankle*, I reminded myself.

I hated to lie, but I couldn't tell him. I felt bad enough that some random guy I'd just met knew about my problems. It would be better to get home and forget this ever happened.

Forget this ever happened? Not likely, I thought as I chanced a sideways glance at Daniel. How could I forget him?

As we were stepping down from the paved area that housed the tables and chairs, I saw someone from the corner of my eye. I did a double-take and felt a stabbing sensation through my ribs, which nearly caused me to fall over. Daniel caught my arm to steady me and lightning surged through me again. I saw the man duck down an alley. I couldn't see his face, but was sure this time that it was Malvolio.

Well, almost sure...

I looked at Daniel and he could probably see the fear in my eyes.

Maybe it wasn't him, I told myself. *It's very unlikely at this time of day and in this area of the station.*

It didn't help. There was no way I was going to convince myself I was safe from him. I needed to get out of here. *Now.*

"Hey, what's wrong? Are you sure you're alright?" Daniel asked. To him, I'd only bumped my arm and twisted my ankle, but he'd probably figured there was a lot more to it than that.

"Yes," I lied. "I just thought I saw someone I knew."

Well, that last part was true. But if it was just 'someone I knew,' I wouldn't have fear in my eyes. I knew Daniel was smart enough to work it out, but I didn't want to talk about it and was glad when he didn't push it.

I looked back to where the man had been. What if it was Malvolio? What could I do? He would be absolutely furious after seeing me with another guy. Now I couldn't go home at all. If it was him, there was no telling what he'd do to me. I had to think of something, and fast. I couldn't go home and lock myself in permanently. I imagined him waiting outside my door for me to leave my apartment.

As I looked into Daniel's eyes again, it was like he was asking, "Was it him?" I could almost hear him say it. I couldn't answer.

After assuring Daniel again that I was fine, even though I was far from it, we walked slowly along the streets until we stood across the street from one of the smaller hotels on the station: The Olympia Hotel. I'd decided that this was a better option than going home.

Daniel frowned. "You *live* here?"

"Yes. Well, temporarily. Umm, I'm moving house and the new apartment needed repairs."

I mentally kicked myself. I hated all this lying. Once you start lying, you have to keep telling more stupid lies to support the first stupid lie...

If I see you again, I will *tell you the truth,* I promised him, *but not now.*

I sighed and started forward, but dizziness whooshed through my head, making me stumble.

Daniel instantly grabbed me around the waist to steady me. "I got ya."

I felt the electricity and pain from my ribs shoot through me simultaneously and fought the wave of nausea that followed. His breath tickled my ear, doing funny things to my chest and sending shivers all over my body.

He put an arm around my shoulders to keep me steady and I tried to walk forward, but he stopped me. "Whoah, hang on there. Let's just get you steady on your feet first, before we go anywhere."

He was right. I needed to wait for the dizziness to subside and I leaned on him for support. My brain still felt fuzzy and before I realised what I was doing, I found myself turning so that my head and hands were on his chest. He smelled like freshly washed clothes and a kind of woodsy aroma. It was nice.

As we stood there, I felt a strange calm sweep over me. I felt safe in his arms. It was crazy... I was crazy. We'd just met and here I was, wrapped in his embrace, with weird tingly sensations shooting through my body... I was being really stupid. And it was... *amazing.*

I could feel the hard muscles across his chest; he must've worked out or something. His body was too toned for someone with a desk job.

He stroked my hair and it felt wonderful. It took a few minutes for the dizziness and fuzziness to subside, but when it did, I didn't move away from him. I knew I should. But I felt so comfortable. Wanted. Needed. Loved. *Loved?*

CHAPTER 23

Now what?

What are you doing? You've lost your mind! You don't know this man and you're letting him hug you in the middle of the street!

All common sense and reason had gone out the proverbial window, but I couldn't seem to let go. Only the thought that Malvolio could be watching us made me finally pull away from him. Daniel seemed surprised by my sudden movement, but said nothing.

"I should get going." I still didn't make a move to go across the street.

"Let me help you," Daniel offered, and I found myself nodding.

He put an arm around my back and snaked it around under my right arm and I jerked away before he could put pressure on my ribs.

He pulled away quickly and apologised. I had to let him think I didn't want him to touch me. I felt bad. It was like I was lying to him again.

He settled for putting his arm around my shoulders again and I leaned on him as we crossed the street, while I enjoyed the buzzing sensations running right through to my toes. I probably could've walked by myself now that the dizziness was gone, but it was better to be safe than sorry. That's what I kept telling myself. And there was no harm in letting him help, was there?

We entered the lobby of the hotel and I removed my sunglasses. Daniel dropped his arm from my shoulders and looked into my eyes. "I'm sorry. You can tell me to shut up if you want to. You can tell me it's none of my business, but I have to know... Your ex. Did he give you the black eye?"

I felt my eyes go wide. I'd forgotten about it and wasn't expecting the question, so it caught me off-guard. I shoved the glasses back on and wrung my hands nervously. "Ah... umm... yes..." was all I could manage.

Plus three broken ribs.

"I'd like to give him a black eye..." Daniel growled.

I was surprised by how passionate his statement was. I wasn't sure how to react to that. What could I say? He didn't even know me and he was ready to defend me.

Then I imagined Daniel giving Malvolio a black eye. Although I abhorred violence, I thought I'd like to see that. He deserved it.

Daniel's reaction made me think of Javolo. He'd probably react the same way. He didn't like Malvolio much. Maybe it was just one of those gut instinct things. I wished I'd gotten a gut instinct thing when I'd met Malvolio that had told me to keep away...

Too late now, I told myself.

I couldn't imagine telling Javolo what had happened. And whatever I said would be recorded anyway. I pushed the thought away for later.

"So, I guess walking you to your room is asking a bit too much?" Daniel ventured.

I looked at him and a mental image of him carrying me into one of the hotel rooms and lying me gently down on the bed popped into my mind. I felt a blush form on my cheeks. "Umm... I'll be okay by myself. If I have any difficulties, I can always call on the staff here to help."

"Okay," he said quietly.

"No offence, but I don't know you..." Why did I feel the need to explain?

"I understand completely." I sensed he didn't want to leave. I could see it in his eyes.

Suddenly, I didn't want him to go either. I felt a strong urge to tell him I did need his help, just so he'd stay. So I could just talk to him. So I wouldn't be alone.

Don't be ridiculous! I thought. *You don't even know him! Plus, you don't even have a room here! He'll discover your lies...*

His voice was quiet. "So, I guess I'll be going then."

No. I don't want you to go. I don't want to be alone. "Yes. Thank you for your help." Why did I feel like this?

He smiled. "Any time. Will I see you again?"

"Umm, I guess so," I replied. "I'll be on the station for a while yet. I'm

only a few months into my contract. And you know where I'm staying..."
I waved a hand around me.

He looked relieved.

Why did I feel this way about a total stranger? The thought of him leaving was hard to deal with, which was ridiculous.

Get it together! I ordered. I desperately needed to lie down, so I needed to organise a room. I had to get him to leave.

I will see him again, I promised myself. *When I'm feeling better. Then I can thank him properly for helping me.*

With that settled, I forced myself to say goodbye, with many thank yous thrown in. I watched him walk through the doors and out into the street. It was a pleasant sight. The way his shirt bulged slightly from his muscled torso and arms. And his tight pants... He was just so... perfect.

I'd never gotten hung up on looks. There were more important things than that, but I couldn't stop staring at him.

Malvolio wasn't ugly either — quite the opposite — but that wasn't what had attracted me to him. And now that I could see he was actually ugly on the inside, I didn't want anything more to do with him.

Snap out of it! You need to sort out a room!

I looked around the lobby and saw a young man with short brown hair and baby blue eyes at the desk, looking at me expectantly.

Now what?

I knew I couldn't go home, so I walked right up to the front desk and said, "Hi..." I looked at his name badge, "Nakei. I'd like to book a room for at least a week."

"Certainly," the clerk replied with a smile. "For how many people and how many beds?"

He looked a few years younger than me, but he must have been at least eighteen years old for him to be working here. "It's just for me," I told him.

He gave me a wider smile, showing a row of perfectly straight, white teeth. "We have two single suites available, each with a King-sized bed, from sixty credits per night. One has a spa."

"How much extra for the spa?"

"Ten credits per night. We can give you a discount though, seeing as you are staying for a whole week." Nakei's smile was infectious. I didn't even realise I'd been smiling back at him.

"Sounds good. I'll take it... Uh, the one with the spa." I would probably empty my main account if I stayed any longer than a week, but I was past caring. I didn't have a problem dipping into my savings if it meant keeping myself safe.

So, after finalising a total price, sorting out the formalities and having a retina and thumbprint scan to add my identification to their system, I was taken to my room.

I'd given them strict instructions to let no one through to my room. They were to tell whoever it was that I was unavailable, then contact me after the person was gone to let me know who it was. I told them not to let anyone know which room I was in or if I was even there at the time. The only exception would be the Enforcers, of course. And as an added precaution, if Malvolio was looking for me, they were to say there was no record of me staying at the hotel.

I waited as the retina scan verified my ID at the door. It swished open and the Hotel Computer welcomed me in a deep male voice. "Greetings, Lennina Callista. Welcome to the Olympia Hotel. Please let me know if there is anything I can do for you."

I didn't respond. Thoughts were rushing through my mind. Why had I led Daniel to the hotel? Why had I let him know where I'd be? I could've led him to this hotel and went straight to another one after he'd gone.

I probably wouldn't have made it to the next hotel. Besides, there was something about him that told me I could trust him. All logic told me I was crazy to trust someone I'd just met, especially someone I'd met by tripping over his bag in the middle of a courtyard. So why? What was it about him? I couldn't put my finger on it.

CHAPTER 24
I Had Two Reasons to Stay

I'd always been a good judge of character — well, before Malvolio came into my life. I could see it in their eyes if they were lying. That was probably one of the most puzzling things about this whole mess with Malvolio. Why couldn't I see through him? Was he that good at lying? Or was it that he really believed all the crap he told me?

I think he does, I thought. *He really believes it. He thinks he is such a good person and that I should be happy to be his girlfriend. I should worship him. Everyone else seems to...*

That was something that had always bothered me. Everybody knew him and everybody went out of their way to make sure he was serviced, comfortable, happy with his meals at all the restaurants, or whatever.

I shoved him from my mind and looked around. There was a nice big kitchen/dining/lounge area and a separate bedroom and bathroom. The spa took up a large part of the bathroom and looked inviting. I looked forward to lying back and enjoying the warm bubbles. The King-sized bed was huge, which I didn't expect. Then I had to have a chuckle at myself. What size did I *think* a King would be?

I wandered out of the bedroom. Now why had I rented the room for a whole week? How long did I expect to be here?

I'd already decided that going home was a bad idea, then seeing someone in the shadows had convinced me I needed to be somewhere more secure. At least I would be safer here. There were plenty of people around me and Malvolio would have to come past the front desk and security to get to my room. Failing that, I could press the emergency button if he did get in. Security could arrive much faster than the Enforcers as they were in the same building.

So much for pushing him from my mind...

I shuddered to think of what could happen if I'd stayed in the apartment all alone and he was able to get in somehow...

Stop it.

For a more long-term solution, I thought I should apply for a transfer to another apartment. Actually, forget that — if I was seriously thinking of quitting my job and going back home to Azaeli, I wouldn't need to move to another apartment on the station. I'd be outta here.

Only, the thought of not being able to speak to Javolo every day left me feeling down. I knew we were just friends, but friends like that were so hard to find.

Then I thought of Daniel. I didn't even want to leave him when I was down in the lobby. Now I had two reasons to stay.

But Malvolio was making my life hell, so how could I stay here? I'd have to work something out because I wanted to get to know Daniel and Javolo better. I'd stay here for them.

It was at that moment my brain decided to remind me of how I'd made up my mind that I wasn't going to get involved with any more relationships. How could I have forgotten so easily?

I didn't need any complications or distractions. I had to focus on my career. I would have to keep it to friendship only. I'd had enough hurt to last me a lifetime with Malvolio.

I would get their contact details so I could still call them on the Vid once I got back to Azaeli. I could get to know both of them that way.

I decided that when I was able to go back to work, I would give them notice. Then I could tell Javolo I wanted to meet him. They couldn't forbid it, because as a citizen living on the station, I could go wherever I wanted. I could live on my savings for a while and go home to Mum and Adamo before I ran out.

The more I thought about it, the more I liked the idea. I could always find another job, but a friend like Javolo was like gold. I needed to do whatever it took to hold onto him. I was pretty sure there would be no restrictions on me going into the Diggers' Section once I quit. If there was, I'd just have to be happy with Vid calls. At least I'd find out what he looked like.

After making that decision, I felt a great sense of relief. Part of the burden had been lifted from my shoulders. My mind raced, thinking of all the things I could do once I finished up at work. All the things I could do with Javolo. And maybe Daniel, too. I wondered if they would get along with each other...

I gave myself a mental shake. I wasn't sure if we would be able to spend time together. It might only be possible if Javolo quit his job as well. And I didn't want to be responsible for that.

If I was really going to do this, then there was some organising to do. My apartment was only let out to me as an employee, so I would need to transfer to the apartments for non-employees. There weren't many unoccupied apartments on the station, but I was sure I could find one without too much trouble. So I'd be moving to a different apartment after all.

I sat down gingerly on the lounge to think. Moving to another apartment would be easy. I didn't own much — the biggest thing being my keyboard — and the things Malvolio had bought me could be given away or thrown away. I didn't want any of them. I didn't want to be reminded of him in any way.

Malvolio wouldn't give up so easily or leave me alone. There was definitely something wrong with him. He needed some professional help to deal with his violent nature.

Now that I'd relaxed a little, I felt a wave of exhaustion sweep over me. I needed to lie down. I sat down on the huge bed and took a painkiller.

Lowering myself down carefully onto my left side, I started some relaxation exercises. Breathing slowly and evenly, I reminded myself of the extra security close at hand.

Tomorrow, I would duck into my apartment and pack a few things, then come straight back to the hotel.

—— *·☆·* ——

I'd been hiding in my hotel room for two days after I'd grabbed my keyboard and some essential items from my apartment. I took a taxi to carry the keyboard.

Staying here was a bit of an adventure at first — especially the spa — but the novelty was wearing off and I was starting to go stir crazy. Again.

I decided to break my own rule. I went downstairs to the restaurant in the hotel for breakfast. The smell of waffles, toast, and bacon cooking reached me as I walked in, making my mouth water.

I picked a corner that wasn't visible from the entrance and ordered bacon, eggs, toast and a cup of tea, which reminded me of Daniel, and I found myself sitting there with my eyes closed, savouring the taste and visualising Daniel's face. I wondered if I'd lost my mind. Maybe I was already crazy before all of this even started. That brought a silly smile to my face. I could imagine Javolo saying some smart-arse comment about that.

Malvolio kept flashing into my mind and I kept pushing him out. It was grating on my nerves. I had to keep thinking of something else. It was hard to enjoy breakfast without worrying about Malvolio finding me.

My brain wouldn't stop thinking about everything and I sat there fidgeting with the last piece of toast.

"Everything okay?"

I flinched as I looked up to see the waitress who'd brought out my breakfast. "Uh, yes. Thank you."

She smiled down at me. "You look like you got a lot on your mind." I nodded and hoped she hadn't seen me sitting here with my eyes closed like an idiot. "Want to talk about it? I mean, you don't have to, but if you want to, I'm here." I must have had a blank look on my face. "I mean, you don't have to tell me names or nothin'. Just the general stuff. It helps to get it off your chest, you know?"

I frowned. It was so similar to what Daniel had said. I opened my mouth to tell her I didn't want to talk about it, but found myself agreeing instead.

Her whole face lit up. "Great! Mind if I sit?"

I gestured to the seat opposite me. I didn't know where to start. Her eyes darted to my face and she seemed genuinely interested.

"I'm Sia," she told me.

"I'm Lennina." I tried to return her smile.

I cleared my throat. I told her I'd only known Malvolio for a short time, leaving out his name, and told her about how he'd changed. Then I just poured out everything about how he'd accused me of cheating and how he'd hurt me. Once I started, I couldn't stop myself. I obviously needed someone to talk to about this.

Her eyes were wide as she listened.

She looked me in the eye. "You know, you don't have to put up with domestic violence, Lennina. Doesn't matter who it is. Even if you guys were married. It still don't make it right."

CHAPTER 25

He's Not a Good Man and He Don't Love You

I'd never thought of it that way — that it was actually domestic violence. Putting that label on it made it seem so much worse. How could I not see it? How could I let him do this to me? I felt so stupid for letting him do these things to me.

"I'm such an idiot!"

She reached out and touched my arm and my first thought was that I didn't feel the lightning racing through me. "Hey. Don't do that to yourself. It's okay. You're not an idiot. You've been manipulated by an expert by the sounds."

Her words made me feel a little better, but I still felt stupid.

As we talked, I tried to explain that I hadn't wanted to give up on our relationship like some people do and I'd wanted to stick with it and not give up, but he'd made it impossible.

She thought about that for a while. "You got the right idea, but you have to make sure you got the right person first. You can't just grab the first guy what kisses you. You need to make sure he's a good man and that he really loves you and you really love him. If that's the truth, then you gotta hold on and fight to stay together, no matter what."

When I thought about it, it made perfect sense.

"And if you ask me, he's *not* a good man and he *don't* love you."

She was right. He didn't love me. I'd been so determined to not be like my father that I'd failed to see that I was doing the right thing for the wrong guy.

It proved once again that relationships weren't worth the hurt. I was more determined to stick to my commitments and stay focused.

"Thank you so much, Sia. You've really helped me."

She smiled warmly as tears glistened in her eyes. "Don't mention it."

—— ★·☆·★ ——

After talking to Sia, I felt a bit better.

As I sat on the lounge trying to watch a HoloMovie, I started thinking about Daniel. Again. It was his fault I'd tripped, but he'd helped me afterward. I had to admit it probably wouldn't have happened if I'd been looking where I was going instead of looking for the man in the shadows. It was partly my fault. *And partly Malvolio's,* I added hotly.

Watching the movie was a waste of time. I couldn't remember anything I'd just watched. I looked around the room as if something to do would appear out of nowhere.

It's so boring here! And lonely... I've got to get out. Get some air... Get to the park... I wish I could call Javolo on the Vid and talk about how work is going. Something. Anything!

The decision was made. I wasn't sure where I would go, but I needed to be out of this room. The park seemed like a good idea. I wanted to simply lie on the grass and enjoy the sunshine — even if it wasn't real sunshine. I decided to wear what I already had on — three-quarter pants and a casual top. I didn't want to be lying on the grass with a dress or skirt on.

Javolo, Daniel and Malvolio had been constantly creeping into my thoughts over the last couple of days. The only reason I'd even been watching the movie in the first place was to try to block it all out. It hadn't worked. Nothing seemed to work. Even though I'd made some decisions about what I was going to do, doubts crowded into my mind and memories of being punched and kicked kept playing on a loop. Being alone with my thoughts was a bad idea.

Talking to Javolo was so free and easy and I needed that right now, but talking to Javolo was not an option, and finding Daniel would be a needle-in-a-haystack kind of deal.

The bruising on my face was gone and my elbow was much better, so I was planning to return to work the following day. I'd be able to talk to Javolo then. But I needed someone to talk to now. Everything was too much.

As it was mid-morning, I thought I'd go to the park for a while, then attempt to somehow find Daniel closer to lunch time. It would be next to impossible, but that wasn't going to stop me. It would be so nice if I could talk to him.

There was something about him. Something that made it seem so natural and easy to be around him. I couldn't get him out of my head.

I reminded myself that I only wanted to be friends. No more relationships. No more chances of my heart being ripped out again.

My thoughts drifted back to Javolo as I brushed my hair in front of the large mirror in the hotel's bathroom. I was determined to quit and meet him at last. I didn't care what The Company said or thought about it, or even what he looked like. That wasn't really important. As long as he stayed the same on the inside, I didn't care. I knew that people who were native to Taon were human, just as they were on Azaeli. Then I remembered that Daniel was from Taon and he looked... well, *absolutely amazing*...

Oh... What if Javolo was as handsome as Daniel? That would be weird. I could handle two best friends that were also eye candy.

Under the brighter light in the bathroom, I could see that the bruise cream had done its job. There was nothing to indicate that I'd had any injuries to my face. *Thankfully*...

My ribs were a different story, however. I carefully removed my top and unwrapped the bandage to see. The worst of the purple bruising was gone, but it had been replaced by lots of other colours, mainly yellowish brown and yellow. I applied the bruise cream, wrapped the bandage back around myself and pulled my top back on. The cream's numbing effect did a good job on my skin, but it couldn't really do anything to ease the pain of broken bones.

The scene replayed in my mind again and I clenched my fists. The punch to the face that put me on the floor. The kick. The pain...

Movement caught my eye and when I looked down, my hairbrush was on the floor. How did that happen? Had I put it too close to the edge? I picked it up carefully so I wouldn't hurt my ribs. I was sure I'd put it closer to the mirror...

I shook my head as I walked back out to grab my bag from next to the Vid. As I touched the bag, I saw a spark jump from my fingers to the keyboard and jerked my hand away.

CHAPTER 26

Why Did I Ever Believe That He Was a Good Person?

What was that?

That static spark was bigger than any I'd ever encountered. It made me think of when Daniel touched me... A sinking feeling spread through my stomach. What if this was related to the lightning — or whatever it was — that I'd experienced with Daniel?

But I couldn't still be feeling it two days later. It made no sense.

My next thought was to check the Vid. Electronic devices couldn't tolerate static shocks. I pressed the power button to bring it out of sleep mode. Nothing. I tried again. Still nothing.

Uh, oh.

I'd killed it. I'd have to tell them at the reception desk on my way out. I couldn't tell them the truth, though. I decided to tell them it wouldn't turn on this morning.

How could I tell them what really happened? No one has that much static electricity in their bodies. I reached my hand toward the keyboard again, but nothing happened. No spark.

Did I imagine it?

I wandered down to the lobby. After I'd reported the dead Vid, the tall woman at the desk told me there'd been a gentleman asking for me. My heart locked up and I felt the blood drain from my face.

"When?" I asked quickly. He couldn't have found me, could he?

"Let me see..." she replied casually. "Yesterday afternoon."

What? "Why wasn't I told earlier?"

"I'm not sure. I wasn't in yesterday. I'm sorry for any inconvenience it may have caused you." That last bit sounded like an automated response from a Home Computer.

"Oh," was all I could say. What else could I say, besides maybe ranting like Malvolio would have?

"Were you expecting someone?" the woman asked. I noticed the name "Simi" on her name badge.

"No, not really... Did he leave his name?" I winced, waiting for her to say Malvolio.

"Let me see..." she said again as she twisted a lock of blonde hair around a finger. "Yes, he did."

Please, not Malvolio. Not Malvolio.

"Daniel. No surname given. No other details."

My heart skipped a beat. Not only was it *not* Malvolio, it was Daniel wanting to see me again.

"Thank you, Simi!" I almost shouted as I headed out the door. "Good-bye!"

"Have a nice day!" Simi called after me.

I strode out of the hotel with a huge smile on my face and a warm feeling in my chest. I couldn't remember when I'd last smiled. I was going to find Daniel. Yes, I'd probably have to wait till lunch time, but that was just a formality.

The Olympia was further from the park than my apartment, but I stuck my sunglasses on my face and strolled along, soaking up the fake sunlight. Once I reached the edge of the grassed area, I wandered over to the fountain and sat down on the edge. It had three circular tiers above the main base, with the water sprouting out from the top and filling the first one, which overflowed into the second and third till it reached the bottom where I sat.

I breathed in and could smell the fresh water, and the scent of the flowers that were scattered around near the base of the fountain. Jasmine, roses, and something I didn't recognise. It reminded me of home.

Birds flitted in and out of the trees and I sighed, trying hard to push all the troubles from my mind. The birds didn't have a care in the world and I wished I could be like that, even if it was only for a short time. Watching them helped me to relax.

I had a sudden urge to play a song I'd learnt on the keyboard not long before I left for the space station. I wished I could bring my keyboard here and play next to the water. Of course, if I did, everyone would stare and think I was weird.

One bird flew down to the fountain and perched itself on the rim of the upper tier. It had green splashed across its wings and tail and red on its head and chest. It looked at me warily before taking a few quick drinks. I smiled. I loved coming here to see the wildlife. If I had a camera with me, it would've been the perfect shot.

A little voice in my head said that if I still had the personal Com Malvolio had bought me and had actually brought it with me, I would've had the perfect camera to take that perfect shot. I told the voice to shut up.

The bird stood there with the water running over its feet and I wondered if it had any idea that this was all a fake park, with fake sunlight, and fake rain, millions of kilometres out into space. Of course, the bird would only look at its surroundings and feel at home and that would be enough for him to be happy. I watched as he took some more quick gulps of water. Then, with a flick of his wings, he was gone.

This was my cue to go and find a nice grassy spot and lie down. I was determined to do what I'd planned. The trees to my left provided patches of shade and would be ideal as I didn't really want to be in the full sun.

Once there, I stretched out on the soft grass and stared up at the branches and the fake blue sky. It was relaxing and exactly what I needed. *I should've come here sooner.*

But I'd been too afraid to venture out.

I closed my eyes and imagined myself becoming one with the ground. The scents from the flowers over here were stronger than the ones near the fountain. These smelled like honey. An almost sickly-sweet smell. It was heavenly.

I listened to all the sounds. The birds, the fountain, the voices of passersby and the young couple that sat on a picnic blanket to my right.

I must have dozed as the noise from a shrieking bird overhead woke me and made me jump. I managed to keep from crying out at the pain in my side. I lay there on my back for a while, breathing slowly, till the adrenalin subsided and the pain dulled.

I'm sick of all this pain! I can't even do anything without it hurting! Why did he do this to me? Why did I ever believe that he was a good person?

I sighed — carefully. I would have to put up with it till the broken bones healed. Which was going to be a long time. That thought almost brought tears to my eyes. I needed to be patient. The only way it would heal without a miracle was with time. And if I took it easy.

Getting up was difficult, but I managed it and headed off to find Daniel.

Where do I even start? I thought.

I tried the area for the Galaxy Mech employees and worried that I might see Malvolio, but then I remembered he was too good to associate with 'middle-class' workers. There was no way he'd be there. But Daniel wasn't there either.

I wandered around through all the areas for the different employees, but there was no sign of him anywhere. I thought of asking someone, then realised I didn't know his full name. How many Daniels would there be on the station?

As I walked along, I felt frustrated. I just wanted someone to talk to. Was that too much to ask for?

I tried a few other places, but was disappointed. Yep. It *was* too much to ask for.

All of the girls I knew from work were at work. I didn't really know anyone else besides Malvolio's friends, and I sure as hell didn't want to talk to them.

How hard could it be to find someone willing to spend some time and have a meal and a chat? I wondered. *I just want to talk...*

I found myself fighting back tears. I didn't realise how much I missed talking to someone — mainly Javolo.

It wasn't just boredom; I was so distressed about what Malvolio had done. I didn't have to talk about any of that stuff to anyone, just talk to someone and get my mind off it all.

I hadn't realised that a huge part of my day at work was spent talking to people. And most of that time, that was Javolo. For the last few days,

I'd been thinking about everything and playing it back in my head, trying to work out if I could've done things differently, which I knew wasn't good for my mental wellbeing.

So I needed to find someone to talk to. And tomorrow wasn't soon enough.

I stopped walking. My ribs were feeling worse, but I needed to focus. Forcing myself to take a few careful deep breaths, I tried to think about where Daniel might be. I'd met him in the Navs' Section, so I headed in that general direction. He was probably working today, but I hoped he would be having lunch somewhere in the area. Or something. This was getting to be too hard. The chances of finding him were so slim.

I weaved my way through the food shops, but with no success. Walking didn't bother me. I was fit enough to walk around the station without any problems, but the pain was getting to me.

Hunger drove me to seek out somewhere decent to eat. Before I knew it, I found myself heading back towards the place where I'd met Daniel. They served good meals, so why not?

As I rounded the corner and the courtyard area came into view, I gasped. There he was, at the same table he was sitting at on the day we'd met.

CHAPTER 27

You Sure Moved On Quick

I stopped walking and my heart soared. Was he looking for me too? Surely he was. Why else would he be sitting right there in the same spot?

I tried to pull myself together as I walked toward the table. My mind raced. What if he wasn't there for me? What if I was about to make an epic fool of myself? What excuse could I use for being there? I couldn't think of one. But I kept walking.

But he came to the hotel yesterday. He must want to see me again...

I became more nervous as I got closer.

What if I'm wrong? What if he's waiting for his girlfriend? What if—

He looked up from his lunch and saw me. My heart was in my throat. Those amazing green eyes greeted me as he smiled and jumped to his feet. I felt relieved when he seemed happy to see me and tried to keep up a steady pace and to act natural.

Daniel started walking toward me and I felt a little light-headed.

What's wrong with me? I hardly know the guy!

"Hi, Lennina," he said warmly as he put out a hand to greet me.

"Hi," was all I managed to say in return. I took his hand, thinking that I needed to sit down.

Lightning struck and the electric sensation raced through my veins, startling me and making me go weak at the knees. His eyes widened and I knew I wasn't the only one feeling it.

"How are you?" he asked, as if nothing out of the ordinary had happened. "I haven't seen you around. I was wondering if you were okay."

I smiled. His words warmed me. It was nice to know that someone cared. Really cared. He still had hold of my hand and was looking into my eyes. I relished the buzz running through me, my heartbeat racing a little.

"Oh, I'm a lot better now," I managed to say. "I had a few days off work. Told them I was sick."

He looked relieved. "Okay. That was a good idea. You really didn't look well the other day. You definitely needed the rest." He looked down as if he just realised he still had hold of my hand, then released it. The tingling faded and I wanted him to take my hand again. "Please, come and join me," he said, gesturing for me to take a seat back at the table.

Relief flooded me as I walked with him to the table. "Thank you." Then I added, "Is it okay? I mean, were you waiting for someone? I—"

"No. I'm here alone," he assured me, and a grin pulled at the corners of his mouth. "I was hoping to catch you here."

My heart skipped a beat. I had to sit down. *Now.*

I sat slowly and let out a sigh, trying to relax and get my breathing and heart rate back to normal. I felt strange.

"Are you sure you're alright?" Daniel leaned toward me. "You've gone pale."

"Yes. I'll be okay in a minute or two." At least I hoped I'd be okay in a minute or two.

It was unusual for me to be sick or dizzy. But that was before Malvolio broke my ribs.

I'd probably overdone it by walking all over the station. I was sure I still had a concussion. How long did the doctor say the symptoms could last? I couldn't remember.

Daniel offered to buy me some lunch and a drink, but I insisted on paying for it myself. He reluctantly agreed, then gave me a sly smile. I ordered a salad sandwich and a Tova juice and put my thumb to the scanner before he could beat me to it. Then I changed the order to tea instead. Hopefully the tea would do a better job of calming my stormy insides.

We talked about the weather back on our home planets and other small talk while we ate. It was so good to talk to someone. It felt like the stress was draining from my body and the lightheadedness faded away.

I felt better with each passing minute. This was a good idea.

But then Malvolio kept creeping into my thoughts and I found myself looking for him in every shadow. It was getting on my nerves. Daniel would have noticed it, I was sure. He would be wondering what I was looking for. Was I being paranoid, or did I have good reason to be looking over my shoulder?

I needed to go somewhere safe. Well, *safer*. Somewhere on the station that I knew Malvolio would never go.

Then I remembered a place we'd gone to a few weeks back. The Ambrosia Restaurant. Malvolio hadn't been happy with the service or the food and had told them, very loudly, that he would never go there again and would not recommend their restaurant to any of his friends and blah, blah, blah. That would be the perfect spot, so I asked Daniel if we could go there once we'd finished our lunch.

I could see the question in his eyes and my chest tightened. Should I tell him? *No lies this time*, I told myself. I'd promised myself and I was determined to keep that promise.

"I... ah... don't want to run into my ex..." I bit my lip and hoped he would understand and not ask a lot of questions.

Daniel nodded. "Okay."

I let out the breath I'd been holding. He was as easy-going as Javolo. He'd probably go anywhere I wanted to go and talk about anything I wanted to talk about. We finished up our lunch and headed off.

I was sure there was no chance we'd run into Malvolio in that area.

Daniel insisted we take a taxi so I didn't have to walk so far, and I gladly agreed.

The taxis used on the space station were small open-topped vehicles that were computer-driven. We hailed one by pressing a button on a pole at the taxi waiting station not far from the courtyard. It arrived in less than a minute. Daniel opened the door for me and made sure I was comfortable before climbing in beside me.

"The Ambrosia Restaurant," I said. The taxi started moving as soon as I'd finished speaking.

As the taxi slowed for a corner on the way there, I heard a woman's voice call out my name, so I ordered the vehicle to stop. It turned out to be Moira, the manager of The Golden Palace. Malvolio and I were regulars, so she knew me fairly well.

Moira looked surprised to see me. "How are you feeling today, Dearie?" she asked.

You have no idea... "Not too bad, thank you," I answered automatically. "How are you?"

Moira smiled. "Oh, fine, dear." She glanced at Daniel. "You're not with the other half today?"

No, and I won't be ever again. "No. I, um... I'm not seeing him anymore..."

Her eyebrows shot up. "Not seeing him? Since when?"

I had to think about it for a moment. "About six days ago."

Her frown deepened. "When I saw him last night, he didn't say anything about that... He told us all that you weren't well."

I clenched my fists and felt the heat rise in my cheeks. He was pretending nothing had happened and that we were still a couple, and he was the reason I was 'not well.'

"Well... I don't know why he didn't tell you..." I was finding it hard to keep my response polite, but reminded myself that this woman had nothing to do with any of it. "But we're not together anymore."

Moira's round face moulded itself into a smirk as she looked over at Daniel again. "You sure moved on quick."

Chapter 28

I Have Three Broken Ribs

And with that, she flicked her long curly hair behind her and stomped off, not even giving me a chance to answer.

I sat there with my mouth hanging open. How could she presume we were together, just because we shared a taxi?

"Don't worry about her." Daniel gave my arm a gentle squeeze and sent sparks racing through me. I sucked in my breath and he pulled away immediately. "Sorry..."

I looked into his eyes. I wanted to tell him not to be sorry, but no words came out.

There seemed to be no escape from his gaze. I was somehow spellbound whenever our eyes met. I wasn't sure how long we sat there for before Daniel cleared his throat and ordered the vehicle to continue. I watched the scenery pass by, hoping we didn't run into anyone else I knew.

There was a warmth in my chest as I thought about her assumption that we were together. Any anger I'd felt for her saying it had melted away.

Daniel turned to face me. "Hey."

"Hey."

"Don't worry about her," he said again.

Moira had decided that Daniel was my new boyfriend without even stopping to think about it. Some people could be so judgemental. I hated that.

"I can't help it. She's the manager of the Golden Palace. She'll... She'll tell my ex..."

It still felt weird calling him my 'ex.'

My blood ran cold as I thought about Moira telling Malvolio about our meeting next time she saw him. He was so convinced I was seeing Javolo and now I'd been seen with Daniel. I could hear him now, accusing me of sleeping with every guy in town... space station. I pushed those thoughts aside as we approached the restaurant.

Daniel leaned closer, but didn't touch me. "There's nothing you can do about that now. Don't worry yourself sick over it."

"I know." What else could I say? Daniel didn't know the full story, but he was right. There really was nothing I could do, so worrying would be pointless. I probably *would* make myself sick.

We managed to get there without seeing Malvolio and without me falling over once we'd stepped out of the taxi. I was pretty sure we hadn't been followed. I was getting paranoid again. The pain reminded me that I had good reason to be worried.

The place was dimly lit and quite crowded. There were so many delicious smells wafting through the place that I wished I hadn't eaten already.

I felt relief wash over me once we'd entered and I'd made sure Malvolio wasn't sitting in one of the darkened corners. Maybe now I could relax. Even if it was just a little bit.

As we searched for a table, I recognised the young waitress behind the counter. Her eyes went wide as she recognised me. She'd bore the brunt of Malvolio's tirade. I wanted to tell her I was sorry; that it wouldn't happen again today. My cheeks flushed and I quickly looked away.

The only vacant spot was small with a bench seat on one side of the table. The chairs that belonged on the other side had been moved to accommodate a large group of people sitting together at a nearby table, so Daniel and I would have to sit side-by-side. I didn't have a problem with that. It meant we could sit together and enjoy the view out the windows.

The table was in a darkened corner, which looked cosy. Maybe a little bit too cosy. I told Daniel not to get any ideas. He smiled at me, his eyes sparkling. He looked so... what was the word? So captivating? Amazing? Gorgeous? ... when he smiled.

We sat down together — not quite touching — as we looked out at a small courtyard that had grass, some flower gardens, and a small fountain containing several ornate statues, which I found refreshing. I remembered my trip to the park earlier. It had been so relaxing. I imagined myself out there lying on the grass. Daniel would think I was crazy. Everyone here would think I was crazy. But it was still better than being cooped up in that hotel room with no one to talk to and not much to do.

"I was going a bit stir-crazy at the hotel and just needed someone to talk to," I blurted out as I tapped my fingers on the side of my leg.

"I'm already crazy, so we should get along just fine," he chuckled. That brought a smile to my face. Then he turned and looked me in the eye. "But seriously, I will be here for you whenever you need me. *Any* time you need someone to talk to, I'm here."

His expression was sincere and it warmed my heart.

"Thank you," I breathed as I tried to hold back tears.

Don't cry again! I commanded silently. Too late. A tear escaped and ran down the length of my cheek to my jaw line.

He gave me a sad smile as he watched the tear's progress. It was a gentle smile that melted my heart. Then he reached out and wiped the tear away with his thumb, sending jolts of electricity across my face and making me gasp. His hand lingered for a moment before he pulled away. I wanted him to keep it there. I wanted him to stay close and to keep feeling the lightning dancing through my veins.

I wasn't sure what to do, so I smiled at him and turned back to the window. We talked about the fountain for a while. How peaceful it looked.

"The guy I work with," I began, suddenly needing to talk about it, "we have to work closely together as a team and he's so easy-going, so easy to talk to. There's never any stress, except the everyday stresses that come from our work. I can talk to him about anything, and I can have a dig at him or joke with him."

Daniel had a far-away look in his eyes. "I have someone at work like that, too," he told me.

I watched him for a few moments. "He never loses it like my ex does. Even when the pressures at work get too much, you know... he always keeps his cool, even sometimes when I can't... Always the level-headed one..." I sighed. "I don't understand it. Where did I go wrong? Why did I have to pick such a self-centred, egotistical pig for a partner?"

He turned to me again. "Hey, it's not your fault. Don't blame yourself."

"I can't help it. I feel like such an idiot. He was really nice at first, you know? He was always a gentleman when we went out, paid for everything, and bought me gifts — even when I told him not to. I don't care about money. It's not important."

He smiled. "No, it's not."

"It is nice, though. An added bonus..." I twirled a piece of hair around my finger absently. "He *was* nice to me... Then things changed. I'm not sure when, but I didn't notice at first. I thought maybe he was just stressed at work or something... I don't know..."

I knew I was rambling... Why was I rambling to someone I barely knew?

Even after talking to Sia, it seemed I still needed to tell someone... but why the hottest guy on the station? I'd scare him away if I didn't shut up soon.

Daniel smiled sympathetically. "These guys are experts at what they do. Master manipulators. They have everyone fooled. You weren't to know."

That was true enough, but it didn't make me feel any better. "I'm usually a really good judge of character, you know, but he really had me thinking he was a genuinely nice guy..."

If I say 'you know' one more time... My cheeks flushed as I thought about how silly I sounded.

Daniel nodded. "It happens. They are manipulative and domineering. And it's always good people who suffer..."

My eyebrows shot up. "You sound like you're talking from experience."

He winced slightly. "I've seen them in action. A good friend of mine was so taken in by him that she even went as far as marrying him... They are divorced now..."

"Oh..." I shuddered. I didn't know what to say. I turned my attention back to the bubbling fountain, watching the water dance over the sculpture of a naked woman. The woman looked so peaceful and happy, and my insides churned while I thought about Malvolio and about what happened to Daniel's friend.

"Getting out before it was too late was the best thing — the only thing — you could've done. My friend wasn't so lucky. Her husband gave her a severe beating and broke her arm in several places and shattered her cheekbone before she left him."

"Oh, that's... horrible." The warmth drained from my face. I thought about what Malvolio did to me and cringed at the thought that he could've done so much more before he left the apartment. Maybe even killed me... Was he capable of that? I didn't know.

A little black and white bird perched on the statue's head out in the fountain. "Can you see that bird?" I asked, pointing toward the window.

Daniel turned and looked in the direction of my outstretched finger. "Yes. Looks like a Fantail. Must have been imported from Earth."

It was gorgeous. It stood on the statue's head, looking this way and that, while its tail fanned out and wagged from side to side.

Before I realised it, I was making a move to get up out of my seat. "Let's go outside," I said. I wanted to see the bird more clearly, and the idea of lying down in the grass again was looking very appealing. I must've been losing my sanity. I didn't care.

As I went to stand up, pain shot through my side and I gave a weird little yelp, and as I sank back into my seat, Daniel's elbow collided with my ribcage as he was moving to stand up. I cried out even louder and practically fell onto the seat, a wave of nausea accompanying the pain.

"Sorry!" he said quickly, but must have realised that his elbow couldn't have hurt me that much. "What's wrong?" He instinctively put a hand on my arm and added the electricity to the mix, causing me to jump. He quickly let go. "Sorry!"

The blackness at the edge of my vision told me I was close to passing out and the pain was making it hard to breathe. I closed my eyes and tried to take steady breaths.

"Lennina! Are you okay?"

He sounded so worried that my eyes flew open and I looked at him. *Might as well tell him now so he doesn't think there is something else wrong... Something worse...*

And of course, there was my promise that I wouldn't tell him any more lies. "I... ah... I have three broken ribs..."

CHAPTER 29
Did I Just Sigh Like a Lovesick Schoolgirl?

His expression turned dark, his eyes wide. "WHAT? As well as the black eye? Did it happen since I saw you last?" I could see it all coming together in his mind when I didn't answer. "Or do you mean... Why didn't you tell me?"

It didn't take a genius to figure out why I was so sick the day we met.

I was tingling all over. I needed to calm down. "I... I didn't know you..." I stammered. "It's... private... humiliating... It's not something you tell a complete stranger..."

His eyebrows turned upward. "I guess... But I could have helped ... done something more... if I had've known..." He raked his fingers through his hair, making it stick up even more, but somehow it still looked perfect. "*Shit*. I caused you to trip and you had broken ribs!"

"Don't... Don't do that to yourself. You didn't know. And you did more than enough to help me. And thank you for that. But I didn't want to have to answer a whole bunch of questions, you know..."

His eyes filled with unshed tears. "But I caused you to fall. You must have been in agony..."

"You weren't to know..." I told him again. I noticed that people were staring at us.

He raked his hand through his hair again. "But that doesn't change the fact that it caused you so much pain..."

I kind of squirmed in my seat. Without mentioning Malvolio's name, I told Daniel about the assault. I told him he thought I was cheating on him.

I didn't tell him I'd hit Malvolio. I was too ashamed.

Tears streamed steadily down my cheeks and Daniel put an arm around my shoulders. The now-familiar electricity ran through me and it took my breath away. But it was his gesture of kindness that seemed to be the trigger to open the floodgates. I'd been keeping all of my emotions bottled up, but now they came pouring out. We were in a public place, but I didn't care. He put his other arm around me and I turned into him and leaned my head against his chest. He said some words of comfort and held me while I sobbed. My ribs screamed at me with every movement, but I couldn't stop myself. The electricity buzzed through my whole body, and somehow it seemed to comfort me.

Was it my imagination, or did the buzzing cancel out some of the pain?

Someone at a nearby table asked if I was okay and I heard Daniel tell them I'd had some bad news and that I'd be alright. I felt the vibrations in his hard chest as he spoke, but his voice seemed far away somehow.

I could feel his pounding heartbeat and that comforted me as well.

When the sobs had slowed and finally stopped, I made myself look up at him. I had to see his eyes. For some strange reason, I drew comfort from him. I didn't know why. And I felt better once I'd simply let everything pour out of me.

"Feeling better?" he asked.

I nodded. I couldn't speak yet.

"I can't believe he did this to you," he said softly. It was almost a whisper. "How could he hurt you like that? I could never do that. Could never hurt you. I want to protect you from him. I know we've only just met, but I... I can't help it. Can't explain it. I feel I need to just... help... any way I can."

There were tears forming in his eyes again as he spoke. My heart swelled and I put my head back down onto his chest. I gave him a light squeeze as a kind of thank you and felt the slightest squeeze in return. He was probably worried about hurting me.

I closed my eyes and willed myself not to cry again. It was hard to believe he would say those things when he didn't even know me. I didn't know him either, but it didn't feel that way. I had to keep reminding myself that this was only the second time we'd met because it seemed like we already knew each other. Something about him was familiar to me. The fact that he'd grown up within the same culture as Javolo and that Taon and Azaeli were similar were the only things I could think of to explain it.

I sucked in a slow, deep breath and could smell him. The smell of clean fabric mixed with that woodsy aroma that reminded me of the outdoors. The park. It was hard to describe, but it was... nice. I felt a kind of comfort in his arms that I'd never felt anywhere else. I could stay here forever. Hide from my problems. Hide from the universe.

Daniel held me just that little bit tighter and it seemed to solidify what he'd said. That he'd meant every word.

Why didn't I find you instead of Malvolio? I wondered. *These last few months would have been so different... and I wouldn't be sitting here now with broken ribs... with all this pain...*

I wanted to stay in Daniel's arms and wipe Malvolio's existence from my brain forever.

What was happening here? Was I developing feelings for Daniel? No. Surely not. Love at first sight was just a fantasy.

I wasn't sure what I felt. I wasn't sure about anything anymore. After being hurt by Malvolio — and it was more than just the physical injuries — the last thing I needed was to be thinking about starting a relationship with someone new. I was crazy to think it would work out. I needed to get over Malvolio first. Needed to really sort through everything in my mind and my heart.

It was probably just a physical thing because he was good looking and because I was a total emotional wreck. Not a good basis for a relationship.

I moved my mind away from those thoughts. I couldn't think about that right now. I needed to move away from Daniel's strong embrace so I could think clearly. My head gave the order, but my body didn't make a move. I couldn't do it.

Right now, I needed comfort and someone to talk to. My mind kept telling me I should move back to my side of the seat and talk to him from there. *I can't... I don't want to let him go...*

I clung to Daniel as if he provided the very air I breathed. I didn't want to look up. I didn't want to see the world around me. I just wanted him to hold me. How did I get like this?

I'd always been strong and independent, but I needed to lean on someone for a while.

Eventually, I forced myself to shift around so I could see the courtyard again. I needed to distract myself and avoid bursting into tears again. Daniel adjusted his hold to suit my new position, but made no move to let me go. The electricity seemed to be a low hum now. It was still a mystery to me as to what it was and why it was happening to us. I'd never heard of it before.

I decided to tell him about the Enforcers and the problems I was having with them. I told Daniel that the Enforcers' investigation was going slow because my ex was in a high-credit position on the station.

"His status shouldn't make any difference. He assaulted you. He has to pay the price like anyone else."

Somehow I doubted it. There didn't seem to be much being done to help me. Or maybe I was imagining it. Being paranoid. But I remembered the look that Malvolio shared with Sarkozy.

I turned back to see Daniel looking at me. I could still see tears in his eyes, glistening in the low light from the nearby lamps. My heart melted. He slowly leaned closer to me. A sigh escaped my lips.

Did I really just do that? Did I just sigh like a lovesick schoolgirl? I felt the warmth rush to my cheeks.

He was so amazingly beautiful, both inside and out. So perfect. My gaze shifted from his eyes to his full lips. I wondered what it would be like to kiss him and have him hold me and run my fingers through his hair.

What? Where did that come from? What was I doing?

This was only the second time we'd met. And yet, here I was, in his arms, as if we were a couple.

What was I thinking? Just because he knew the right things to say, just because he was so... stunningly handsome... didn't mean that he was really, genuinely a good person deep down... I didn't even know him... He could be like Malvolio... But then, I felt like I *knew* him. Like we were kindred spirits...

Snap out of it! I ordered. Why was I listening to my heart and not my head? Where was my common sense and good judgement?

He was so close I could feel his breath on my face. I closed my eyes briefly, then looked back up into his eyes. The lightning buzzed through me, stronger now.

Then I stammered like an idiot. "But... they won't... He's..."

Daniel leaned his forehead against mine and I stopped talking. It felt strange to have the buzzing running through my head like that. "Shhh... Don't talk about that now..."

Our noses touched. My breathing stopped. Our lips were so close. My heart was pounding in my ears. My eyes closed without any command from my brain.

"Shhh," he said again when I opened my mouth to speak. How did he know what I was going to say? It didn't matter. "Breathe."

I forced myself to breathe again. We stayed like that for a while and I kept my eyes closed. I was having trouble breathing. His mouth was so close to mine. Was he going to kiss me? Did I want him to kiss me? Should I let him kiss me?

We were strangers, but there was a certain amount of excitement at the prospect of kissing a stranger. Well, not quite a stranger anymore...

He closed the small gap and gently pressed his lips to mine.

CHAPTER 30
I've Lost My Mind... And it Feels Great

Lightning shot through to the tips of my fingers and toes. It was such a soft kiss, but the electricity was so strong and explosive, and it made me feel alive. I gasped against his lips.

And that answered the question of whether I'd let him kiss me.

He pulled away only long enough for us to take a breath, then kissed me again. Warmth spread throughout my body. Everything else fell away. The sounds from the restaurant. The entire universe. The kiss started slowly, then became more urgent. This felt so right. I never wanted it to end.

I was melting and drowning and my mind was drifting away. I didn't want to let him go. I wanted him to kiss me forever. It felt like it was too much and not enough and I wanted more of him. I reached a hand up into the hair on the back of his head and pulled him closer.

He made a growling sound in the back of his throat. The kiss changed to something deeper. Something hungry. Like he couldn't get enough either. I needed to get closer to him. I felt like I was losing all control.

Then he slowed things down. When he pulled away, I was frozen to the spot and gasping for breath. I stayed there with my eyes closed for a few seconds, then realised I was just sitting there like an idiot, and opened them again.

Daniel was looking into my eyes again. Searching. For what? Maybe he thought I'd be upset with him for kissing me. But there was a whirl-wind running through my head and my heart. I was warm and cold, exhilarated, but scared, happy, but shaking. He would probably see it in my eyes. I watched the emotions play out in his. Could feel it somehow. I couldn't believe that I could feel so much from kissing someone, and that Daniel could feel the same. It was so strange. I wanted to laugh, but at the same time, I wanted to cry. Tears threatened to come. Happy tears. But I wouldn't let them.

"Your eyes are so blue," he breathed.

I melted. *And yours are so green...*

Kissing Malvolio had never felt anything like this. *Ugh!* I didn't want to think about him. Not now. Not ever.

What was I doing kissing Daniel? We'd just met. I was crazy. But how and why did he make me feel this way? Surely there was some rational explanation for it. Something that could explain my reckless behaviour and my wild emotional state. Malvolio had ruined everything. I couldn't even think straight.

Daniel's face suddenly lost a bit of its colour. "I'm so sorry. I shouldn't have done that. I don't know what came over me."

Oh, no. I felt my cheeks go cold. He regretted kissing me. Maybe he didn't really care about me. He was going to tell me it was all a big mistake and then make an excuse to leave. The thought of him leaving left me feeling empty inside. I needed his support right now. Tears stung my eyes.

"After— I mean— You must think I'm— Ugh, I'm not explaining this very well." He paused. "After what he did to you, the last thing you'd want is me... Please don't get the wrong idea. I don't want to upset you. I just... I couldn't help it..." He trailed off. His eyes were pleading. Worried.

Relief swept through me. I'd never been so glad to be wrong. "It's okay," I told him. "You haven't done anything wrong."

I leaned forward and kissed him again. It was only meant to be a quick kiss to put him at ease, but my lips lingered on his and I couldn't bring myself to pull away. His arms were around me again and my entire body buzzed and flushed with heat. His lips parted and I felt his tongue dart out, testing. I opened my mouth and let him in, and felt a shiver run down my spine as his tongue explored my mouth. I pulled him closer, but somehow he wasn't close enough.

He pulled back away from me and I gasped. The pupils in his beautiful green eyes were huge. We were both breathing hard and the sounds of the restaurant came flooding back to me. I felt my cheeks flush hot when

I realised we had an audience.

I closed my eyes and buried my face into his neck, hoping our audience would go back to whatever they were doing before.

Was I crazy? Why did I tell him it was okay to kiss me? Why did I kiss him back?

Because it was the most amazing thing I'd ever experienced and I wanted him to make me feel that way for the rest of my existence. I wanted to tell him he should never be sorry for doing that. But I couldn't.

I've lost my mind... And it feels great...

I kept my eyes closed and he held me close for a long time. I felt so safe in his arms. I needed to feel safe after all that had happened. After Malvolio...

A little voice in my head was telling me to stop this. To stop leading him on. To stop giving him the wrong idea about what was happening. But I couldn't help it. The thought of letting him go and going back to the hotel room to be alone again was something I couldn't bear. My tears fell silently onto his shoulder. I needed this. Needed to feel like someone cared. Needed to feel loved.

Loved? But how could he love me after us knowing each other for such a short time? Love at first sight was something that happened in romance stories. It wasn't real. This was crazy.

If I was crazy, then I'd be happy being crazy. They could lock me up. I wouldn't care, as long as they locked Daniel in the cell with me... Now that really *was* crazy.

So many questions flooded into my mind. I needed to sort through them, but there were too many. What was going on in that stupid, reckless brain of mine? What was I doing in the arms of a stranger? Why did I need him so much? Why couldn't I bring myself to let him go? What would he be thinking right now? What did he think of me? Why did he kiss me? Was it because he cared, or because I was there and the opportunity presented itself? Why did I let him kiss me?

It felt so good, though, to feel his lips against mine. To feel loved. To feel the desire run through my body in reaction to him. The sparks we experienced every time we touched were incredible, and they were enhanced when we kissed. It was strange, but it felt somehow like we were meant to be together.

None of it made sense. I knew so little about him, but I knew he was kind and sincere. Maybe I only felt like this because of what had happened with Malvolio. Maybe it was just the trauma.

If that was true, then I shouldn't be in Daniel's arms right now. I would be leading him on, making him think I had strong feelings for him — maybe even love him — but it might not be true. It *couldn't* be true. I needed to be more careful. I needed to exercise some self-control. That made me want to laugh. I didn't have any right now.

I thought about everything that had happened, turning it all over in my mind, and I started thinking about Javolo. I missed him. I wanted to go to work to apologise to him because I hadn't been at work to be his eyes and ears, and I wanted to tell him I hadn't really been sick. I felt like I'd let him down. Like I was being selfish. But that was silly. I'd needed the time to recover. I wasn't just sick, I had broken bones.

Man, I really need to get my head straight...

I realised I couldn't tell Javolo over the Com that I hadn't really been sick. They were always listening. And if I told them the truth, there would be too many questions and maybe some trips to counselling... And I'd be in trouble for lying...

I wanted to tell Javolo about everything that had happened and especially about Daniel. Although, I felt weird even thinking about telling him about Daniel and what had happened since I'd met him. But why? Why would it be weird? I suddenly didn't want to tell him. I'd told him about seeing Malvolio and it had been fine. I hadn't had a problem with it, although it was clear almost from the start that Javolo didn't like Malvolio. So why was this different? He was my best friend, so why would I feel this way about telling him I'd found someone as wonderful as Daniel?

Daniel's heartbeat was racing. I sat listening to it and I wondered why. He seemed so calm on the outside. My heart was racing too, thinking about everything.

Daniel kissed me on the top of my head and I felt like I would melt into a puddle on the floor, but I could sense that he was hesitant — like he was as confused as I was. I could feel it somehow. There was something in the air — I couldn't explain it. How could I know what he was feeling? I looked up at him and I could see it in his eyes. I thought of how I felt about Daniel and how I felt about Javolo and there were so many similarities.

While I looked into Daniel's eyes, I felt... Was I was falling for him? No. I couldn't be. But I could feel my emotions sweeping me away.

I'm losing my mind... I thought. *It has to be something else... Some other explanation...*

My thoughts returned to Javolo again and how I felt when I spent hours talking to him. How happy he made me feel. And I realised why the thought of telling him about Daniel was so weird. All the pieces clicked into place in my head. All the good times. All the joking around and laughing and how terrified I felt whenever there was ground movement in the tunnels. Why I felt so sad every time I thought about working with another Digger and never getting to talk to him again.

It hit me hard. I was in love with Javolo!

CHAPTER 31

Malvolio is the Biggest Jerk in the Universe!

That was why I felt so at ease and so full of life at the same time when I was working with him and why I was so desperate to get back there and talk to him over the Com. That was also why I was planning on quitting my job so I could meet him. He was more than a friend to me.

I love him! I really love him! I screamed in my mind. *I think I've loved him for a long time! Why didn't I see it before? I'm so stupid!*

I could see it in Daniel's eyes. Felt his body tense. He knew something was different. Something was wrong. It would have been written all over my face.

What was I going to do? What had I gotten myself into? To maybe, possibly, be in love with both of them... My mind raced and my heart felt like it was going to burst.

No, no, no, no, no! This can't be happening. Maybe I'm just imagining my feelings for Daniel. How can I be in love with two guys? Well, probably in love. Maybe. I don't know. This is... so wrong...

I could feel new tears forming and tried to blink them away.

Daniel's eyes were searching, questioning. "Lennina? What is it? What's wrong?"

My head was going to explode. I started to pull away from him. How could I even *begin* to explain? "I... I've got to go... I've just realised something... I have some serious thinking to do."

Daniel grabbed my arm. "What? What do you mean? Did I do something wrong?" He looked down at his hand on me and gasped. It seemed to have freaked him out to realise that he was holding onto me like that. He released me quickly. "Sorry."

He was clearly confused by the sudden change and my need to leave.

I looked into those dreamy green eyes. What to tell him? The truth? I'd promised myself. No more lies. "I... I like you... a lot. But like, more than just friends." I blurted out.

His eyes widened and he raised his eyebrows. But then a smile lit up his face. "What's so bad about that?"

What's so bad? Well, I just ended a really bad relationship. Don't they say you shouldn't just grab the nearest guy? Something about a rebound relationship being really bad... And then there's the fact that I don't know you... And then there's the other fact that I think I love my best friend... "I... I think that... I just realised... that..." *Spit it out!* "I'm in love with... someone else... I think I have been for a while... a long while... I... just didn't know it..."

Tears streamed down my cheeks. How could this have happened?

I could see the hurt in his eyes and I felt so bad for doing this to him, but I had to say something. And not lie. No more lies. It only made things worse.

"What are you saying?" he asked. "Who are you talking about? You mean your ex?"

My chest tightened. "NO! Not him! *No way!* Malvolio is the biggest jerk in the universe—"

"Malvolio? Did you say Ma—"

"It will never be him! Not after what he did..." I shuddered at the thought of all the things he'd done, and the movement hurt my ribs. Daniel touched my arm to comfort me and I relished the warm buzz.

I felt confusion and a sort of elation fill me, but they weren't my feelings. I didn't know how, but I knew they were flooding through from Daniel. But that was impossible. How could I feel someone else's emotions? And how could I know they were from him? The elation was growing by the second and he was looking at me with a smile spreading across his lips.

Why was he smiling? I shook my head to try to get those feelings out of my mind and my heart. Then I realised I'd told him Malvolio's name. It didn't matter anymore.

I looked into Daniel's eyes and could see the emotions I'd been feeling... The emotions that weren't mine... But how?

"No," I continued, more calmly than I felt. "It's the guy I work with. I've known him for like four months and I didn't realise I loved him till just now." Daniel's eyes widened even more. "Which is crazy because I've never met him because he's a Digger..."

His eyes glistened with unshed tears. "What?"

I shifted uncomfortably. "I don't know why I didn't tell you I'm a Nav Operator—"

"What?"

I felt so terrible for lying to him, even if it was only by omission, but it was too late.

"I didn't know what to tell you... I didn't know you... Anyway, I have to go. I have to think... Sort my head out..." I moved further away from him and he kinda sat there staring. "Please understand... I have to tell him I love him... even though I'm not allowed to." My heart was twisting inside my chest and I raked a hand through my hair. "I'm sorry, but I do — but... I think I'm... I can't! Not both of you! I've got to get outta here!"

I shifted to the edge of the seat so there was no chance of touching him. Maybe if I touched him and felt the lightning race through me, I might not be able to leave. And I had to leave. *Now.*

"Lennina, I..."

My heart felt as if it was being squeezed inside my chest. It was a horrible feeling. How could this happen? How could I fall for them both? How could I just tell him all this? Just rip his heart out? I was a monster and I was totally disgusted with myself.

I hadn't used physical violence like Malvolio, but I'd hurt him anyway. How could I be so cruel?

I looked at Daniel and could hardly see the incredulous look on his face through my tears. I knew it had to be hurting him, but I couldn't help it. I'd loved Javolo for maybe a few months and not even realised it!

This was all too much. I couldn't deal with it. My ribs ached and I realised I'd been hardly breathing. I forced myself to take in some slow breaths.

I needed to clear my head, but then I had to tell Javolo. I would have to wait and tell him at work tomorrow. Somehow. I didn't care if people from The Company were listening in. I was giving them notice anyway, so it wasn't like I would lose my job over it.

I realised that Daniel was speaking to me. He had tears in his eyes, which didn't surprise me. "... please, listen to me. I need to talk to you... Tell you—"

"No! I have to go..." My heart was trying to jump out of my chest as I stood up and it felt like there was no air left in the room. I needed air. Needed to breathe. My ribs screamed in pain and I felt faint. I wondered how I was going to make it back to the hotel.

He tried to say something more, but I didn't want him to say anything that would make me feel worse than I already did, so I cut him off. "No. Don't. I'm sorry. I'm *really* sorry. I have to go... Don't look at me like that... I *have* to. I need to think..." I looked away from him. I didn't want to see the pain I was causing him. "I have to go!"

CHAPTER 32

I Quit

I practically yelled out that last bit, then I stumbled through the restaurant to the door, my ribs feeling worse by the second. My surroundings were starting to spin.

"Wait!" he called after me. I could hear him following behind me as I made it outside. I didn't know what he was talking about, but didn't stop to think about it. I had to escape. "Lennina! Wait! I have to tell you something! *Wait!*"

It was too late. I could still hear him calling as I ran, but couldn't hear what he was saying and after a while, his voice faded away as I ducked into a shop that I knew had a back entrance into an alley, then crossed the alley and headed into another shop, almost blinded by my tears. The pounding of my heart in my ears made it hard to hear.

I thought I could hear footsteps coming closer, so I rushed into the change room and closed the door. I sat on the little shelf where you put your bags and waited there for a long time before coming out and looking around outside the shop. There was no sign of him.

I ducked down a narrow alley that ran between two shops. I looked back a few times, but couldn't see Daniel anywhere. There was a side entrance to a shop on my left, so I took it and hurried through and out the front door, which opened onto another street.

The park was straight ahead, so I thought I'd take a shortcut through it to the taxi waiting station. I was halfway across the grassed area when I noticed that the sunshine had been dimmed.

Uh, oh.

I knew what that meant.

Rain.

I couldn't run. I tried to walk faster, but I was in too much pain. The drops were light at first, but within seconds, I was wet through to my skin.

I groaned. *This day just keeps getting better.*

Once I reached the edge of the park, I stepped out of the downpour and pressed the call button at the taxi waiting station. Water pooled around my feet while I waited. My clothes and hair were stuck to my skin. I was thankful that my bag was waterproof, but the new clothes I'd bought were sopping wet.

I didn't have to wait long for a taxi to stop for me. I practically fell into it — not caring about wetting the seat — and it took me back to the hotel while searing pain ripped at my side. And my heart.

I ignored the questioning look from the desk clerk at my drowned-space-rat appearance and headed up to my room.

Once inside, I peeled off my clothes, wrapped myself in a bathrobe, put a towel on my pillow, and carefully climbed into bed. Another flood of tears followed and I let them come. The guilt ate at my gut. How could I do that to him? I could have lied — made up some excuse to leave — without telling him something like that.

I lay there afterwards feeling drained and exhausted, and somehow, I finally managed to fall asleep.

—— ⋆·☆·⋆ ——

The unusual tone of the alarm clock jolted me awake. Pain shot through me with the movement. It took a few seconds for me to recognise where I was. For the memories to come flooding back. I felt like crying all over again.

I almost turned the alarm off. I didn't want to face the day ahead, but I knew I had to.

As I lay there trying to will my body to get up, I saw a flash of light in the rough shape of a human in front of my vision and realised I'd been dreaming about it. It made me think of the rumours of the Ghosts that supposedly haunted the tunnels down on Kronos. Rogan told everyone he'd seen one the day he'd lost it down there. They say if you see a Ghost, you've been down there too long. Being underground can affect some people like that.

It had happened when I'd been off sick. He'd gone crazy insisting there was something down there and I'd lost him as my Digger. And on my next shift, Javolo had been assigned as my new work partner.

I'd felt a pull toward the being in my dream. Like it was calling to me.

The sound of the alarm reminded me that I needed to get moving. I forgot the dream and headed to the kitchen with a new conviction. I had to do this today.

I was famished. I hadn't eaten dinner the night before.

As I ate breakfast, I searched my feelings. I needed to be sure of how I felt about Javolo before I said anything to him. I still came up with the same thing. I loved him.

Guilt clawed at my chest when I thought of the disaster that was yesterday. I'd kissed Daniel, told him I thought I was developing feelings for him, then told him I loved someone else and had run out on him. He probably thought I was a nasty, manipulative person. Like Malvolio. Or like his friend's ex-husband. Who wouldn't?

I'm such a bitch! How could I do that to him? How could I be so cruel? Why didn't I just make up some excuse for why I had to go? Why did I do that?

My heart sank. Daniel would probably never speak to me again. I'd stuck a knife in his heart and twisted it for good measure. I wiped my eyes and forced myself to eat some breakfast. As I drank my tea, it reminded me of Daniel. Then my thoughts turned to Javolo and what I had to do. It was so hard to stay focused.

One of the biggest disasters of all was that I'd resolved to stay away from relationships and as soon as I'd made that promise to myself, I'd broken it. Smashed it into tiny pieces.

Re-wrapping the bandage after my shower proved to be a nightmare. It should have been getting easier to do. I really needed someone to help me... or a third arm...

Finally, I was ready to go. I headed off to work with renewed conviction.

I had to tell Javolo. I didn't care about the consequences. I had to tell him everything. I hoped it didn't ruin our friendship, but I was sick of the lies, sick of the pain, sick of The Company and their stupid policies, and sick of living in fear of Malvolio.

Today, things were going to change.

——— ⋆·☆·⋆ ———

I arrived early and went to see the head supervisor, Mr Sonrisa. I didn't want to deal with Janga today.

Sonrisa was surprised when I told him I wanted to quit. It was unusual for someone to terminate their contract early with Katoa, but I cited health issues as the main reason.

It was more lies, but what could I do?

He told me I'd have to submit a formal resignation in writing, stating the reasons and providing medical certificates. I simply nodded.

I was flooded with a mixture of relief and sadness and I vowed to get Javolo's contact details before I left.

I'd have to work for another two weeks before finishing up, but I wished more than anything that I could leave at the end of the day.

Before I left the office, Sonrisa told me Janga had put in a recommendation for me to be assigned to a new partner for the rest of my Rotation.

My chest tightened. "I have a new partner?"

CHAPTER 33

This is Going to Be a Really Long, Awful Day

"No. Not yet, anyway. But we both agree that you need to have a Psyche Eval. It's been booked for tomorrow."

A Psyche Eval?

The last thing I needed was to be forced to go to counselling. But I wouldn't have to now that I'd quit. I tried to calm my rattled nerves.

"Well, you might as well cancel it now that I'm quitting."

He didn't answer.

I hoped they would at least let me work with Javolo till I finished up, though it didn't seem likely.

Once I'd logged into my workstation and the Com system, my nerves went into overdrive thinking about what I'd say to Javolo.

I performed the routine checks that were needed before we could get started for the day. It was so hard to get back into the swing of things. Much harder than I thought it would be. It had only been a week, but that wasn't the reason I was finding it so difficult. My mind wasn't on the job and my heart wasn't in it anymore. So much had happened in those seven days.

I had to push hard to keep focused on all the mundane things like checking the equipment and working out where to begin mining for the day.

I flipped on the Com system and stated my name and Nav ID.

"Hey, you!" Javolo said as a greeting. It was so good to hear the enthusiasm in his every word — even though he'd only uttered two of them — and to hear his voice. I felt like I'd come home after a long holiday.

"Hey, yourself!" I was dying to say more, but we had to work. If I didn't complete all the necessary groundwork, I could create a very dangerous situation for him. So I pushed myself harder.

I wondered how I would tell him. How to even start? What could I possibly say?

He continued on in his cheerful tone. "How're you feeling, Cal?" I could tell he genuinely wanted to know how I felt. It wasn't the usual empty greeting people gave out of habit.

"I'm much better now. Thanks. Who did they give you while I was gone?"

"Salvani. She's cool. We get along pretty good."

"That's good. Nadesha is pretty easygoing."

"Is that her first name? It's pretty."

"Yeah."

I started us on the usual equipment checks on the Mech-suit before he could say any more. We couldn't afford to talk too much after the last day we'd worked together. That had been a disaster in so many ways.

As I listened to his crackly voice, I thought he sounded different somehow. Maybe I was imagining things. Maybe he sounded so happy because I was so down. Was it because I was finally back at work? Maybe he hadn't gotten along with Salvani as well as he'd said and was relieved to have me back.

No... It was more than that. He was way too happy.

Maybe while I was away, he'd met the beautiful woman that he'd talked about the other day. My heart sank. What if he had finally met the 'girl of his dreams' and was now in a relationship? I hadn't thought of that. What if he didn't feel the same way about me?

I ran a hand across my forehead and through my hair. I was confused. Should I tell him? What if he laughed at me? What if he thought I was joking? We hassled each other all the time. He could just take it that way.

How could I cope with that? What would I even say to that? Should I laugh and pretend I was joking, or should I tell him it's true? I couldn't just laugh it off. I'd made up my mind to let him know how I felt, regardless of the consequences.

My attention was jolted back to reality as the Nav Computer gave me the information needed to get started. I was finding it so hard to do my job, but somehow managed to give him directions for his first run.

"I'm on it," he said cheerfully.

What was that? Was he actually humming? My heart deflated a little more.

I swallowed hard. Once I told him how I felt, it could ruin all we had together.

This is going to be a really long, awful day, I thought.

Despite all the questions and negative thoughts racing through my mind, in the end, it boiled down to the fact that I loved him and that I *really* needed to tell him.

I was determined that whatever happened, I would be honest with both Javolo *and* Daniel. That was the least I could do. I would have to live with whatever outcome there was after that.

If Javolo was involved with someone else, then I would have to find a way to deal with it.

What if he did love me, but loved the other woman too?

That would be an even *bigger* mess. I'd heard of love triangles, but that would be beyond ridiculous with Daniel thrown in too.

"Turn left at the second intersection," I told him. Concentrating was so damned hard.

"Yes, Ma'am."

I smiled, but my mind went straight back to what I'd been thinking about and it disappeared from my face.

I didn't know how I was going to tell him I loved him, but then tell him I had strong feelings for someone else. It seemed so nasty, and I already felt so bad for doing it to Daniel, but it was the truth. He deserved that much. They both did. I had to at least tell him what was going on inside my heart. There was a strange feeling of déjà vu. I'd done this once already this lifetime, and once was way too many.

I was dreading it, but I'd made up my mind.

No more lies.

Once it was all out in the open, then we could start to sort everything out from there.

How did my life get to this? I wondered. My life had been so simple.

All the troubles started when I came to this tin can floating around that chunk of rock out there. I wanted to go home. For the first time since I'd arrived, I really wanted to go back home.

But I pushed on. I had to. What else could I do at this point?

I checked my screen. "Okay, the computer says you're on the right track," I told him. *But I really want to tell you something... I need to talk to you... right now...*

"About what?"

I gasped. "What?"

CHAPTER 34

Just Do It

"Didn't you just say you wanted to tell me something?"

"I — ah, no."

What was that? I didn't say those words out loud. Did I?

I watched as the dot with Javolo's Digger ID above it moved forward on the screen. Six eight nine six. The number was burned into my memory. I doubted I'd ever forget it. Salvani must have changed the settings so it would display the number instead. I quickly changed it back to his name. I preferred to see his name rather than a number. The Company seemed to forget that the Diggers were actually people.

He gave a huff. "Yep, this looks right."

I remembered to double-check the information. "Yes. Just head down and around to the right." I felt so frustrated. I didn't want to be doing this. *I wish we could just stop and talk...*

"Me too."

"What?"

"I didn't say anything."

"Oh. Must have been a noise over the Com."

That was weird. I could have sworn I heard him answer me. Answer something I only thought and didn't say out loud. I shook my head. I must have imagined it.

The Nav Computer gave me a definite location. "Got some new info. It confirms the stuff we already had. Keep going that way."

"Got it." I could hear his breathing and the hydraulics in the suit as he walked. A rare few seconds of clarity across the Com.

Tell him. Tell him. Say something... "Umm..." I ventured.

"Yeah?" was his enthusiastic reply. He had no idea.

Say something. Now. Don't keep putting it off. "Javolo... I... umm... need to talk to you later..." There. I said something. I'd started the ball rolling.

"Okay, sure."

Huh?

It was weird that he didn't ask what it was about. It was usually immediate with him to ask what I wanted, like a reflex action... Maybe he was too preoccupied with what he was doing...

I doubted it — he was just walking.

"Me too," he added quietly.

I gasped. So Javolo had something to talk about as well?

Now I was curious... and anxious. All sorts of possibilities ran through my mind... My heartbeat picked up. Had he gotten to know that woman from the grav shaft? Even if he had, I had to tell him my stuff first so I wouldn't lose my nerve.

I ran a hand through my hair. *This is so hard. How can I do this? We need to talk, but when? Maybe when he's at the shuttle dumping the load... Yes... He won't need to be concentrating much on what he's doing... That'll be the safest time... otherwise I can't talk to him at all.*

I kept giving directions until he was finally able to start work on a large vein. The rock-breaker hammered away, and so did my heart.

I started to chew on a fingernail. My insides were churning.

How do I even start a conversation like that? Hey Javolo, I think I love you even though we've never met, and by the way, I think I love this other guy I've only met twice... How stupid does that sound?

The waiting was driving me insane. Maybe I could tell him part of it once he'd finished the noisy part of the digging — but which part? I couldn't say I loved him and then wait till he reached the shuttle to tell him there was someone else too. That would be more than cruel. My heartbeat thundered in my chest and I realised I was wringing my hands, so I made a conscious effort to put them in my lap and keep them there.

Maybe I should ask him about the woman from the grav shaft first — find out what was going on there? I could at least see what was happening before telling him how I felt about him. It wouldn't make it any easier, but if I knew, I could word things differently.

Yes. That was a better way to approach things. Maybe I could ask casually. He was raving about her on our last shift together. It wouldn't seem like a strange question to ask him.

My palms were sweating and my hands began to shake. I had to somehow keep control and just ask him.

Finally, Javolo finished digging. This was my chance. My heart thrummed in my ribcage and my bottom lip quivered. And I hadn't even said anything yet...

Umm... That girl you saw the other day with the long, dark hair. Have you seen her again? Have you met her? I sighed heavily. *Just do it.*

Just as I worked up the courage and opened my mouth to say something, Javolo swore loudly.

My heart slammed up against my ribcage. "What? What is it? What happened? Are you hurt?"

"No. Nothing like that. There was this really bright flash of light from out of nowhere... Blinded me for a few seconds... It's gone now."

There was a lot of interference coming through the Com and it was hard to hear him.

"What do you mean? Is there another Digger in there?" I checked the Nav Computer for signs of other Diggers in the area. "There's nothing on my screen."

"No. No one. There's nothing... No more light from any dir..." The static wiped out his voice.

I continued to scan the information on the screen. "It's hard to hear you. I have nothing in that area on screen. There should be no one near you at all."

He sighed heavily. "Then I don't know what it was."

I sighed too. It didn't make any sense. What could have caused a flash of light so far underground? Was there some kind of malfunction with the Mech-suit? Maybe he needed to get out of it before something caught alight—

"Whoah!"

I heard a loud crash through the Com and my heart skipped a beat. "What was that?"

CHAPTER 35

It's Right in Front of Me!

"That was freaky... It just... Whatever it was, it—" Static took over for a few seconds. "—at me like it was going to attack me... knocked me over!"

I tried to imagine the scene with the Mech-suit lying on the ground. "You're breaking up. Are you okay? What was it? Did you get a better look this time?"

I could hear the alarm within the suit telling him it was in a horizontal position. "I can't tell you what it was. It was a mass of bright coloured lights. Man, it was so weird — it went straight *through* me!"

Wow... "How is that even possible?"

"Uh, I don't know."

I tried to calm my breathing. "Are you okay, though?"

"Yeah, I'm fine. Suit's rep... all systems norm... Just need to get up."

There was a pause as he wrangled the Mech-suit into a standing position. I tried to picture it as I heard him grunt a few times with the effort. The suits were large and heavy and although the hydraulic system made it easier to move the heavy arms and legs, it still took some effort to do something as drastic as getting up off the ground.

I thought about what he'd said. A mass of bright coloured lights in the tunnels, and it went straight through him. It couldn't be a drone or anything from Katoa. A drone would be solid. It wouldn't be able to pass right through a guy in a heavy metal Mech-suit.

Then I thought of the Ghost sightings. What else could it have been? The Ghosts supposedly didn't exist, so was Javolo starting to lose his mind like Rogan? Or were the Ghosts real and there was nothing wrong with Rogan?

Uh, oh. Katoa recorded all of our conversations. They would recognise this as a sighting and act accordingly. They would take him off active duty and give him some counselling. I wished I could do something, but there was no way to undo what had already been said.

"Okay," he said finally, "I'm up."

"Javolo?" I asked quietly. I couldn't keep the tremor out of my voice.

"Yeah?" His voice was just as quiet.

I fidgeted with the edge of my keyboard. "They're listening..."

"I know."

I could hear it in his voice. He knew what would happen to him. I extended the view of the surrounding tunnels on my screen. Nothing. No one. My hands were trembling. I could feel the tears. I wouldn't let them come.

His voice sounded oddly hollow. "Do you think I'm losin' it?"

"No!" I answered firmly. "There's no way!"

He could still hold a coherent conversation and had done nothing to make me think there was something even remotely wrong with him. He'd never shown any of the symptoms that I'd been told to look for. But now he was reporting seeing bright lights. Bright lights that had travelled *through* his body. Had even caused him to fall over in the very expensive Mech-suit. The Company wouldn't like that.

"Hey!" he shouted.

My eyes went wide. "What?"

"It's back! It's right in front of me!"

There goes your career out the window, I thought as I bit my lip.

"What's it doing?"

I was scared, but really curious. If it *was* a Ghost — a real entity — there were all kinds of possibilities. It would have to be extra-terrestrial. Possibly native to Kronos. Maybe even sentient.

"Nothin'. Just kinda floatin' there... Whoah... It's really close..." His voice had reduced to a whisper.

"What does it look like?" I asked. My fear was quickly turning into excitement. I really wished I could see what he was seeing.

"It's really bright and it's all different colours. It kinda has a shape. I can see arms and legs. A head. I can see right through it. It's moving around slowly. It must be some kinda life form. It's checkin' me out..."

There was a long pause and all I could hear was static. I couldn't keep quiet a moment longer. "What's it doing now?"

It was amazing. This could be First Contact with an alien species. And Javolo was right there...

"Just lookin' at me. Its face — if you could call it that — it's like right in front of the shield on the Mech-suit. Wow..." he breathed.

Goose bumps spread across my skin. It was incredible. I stared at the dot on the screen next to his name and tried to imagine being there. I wished I was there...

"It has moved back now. Hey. I put the suit's hand out, palm forward, and it is touching it. Palm to palm. Like he's giving me a high five. That's weird. My hand sort of feels warm and tingly from the touch, even though the suit is the thing touching him."

I tingled with excitement. I realised I'd been closing my eyes while trying to picture the scene. I'd forgotten everything else. I looked at the readouts on the screen. There were still no indicators that there was anyone there with Javolo. No sign of anything at all. Maybe that was one of the reasons why the Diggers who'd seen these creatures were thought to be crazy. No evidence.

"Cal?"

I tapped a fingernail on my teeth. "Yeah?"

"It seems to be calling me or something."

I frowned. "What do you mean?" *What could it want?*

"It's kind of movin' its arm like it's beckoning me. Maybe it wants to take me to its leader." He laughed out loud at his own joke.

I stifled a laugh. "Oh, you're sooo funny..." I couldn't wipe the smile from my face. Trust him to be joking around at a time like this... But that's what I really liked about him.

"Oh... it seems to be getting kinda agitated. It wants something... Trying to talk to me, I think. Maybe I should go with it."

"Yeah, maybe you..." A warning message flashed up on the Nav Computer's screen. My heart was in my throat. "Hey, there's a message coming up on my screen," I told him, my stomach twisting into knots. "It says you need to return to the shuttle immediately. You're in trouble now."

I wasn't joking about him being in trouble.

"But I *can't* go now. I need to... then I can... and find out what he wants... Try to communicate..."

Damned static.

"These are direct orders." I told him.

I felt a sinking feeling in my chest. I needed to somehow convince him to follow orders so he wouldn't get into more trouble, but I didn't want him to lose contact with the alien either.

"Just a bit longer. I can't lose contact with it now... is really goin' crazy over there like it's a matter of life and death..."

There was a whole lot of static coming through. I understood why he didn't want to move, but he was being ordered back. He shouldn't ignore it.

Another warning message came up on the screen. My heart froze as I read it. This one was a warning about ground movement in the area. In the *immediate* area.

"I'm gonna follow him—"

"Get out of there!" I shouted, my mind screaming at me to make him listen. "The computer is reporting ground movement. It's gonna—"

Several things happened at once. Javolo yelled out over the Com, there was a loud roar and crashing sound, and I felt something heavy hit my left shoulder from above, making me cry out.

CHAPTER 36

Javolo? Can You Hear Me?

I was dazed for a while... The pain was unbearable on my left side, but the rest of my body was numb. I opened my mouth to scream, but nothing came out.

What happened?

My vision was clouded and I realised I was staring at the ceiling. Why was I staring at the ceiling? Had I fallen? I couldn't move. It felt like my left side was being crushed — like the roof had caved in on me.

A few seconds passed and my vision cleared some more. I could still see the ceiling, which meant I was lying on the floor. Whatever had fallen on me must have knocked me off my chair. I looked around and saw my chair lying on its side to my right. It didn't seem to be damaged. I looked back up at the ceiling. It looked normal. Undamaged. That didn't make any sense.

What had fallen on me?

I took some deep breaths and tried to calm my erratic heartbeat. I had to look. I had to see what was crushing me. There had to be broken bones. I could feel it. I steeled myself, not wanting to see the blood, but knowing I had to see what had happened. I managed to lift my head and look down at my body, cringing and expecting the worst, but there was nothing there. Everything looked normal.

I gasped. How could there be nothing? What was going on? Why was I in so much pain? It still felt like a heavy weight was pinning me to the floor.

I tried to lift my arm to have a closer look at it, but it wouldn't move. I tried again and was able to raise it a little. I couldn't see anything wrong with it — but moving it caused me more pain, so I lowered it gently to the floor.

I couldn't understand it. There was no blood, nothing that could be causing the intense crushing pain, but I was still feeling it.

The numbness was fading. I started to feel the pain from my ribs as well. It was nothing compared to this new pain, but at least I knew that that was something I could explain. At least it was real.

Panic was creeping into my mind. I was taking fast, shallow breaths and was shaking all over. What was wrong with me? There was nothing there. I had no injuries that I could see, yet I was in severe pain... Why was this happening? It didn't make sense.

I tried to remember what had happened before I ended up on the floor. Maybe I could find some clue as to what happened. There was the report of ground movement and that loud crash over the Com. My heart was suddenly in my throat.

Javolo!

I had to see if he was okay. But how was I going to get up off the floor?

I felt the right side of my head. My earpiece was still there. I was relieved that I didn't have to hunt around on the floor for it.

"Javolo?"

Static was the only answer.

My fingers travelled to the back of my head. There was a huge lump there. Probably from hitting the floor. It didn't feel good.

The thought of Javolo lying under fallen debris from a collapsed tunnel motivated me to slowly drag myself up to a sitting position. I had to do something to help him.

The room spun.

I grabbed the chair with my 'good' arm and managed to pull it upright. After a number of attempts, I climbed up onto it, then carefully placed my left arm on my lap. I could hardly move it, or my left leg. I wasn't sure how I'd managed to get up, but I had to know what happened to Javolo. Was that roaring noise I'd heard the sound of the roof coming down on him? It had to be. Was he alright? Was he alive?

The room spun some more. "Javolo?"

Nothing.

"Javolo? Can you hear me?"

Still nothing.

I read the information streaming down the screen. There had been major ground movement, which had caused the tunnels in Javolo's immediate vicinity to collapse. My heart twisted and I felt adrenalin rush through my veins. "No!"

CHAPTER 37

Get Out of Here!

I could read it, could understand it, but couldn't believe it. This couldn't be happening. I'd just been talking to him.

I took a deep breath. "Javolo? Javolo, do you read me? *Javolo!*"

Tears were already threatening to flow. With a collapse that big, the chances of him surviving were practically zero. My legs became jelly.

No! No, not him! Not now! I thought of all the hours we'd spent together, laughing and joking as we worked... I couldn't lose him. I'd only just realised how I felt about him.

I didn't get the chance to tell him...

I stopped myself. This was not helping him.

Okay... Breathe... Procedures... what are the procedures in the event of a tunnel collapse?

I couldn't think... I'd completed all the training, and couldn't remember any of it. It was all for nothing. I couldn't get my mind to focus. I kept imagining his crushed body...

This is why we aren't allowed to get too close to our partners... Too many emotions... I'm an idiot...

I was beside myself. How was I going to be any good to him like this?

I knew it wouldn't have mattered who was in the Digger's suit, I doubted I would have been able to cope no matter who it was. I cared too much about everyone.

I was in the wrong profession.

Bit too late to realise that.

In my mind's eye, I could see the dirt surrounding me...

I closed my eyes and focused. *Calm down... Breathe... What do I need to do?*

Opening my eyes again, I got to work. I kept calling him on the Com, while punching in requests for help on the screen, one-handed. The phantom pains from nowhere were unbearable and were making it extremely hard to focus and function. The fingers on my left hand wouldn't move properly so typing with two hands was not an option.

If I wasn't able to see for myself that my body was uninjured, I would have sworn I had multiple broken bones in my arm and leg. And maybe my shoulder, too. It didn't feel right.

There must be a rational explanation for the pain, I thought, *But what? Think...*

The 'injuries' were consistent with me being struck from above by something extremely heavy... Like I'd been in the tunnels with Javolo when the collapse happened... Javolo was the only one in there... Could I be somehow feeling Javolo's pain? No. That was impossible. How could I? It was beyond the laws of physics.

Focus...

It was hard to see through the tears and I swiped them away with the back of my hand. I remembered that I had to make sure my supervisor knew all the details — the last coordinates recorded and the section Javolo was in before the incident. They'd be in the system, but I needed to send confirmation from my end. I sent them to him as I kept calling on the Com.

Information came up on the screen about the collapse. Several Diggers in the general area had not been responding to calls from their Nav Operators since the collapse. The Coms were now down and Satellite Navigation wasn't able to pinpoint them as it was estimated that all or most of the missing Diggers had damaged satellite equipment.

How were they going to find them all? How could they possibly make it there in time with all the equipment failures? And how could I help from where I was? I didn't know the answers, but I had to keep trying and do whatever I could.

I tried hard to calm my breathing, but failed.

Another thing I had to confirm was whether he was carrying a load of Amakio and how much air he had left. It was coming back in bits and pieces, but that wasn't good enough.

Think! I ordered myself. *And focus!*

I remembered that he'd just finished digging, so his tub would be empty. The system said he had six hours of air left in his tanks. I gave a shaky sigh. I hoped they could get him out within the six hours. I had to push aside thoughts of what would happen if they didn't.

Finding it practically impossible to concentrate with the constant pain, I reached a shaky hand across to my purse and grabbed some painkillers. The usual dose was one, but I took two. I put them in my mouth quickly and swallowed.

If the pain down my left side really was from Javolo, the painkillers might not work, but I had to do something, even if they only killed the pain in my ribs.

Taking some slow, careful, deep breaths seemed to help a bit, but there was still too much pain. And I couldn't expand my lungs fully without making it worse.

I stared at my screen. For some reason, it was hard for me to see it properly. It was too dark. I checked the brightness control. It was set to its usual setting. I turned it up. It didn't make any difference. Even with it turned up as far as it would go, it was too dark. What was going on? Was it broken? Was I losing my sight?

I tried to take a deep breath and it felt like there wasn't enough air in the room.

—— ⋆·☆·⋆ ——

I opened my eyes. I was lying across my desk with my cheek on the keyboard. I remembered the screen looking too dark, but nothing after that. I'd somehow managed to pass out and not fall to the floor again.

I pushed myself up as the memories flooded into my mind and my head started to spin.

Oh no! Javolo!

How long had I been out? He could have been calling while I was unconscious.

"Javolo? Do you copy?"

Nothing.

The screen was so bright it hurt my eyes. I turned the brightness down and scrolled up to the last piece of information I remembered reading.

They were making progress into digging their way to the men and one of them had regained consciousness. He reported being injured and wedged in by the falling rocks. The panic started to ramp up. Reading that made it more real somehow. I desperately needed to know if Javolo was okay.

I saw a report on the screen that said the Com system had come back online. I tried to call Javolo again in case his was now functioning, but there was still no answer.

The door to my cubicle opened and Sonrisa stormed in. "What are you *doing?*" he roared, the veins sticking up in his neck and his face bright red.

I cringed at the sudden blast. "Mr Sonrisa... I've been—"

"You've been making a mess, that's what you've been doing. Have you forgotten all your training?" he bellowed.

"N-no, I've had some trouble... I'm in a lot of pain and umm..."

I didn't know what to say. They would lock me up and throw away the key if I told them I could feel some horrific pains that I thought might be coming from my Digger.

He ignored me. "Why did you wait so long before calling your Digger? It was four minutes and twenty-seven seconds before you made the first call. After that, it was another forty-five seconds before you entered in your details to confirm that your Digger was in the vicinity of the collapse and was not responding to calls."

Sonrisa hardly stopped for a breath and didn't give me a chance to answer. This scenario was very familiar. I dragged my thoughts away from Malvolio and tried to focus on what he was saying. He let loose with more questions that apparently did not need answering.

Four minutes and twenty-seven seconds. It had taken that long for me to call Javolo. I must have passed out. That would be why I didn't realise at first that I was lying on the floor.

I tried to take in what he was saying, but I zoned out for a while. I couldn't help it. I wasn't bored. The pain was too overwhelming.

Somewhere in the middle of it all, I felt a change in the pain down my left side. It increased sharply, then receded like someone had shifted the heavy weight off me and proper circulation was now getting through to my arm and leg. It was still agony, but it was better than it was. I wondered what it meant.

My attention returned to the present as a woman walked into the room and stood waiting for something. She must have been a new Nav Operator; I'd never seen her before.

Then I caught the tail end of Sonrisa's rant. "... potential risks involved. Are you listening to me?"

"Y-yes," I managed to stammer. Should I tell them I'd passed out? Would it make any difference to him? Probably not.

His face was stern and his eyes bulged. "You're being relieved of your duties, Miss Callista. You are not fit to be carrying out the necessary emergency procedures."

"You got that right..." I said. He would have taken that as me being rude, but it was the truth. And I didn't care what he thought anymore anyway.

I logged out of the system, put my earpiece on the desk, and thought, *How am I going to help Javolo now?*

I suddenly felt like I shouldn't leave. My heart clenched. It was like I would be abandoning Javolo when he needed me the most. I couldn't do that. I needed to stay. I needed to do anything I could to help them find him... I didn't know what else I could do, but I couldn't just step aside.

Sonrisa stepped forward and the other Nav Operator fidgeted nervously. "Miss Callista, you need to vacate your station."

"But... Javolo... I need to help him."

"You are in no fit state to help him. Get out of here!"

"But—"

"GO!"

CHAPTER 38

Where are my shoes?

I cringed and my earpiece slid across the desk and fell on the floor.

"What the—?" I sat there wondering how it had happened while Sonrisa raged at me for throwing company equipment around. "But it wasn't me!"

I carefully picked it up off the floor, put it back on the desk, and slowly rose out of my chair as Sonrisa was telling me to report to Janga. The pains escalated as I walked toward the door and quickly reached an unbearable level... The room tilted violently to the right and everything faded...

——— ⋆·☆·⋆ ———

I came to in a dimly-lit room. The bed I was lying on felt too firm to be mine.

Where am I? What's going on?

I blinked and tried to focus on my surroundings. I was in some kind of Medical Facility. The Infirmary at work? As I was scrambling to figure out why I would be in the Infirmary, the pain returned. First, the pain from my ribs when I moved, then the strange pain from nowhere down my side.

It all came rushing back. The tunnel collapse. The horrendous pain that had hit me and the awful crushing feeling, even though there was nothing there. Passing out. Sonrisa yelling...

I must have passed out again and been taken to the Infirmary.

The fact that the phantom pains were still there was unnerving. I had no way of knowing for sure what they were or whether they were going to stop any time soon. It was scary. What if they didn't stop? What would I do? I would have to tell someone and hope they could help me.

I sighed. Carefully.

I couldn't hear anyone outside the door to my room. I had to get out of here. I checked my arms for a cannula or anything else that would prevent me from leaving and was relieved to find nothing. I didn't want anything to stop me from walking out. I had to somehow help Javolo. I didn't know what I could possibly do, but was determined to do more than lie around in bed.

I sat up slowly and winced at the pain. Sleeping was going to be extremely difficult from now on.

Taking some slow breaths until the room stopped spinning, I managed to get up out of bed to read my chart without fainting and scrolled through the data on the portable screen. They'd done a full analysis and picked up on my broken ribs. They'd also put down that I had a lump on my head, but it hadn't caused any significant damage, so were not sure what had caused me to pass out. They'd also given me an injection of a strong painkiller. It must have been wearing off; the pain in my side felt dulled, but the phantom pains were at full strength.

The floor was cold beneath my bare feet.

Where are my shoes?

I replaced the chart and looked around. I finally found them — and my bag — on a tray under my bed. Grabbing them, I tossed the shoes on the floor and slipped into them and put the strap of the bag carefully over my left shoulder.

It was quiet outside the room. Opening the door a crack showed that the corridor was clear and I assumed all staff would be on alert for any casualties coming from the planet below. I felt a different kind of pain at that thought. I imagined them rushing Javolo in with multiple wounds, heading straight for the ER.

Fighting back the tears that stung my eyes, I headed down the corridor to the left, hoping it led to the way out. Eventually, it did. I was relieved and kind of shocked that something had gone my way today.

The entry was crowded; people had arrived from the planet with minor injuries caused by the tunnel collapse. My heart clenched, imagining Javolo amongst them, but I doubted he would be walking in. He'd be lucky to be alive at all. The thought had me fighting tears again.

I had to push past it and seize the opportunity to get out without being noticed. I resisted the urge to look at each of the patients they were bringing in — I had no idea what Javolo looked like, so it was pointless. The only way I would be able to know if it was him was if someone mentioned his name.

As I wandered down the hallway, I tried to decide what to do. The only way I could talk to Javolo was through Katoa's communications network. I needed access to a Nav Computer.

My brain worked overtime as I thought about my options. I could go back to my station and see if the new Nav would tell me anything, but I was supposed to be in the Infirmary. I couldn't ask at the supervisor's desk for the same reason. The Navs were not allowed to take calls while they were working, so I couldn't call Salvani or Zinta Anterres and ask them for information.

Maybe I could sneak into Anterres's cubicle. It was close to the entrance to Operations, so I might be able to pull it off.

Acting nervous would draw attention to myself, so I walked into Operations like I did on any normal workday.

Anterres was surprised to see me when I slipped silently through the door and approached the station, and I explained that they'd replaced me because I hadn't responded quickly enough when it first happened. Of course I left out the part about me passing out. I told her I just wanted to know what was going on.

Anterres sighed. "Okay, but if they catch you in here, girl, there'll be trouble."

"I'm already in trouble for my mess-up when I was at my station," I told her.

Anterres showed me what was happening and I could see there'd been no significant aftershocks or further collapses, and only one Digger had managed to call in. Her Digger. They were getting close to his location.

"Nazan told me his legs are a mess, but the rest of him is okay."

"Wow. That's good, though, isn't it? They'll be able to get him out and he'll eventually be okay?"

"I hope so, but his legs are still wedged under rocks and stuff. Rescue is worried about crush injuries."

CHAPTER 39
Not a Chance, Girl

"He'll be okay," I told her. What else could I say? My heart clenched as I thought about how dangerous it was to have something crushing your limbs for too long.

"I hope so." Her voice wobbled and tears filled her eyes.

It was a relief to know I wasn't the only Nav who actually cared about their Digger.

"So, is he still talking to you?"

"No. Coms are down again. They keep cutting out."

I ran a hand through my hair and tucked some of it behind my ear. "I hope my Digger can get through soon."

She winced. "It only seems to be Nazan's Com that's working. Sorry."

My heart felt like lead. I had to try to control my emotions in front of Anterres. I was supposed to be a concerned co-worker and nothing more.

"How are they going to reach them all in time with the Coms down? I don't know what I could do to help. I feel so helpless."

She gave me a weak smile. "Me too. I have access to all this," she waved her hand at the computer terminal, "and I'm still next to useless."

The fact that they were close to Nazan made me feel a bit more hopeful, but I still felt an ache when I thought about Javolo. Time was ticking by and they didn't seem any closer to reaching him.

I thanked Anterres, but had to leave before I was discovered. I didn't want to get her into any trouble.

I wandered around, feeling totally lost. I wanted to do something — anything — to help, but without the Nav Computer to give me the information I needed, I couldn't even start to do anything useful.

As I walked and my mind reeled, I saw a Rescue team preparing to depart and recognised one of the men. "Kryson! You got a minute?" I called. I hoped my voice sounded casual.

Kryson turned to look at me. He had 'Team Leader' printed on his shirt and wore a serious expression. His face brightened as his blue eyes flashed with recognition.

"Hi Callista! Listen, I can't talk now, I'm on my way to the surface to help out." He frowned. "Why aren't you at your station?"

"Long story. But I need to ask you, is there any way I can get down there? I do have a basic ticket for first aid—"

"Not a chance, girl. Only the most experienced are being shipped out. You need to be qualified in underground rescue at the very least. Too dangerous down there. Sorry," he smiled apologetically. "Gotta go now. Say hi to Anterres for me, okay?"

I forced a smile. "Okay, I will. Thanks..." He had a thing for Anterres. I wasn't sure if she knew it. *Maybe I should tell her.*

He kept smiling as the team headed down toward the terminal. I watched them until they were out of sight. I had to tell myself to be strong and fought the urge to run after them.

"Hey, Callista!"

The blood drained from my face. I spun around and saw a familiar face. Kabir. I froze. He worked as a nurse in the Infirmary, so I hoped he didn't know I was supposed to be in there as a patient right now.

I plastered a smile on my face and tried to act natural. "Hi Kabir, how's it goin'?"

He continued to smile. "Okay, but we're all on edge waiting for the guys to be found. How're you holding out?"

So, he didn't know. Good. "I'm alright, I guess, but I messed up at my station and they kicked me off... I guess I'm not much good in an emergency..."

He raised his eyebrows. "Oh. Are you sure you're okay? I mean, really? You do look kinda pale..."

My chest tightened. I didn't want to be caught out and taken back to the Infirmary. "I'm fine. Really. Just worried about my Digger and the others, too. I hope they're all okay."

Kabir stooped down to look me in the eye. "You look terrible — no offence. You need to rest, my dear. Nurse's orders. If they don't want you here, then go home. There is nothing you can do here."

Tears stung my eyes again. "I, ah, I guess you're right," I admitted. "Thanks."

He gave me a warm smile and rubbed my upper arm. "Go. Rest. Just watch the Vid for updates. Gotta go. See ya."

I couldn't help frowning. "Okay, bye."

I turned and walked away, thinking hard. He was right — I couldn't do anything here. Maybe I should go home. Well, back to the hotel anyway. I felt a pang in my chest thinking about the reason I was living in a hotel.

I can't leave here, I thought, but knew it was my best option at this point. I had to face the facts. And I needed to rest and eat something...

As I walked along trying not to limp, I kept thinking about Javolo being trapped under huge boulders and covered in dirt and it caused an ache deep in my chest. And a cold fear in my gut. I had to do something to stop my wild imagination. It wasn't helping things.

I closed my eyes, took some deep breaths, and pushed all images of rocks and dirt from my mind.

I needed to know more about their progress. I couldn't stand it anymore. I had to know what was going on. Maybe the reports on the Vid would give me some more information while I rested. I decided I would do anything I could to get there or to help him somehow. But first, I needed to get organised and formulate some kind of a plan.

I made my way back to the Olympia — with the help of a taxi — to gather my thoughts and to pack anything I might need if I worked out how to get down to the surface.

When I walked in the door, I remembered that I'd broken the Vid. My heart sank. How could I get updates? Would I have to go back home?

Maybe they've fixed it.

I crept over to the console, hoping their service was fast, and pressed the power button. It flickered to life instantly and I relaxed.

The reports didn't contain much I didn't already know, so I left it on and turned my attention to what I could organise in the meantime.

The weird phantom pain slowly subsided. That was strange, but very welcome. It was such a relief that I sunk down into one of the lounge chairs for a while and tried to relax now it was gone.

I soon got moving again and filled a drink flask with water, packed some small snacks and dressed myself in long pants and long sleeves. I couldn't remember from my training if we had to wear any special clothing on the planet, or whether we only needed the mask and air tank. I didn't know whether I'd need to pack food and water for the trip down there. I knew it was about a ten-minute flight from the station, but from there, it was anybody's guess as to how long it would take to get to the miners or how long I could be down there helping out. I had no clue what to expect and wanted to be prepared.

Once I'd finished, I started pacing. My mind was working furiously. How could I get down there? My first aid qualification wasn't enough. I didn't really think it would be, but I had to try.

Maybe I would have to sneak down there. Stow away somehow.

I ran my fingers through my hair. *I don't want to be here... I need to be there...*

My breathing became shallow and my chest tightened.

What?

An image of dirt and tree roots flashed into my mind. And crawling insects. If I looked up, I could see the grass above me. The way out. But it was too high. I was stuck. Panic clawed at me.

I pushed the images from my mind and looked around me at the solid walls.

I'm safe. I'm okay.

The thought of going underground brought back memories from my childhood when I'd fallen into a hole in the ground and become trapped. I was too young and too small to climb out and I'd been stuck there overnight, cold and terrified. I shuddered.

I would do it for Javolo. I'd go down there to help find him.

The phantom pain returned with a vengeance and I gasped. It took my breath away and made it hard to even walk.

Not again.

I limped over to the lounge chair and sat down again slowly.

What was it? Why was I feeling this pain? There was only one insane — but in a way, logical — reason for the pain. It was Javolo's pain. But if that was true, then it meant he had some serious injuries. Right from the start, it had felt like broken bones. Somehow, I knew I was right. But it only made it worse that I couldn't help him.

Then I thought, if I really was feeling his pain, that meant he was still alive! Elation filled me.

Alive... but for how much longer? He has to have broken bones. I'm positive of it... definitely in the shoulder... He needs medical attention...

I jumped when I heard a noise from the bathroom. Was someone in here with me? I crept toward the source of the sound, listening for anything more.

I stopped. Had Malvolio found me? If he was in there, I shouldn't be walking toward him. My heart beat so fast and my knees threatened to give way.

Should I call the Enforcers? And tell them what? That I thought I heard a noise? They'd laugh at me. I had to see what was going on first.

I moved forward. The door was open and when I peered around the doorway with my heart in my throat, I was surprised to see the room empty.

What had made the noise then? The cupboard above the sink was open and a packet of bandages had fallen out onto the floor. *Huh? How did that happen?*

I walked in and picked up the bandages. I always closed cupboard doors because no matter how careful I was, I always seemed to bump into the open door the next time I turned around. It couldn't have been me. Maybe someone had been here. The cleaning staff?

I checked the contents of the cupboard, then looked around the hotel suite, finding nothing out of place. I frowned. Maybe the door was faulty and had come open on its own. I checked. It had a magnet holding it closed. It couldn't have fallen open.

I sat down on my bed. I needed to just relax and stop freaking out. The security here was tight. There's no way Malvolio could have gotten past the front desk.

I reached for the ornament I always kept by my bedside — a small wooden Pegasus — but it slid across the bedside table and toppled to the floor.

What the?

As I reached out my hand to pick it up, it moved again, this time toward my hand, and I pulled my hand back in shock. What was going on?

My trembling fingers slowly inched forward and I managed to grab it without it moving this time and I sat there staring at it. It didn't look any different, and I was thankful that it hadn't broken. Adamo had given it to me for my last birthday, so it was precious to me.

But how did it move? Did I do that? Had I somehow developed some kind of Talent I didn't know I had? If that was the case, why now? This had come from out of nowhere.

What was happening to me? Did all this weird stuff have anything to do with the lightning connection I seemed to share with Daniel? Maybe. Probably. I had no answer.

I needed to rest for a while as the pain was too much, so I lay my head down on my pillow carefully.

How could I help Javolo?

The thing that kept coming back to me was that no one at work was going to let me help. They would tell me to go home. I would have to stow away somehow to get to Kronos and steal a mask...

What if I stowed away in the cargo hold and couldn't find a mask in time? They'd open the cargo door and I would die as soon as I was exposed to the toxic atmosphere on the planet.

Brilliant plan, Lennina.

Okay, so I'd have to have a plan that included getting a mask first. Only, I had no clue where they were kept. I'd had no training in that area because Navs didn't go down to the surface. We sat up here in our comfortable cubicles while the Diggers risked their lives.

Maybe I could do some research on the Vid and hope I could get an idea of where these things would be stored.

I had to do something. I was determined to do whatever it took. I would *not* lose my best friend. If I couldn't stow away, I'd try something else. Something I could do from up here in the station. I would *not* give up.

My stomach chose that moment to let me know it wanted food, so I slowly pushed myself up and headed to the kitchen.

The Vid wasn't displaying the news when I went back out and I kicked myself for staying in my room for so long. I could have missed something important.

I went about making myself a sandwich and ate a banana while I worked. I grabbed a Tova juice from the refrigerator before I sat down at the small table facing the Vid.

I managed to finish all of it before the next news broadcast came on. It went through all of the things I'd seen before and I felt frustrated. I needed more information. I changed the channel and didn't have to wait long for their news.

I felt a lot better with some food in my stomach. When was the last time I'd eaten? I couldn't remember.

The phantom pain had faded away again and I felt both relieved and uneasy. What did it mean? It was so good to be free of it, but I still wondered why. There was a dark feeling growing inside me. A feeling of dread. Was Javolo no longer in pain? Had he been found and given painkillers, or was he— I couldn't finish that thought. I couldn't deal with that right now. He was alive. I had to believe that.

I forced myself to stay seated so I wouldn't start pacing again. I took a painkiller for my ribs and the pain started to fade.

The next news update started. Even though I could see the screen from where I sat, I stood up and trudged over to the Vid. They reported the latest developments concerning the tunnel collapse and began to list all the missing Diggers. I leaned forward to hear, focusing all my attention on the person reading out the list. I prepared for the worst. My breath caught at the thought.

No. He wasn't dead. He was still alive and was just hurt.

As I listened, I heard some names I didn't recognise, a couple of names I'd heard Javolo mention before, and Zinta's Digger, Abadal Nazan. But it was the last name that really grabbed my attention: "... and Daniel Javolo."

CHAPTER 40
It Was Like a Knife in My Heart

I gasped. My chest felt tight as the warmth drained from my cheeks. My arms and legs went to jelly.

"Daniel Javolo?" I said aloud, adrenalin rushing through my body. "*Daniel* Javolo? It can't be him... could it? No. It can't be. It's not po ssible... Is it?"

I continued to stare at the Vid screen, no longer seeing or hearing what was being broadcast. I couldn't believe what I'd heard. My mind was reeling and my head felt fuzzy. My legs gave out and I sank to the floor as my hands moved to cover my mouth.

How could Daniel and Javolo be the same person? I'd forgotten Javolo's first name long ago and not even known Daniel's surname. Could they be the same guy?

No... It's just a coincidence... It has to be...

My brain was working overtime, piecing my memories together. The pieces started to actually fit, which scared me. They both had the same easy-going attitude. No stress, no anger issues, and they were both funny and genuinely cared about people. They both came from Taon and were finishing their contract soon...

No. It's not true.

Daniel kept reminding me of Javolo. A lot of the things he said were just what Javolo would've said in the same situation. Maybe it wasn't just the fact that they came from the same planet and were raised within the same culture like I'd thought.

It can't be true.

Daniel had obviously lied about his job. I felt annoyed until I realised he couldn't have told me the truth if he wasn't allowed to be there. He must have found a way through to this section somehow. Even that fit with his sense of adventure.

And besides, how could I be angry with him when I didn't tell him where I worked, either? Well, not at first.

If Daniel was Javolo, did he know who I was? Surely not. I didn't tell him my last name, and I was positive he would've told me if he knew. Even if he was breaking the rules by sneaking into the Navs' Section.

I thought about how I felt like I'd known Daniel for ages, even when we first met. Maybe that's why I'd felt comfortable enough to let him get so close to me...

It all seemed to fit, but there were still many unanswered questions. And what if I was wrong? That would be an embarrassing situation to try to talk my way out of...

If it was true, it would be a relief, in a weird, kind of screwed-up way. I'd been so upset thinking I had feelings for two different guys.

There was no way I'd even think about seeing two men at the same time. I'd been on the other end of that before, so there was no way I'd put someone through that. That scenario only existed in Malvolio's twisted mind.

I thought I'd have to sort out my feelings. And choose. But now... If it was true — I wouldn't have to choose. My head spun thinking about it.

If it was true...

This is too insane, I thought, rubbing my temples. This was so unbelievable.

My heart clenched; if Daniel and Javolo were the one person, then that meant I could potentially lose someone that I'd thought were two people. It was so messed up that a person could get messed up thinking about it.

THIS IS CRAZY! I screamed in my mind. It was too much...

But I had to focus. I had to act. I couldn't stay put another minute. I'd go back and insist I was well enough to help and make up some rubbish about being loyal to The Company or something. Even if I helped out on the Com. Something — *anything*...

Or stow away.

I wanted to go down to the surface and help with the digging, but I

knew that that wasn't possible. I'd dig with my bare hands if I had to...
If they'd let me...

I pushed the images of dirt and roots that stretched out toward me in the dark from my mind. I couldn't think about that now. I couldn't let my fears control me.

I stood slowly and looked around, hoping I'd think of something else to bring. I couldn't think of anything. I knew the things I'd packed were not going to be enough and that my 'plan' was lame, but I was desperate.

The phantom pains returned with a jolt to my shoulder. My brain became fuzzy again, but I was determined. *Just breathe deep... Calm down... Relax...*

Closing my eyes didn't work. The pep talk wasn't working either. But I wasn't about to give up.

Okay, I have to do this, I thought as I broke out in a sweat. *I'll just have to walk around a bit and get through the pain. Once it passes, I'll be able to pretend like nothing is wrong and try to convince them to let me help...*

After double-checking that I had painkillers with me, I tried to hitch the bag that I'd packed up onto my shoulder. My left arm had become useless again with the pain, so I pulled it up onto my right shoulder. The bag swung around and hit my ribs. I gasped as the pain became unbearable. I stood for a few moments, breathing slowly and deeply while holding onto the wall. That was a really stupid move...

Once I thought I'd recovered enough, I headed for the door, but the door started to move sideways and twist violently to one side as it faded from view...

———— ⋆·☆·⋆ ————

I became aware that I was lying on something hard.

The floor.

A few seconds passed before my mind could focus and I could remember what had been happening. How long had I been unconscious this time? I looked over at the clock on my kitchen wall. I'd been out for about half an hour. More time had passed and I was no closer to being able to help Javolo.

Damn it!

I fought back tears.

I managed to slowly drag myself up off the floor and sat leaning against the wall near the front door as I told the Vid to show me the latest news. They had reached Nazan. I remembered Anterres's tear-streaked face and hoped he would be alright.

Daniel Javolo was still listed as missing, along with the others. That was further confirmation that it was actually his name and that I hadn't imagined it the first time, but I still couldn't believe it. I also knew I wouldn't have imagined in a million years that Javolo and Daniel were the same person... Or would I?

There was a small voice inside my head saying, *What if you're wrong? What if they're not the same person? You're reading too much into this...*

I decided to ignore the voice. I had to be right. It all fit together. I just couldn't see it before.

The news program on the Vid had moved on to other things, so I told it to switch to another channel. Maybe I could get some new info.

As it flicked across to the other news, they reported that Rescue had reached Abadal Nazan and were in the process of extracting him safely. It had slightly more detail than the other channel. They followed that by listing the missing Diggers again — this time with *images* of their faces.

My breath caught. Each name was read out, with an image that looked like it had been taken for Katoa to use as ID. They were staring straight ahead, with only a trace of a smile on their lips. As they said Daniel Javolo, his beautiful face appeared on the screen with his name underneath. I sucked in a breath. It was like a knife in my heart. It was him.

Daniel was Javolo.

CHAPTER 41

If I Wasn't Freaking Out Right Now, I Might Even Think it Was Cool

I couldn't breathe properly. It was agonising and a relief and sad and right and wrong and my heart felt like it had been ripped open.

I couldn't move and was glad I was already sitting on the floor. I wouldn't have been able to stand right now. The news had moved on to reporting the weather on Kronos's surface, but I wasn't listening. Maybe I should have been, because it could affect the rescue efforts, but I sat and stared at nothing.

I had to pull it together. Despite what I'd just seen and heard, I knew I had to act. I had to help. Javolo — Daniel — was down on the planet buried underground and needed help.

I struggled to my feet and tried to stand without support, but the room spun crazily. I needed to wait a bit longer. It was frustrating. I was wasting time, but I couldn't help it. So many things kept going wrong.

Javolo could die and there was nothing I could do about it!

That last thought caused a small sob to escape. Then the tears came easily and streamed down my face. There was nothing I could do. I felt helpless. I leaned my back against the wall and slid down till I was sitting on the floor once more, the bag slipping from my shoulder. It was hopeless. If only there was a way for me to contact him outside of the Com system.

I folded my arms across the top of my knees and buried my face in them. The Vid started playing another update, but I didn't look up. The news reporter said they were getting close to the section where Javolo had been when it all collapsed. That made me look up, but they were only showing the reporter's face.

They were getting closer... If I could just find a way to talk to him, tell him to hang on till they got there...

Javolo? I called desperately, knowing it was useless, but willing him to hear me...

I was struggling to stop myself from crying. Pain ripped through my ribcage and I knew that crying would make it worse.

The fact that I could still feel the phantom pains meant he was still alive... but still hurting...

Time seemed to stand still. I couldn't hold back the tears. I cried for Javolo and for all the hurt Malvolio had caused me. I let it all out. And I wished I could go home. I wanted my mum. Physical pain mixed with the pain in my heart. It was too much.

Once I'd stopped, I felt drained and exhausted. I sat still, listening to my slow breathing, my mind feeling numb. I wished I could tell Javolo they were close. I wanted to give him some hope in the darkness.

Javolo. I wish you could hear me...

I seemed to be floating, rather than sitting on the floor. I tried to reach out to him. Something urged me to keep trying to call him.

Javolo? ... Daniel? ... I felt a strange sensation like I was travelling through darkness. Then it was as if I'd come to a sudden halt. *"Daniel... I really wish you could hear me... They're coming for you... Just hang on..."*

"What the?"

The thoughts swirled through my mind in response to my call. My heart stopped beating for a second or two.

"Daniel?" I asked tentatively as my brain shifted into overdrive. I couldn't be hearing his thoughts in my mind. I needed to get it together.

"Lennina?"

It *was* him.

"Yes. I — uh... it's me," I stammered. I needed to pinch myself. I was dreaming, or hallucinating. Or something...

"But how?" he asked me. *"How can you be inside my head?"* He sounded exhausted.

"I don't know! I just wished so much I could tell you that they're close to finding you and you actually heard me! I don't believe it! This can't be real."

Tears streamed down my face again. I was amazed. I felt Daniel's emotions, things moved on their own, and now this. How could I even do this? I'd never shown any signs of Talent before.

"I must have some form of Talent, and if I wasn't freaking out right now, I might even think it was cool."

Focus, I told myself. I didn't want to lose this, whatever this was.

"What's happening with you?" I asked him. *"How are you holding out down there?"*

He seemed to hesitate a bit. *"Okay..."*

"That's good. Hang tight, okay?" I told him. *"The news report said they're getting close to where you are."*

"That's good... But how do you know where I am?" he asked.

I guessed his confusion would be because he didn't know who I really was. *"Well,"* I told him, *"I know because you were talking to me when the tunnel collapsed."*

"What?"

A million thoughts raced through my mind, but I had to put them aside for the moment and tell him who I was. I wasn't sure how he'd react, so I just blurted it out. *"Umm, I... I'm Lennina Callista..."*

I waited for his reaction. For it to hit home.

"I know."

CHAPTER 42

All the Pieces of the Puzzle

"What? You know? How could you know?" A tingling sensation swept through me.

"I know. I just didn't know you'd worked it out..."

"But how do you know?"

How could he possibly know? I found out from a news report, and that was less than an hour ago.

He seemed kind of amused. *"Well, umm, I worked it out when you mentioned Malvolio's name."* I gasped. *"Then you told me you loved the Digger you worked with."*

Oh, crap. I did too.

Now it was my turn to be silent. I felt the heat rise in my cheeks. I hadn't realised I'd basically told him who I was with those two things. And I was embarrassed to think I'd told him I loved him right to his face without even knowing it was him. My head spun.

"Oh, I guess I did... I gave you all the information you needed, really... all the pieces of the puzzle..."

"Yeah."

"And... then I ran off on you." I'm such a moron!

He'd called out to me. He even said he had something to tell me. And I didn't wait — didn't even give him the chance to tell me.

"Damn! I'm such an idiot sometimes! I should have stayed..."

Daniel coughed, which made the pain flare up and I had to bite my lip to stop myself from crying out. Now I knew I was feeling his pain.

"Are you okay?" I knew how bad it was, could *feel* how bad it was, but had to ask him.

"Yeah. Hurts to cough," he told me.

I squirmed. I needed to get him to tell me how bad it was. He needed to report it as if I was still at work at my Nav Station.

"Yes, you should of stayed..." he continued, as if nothing had interrupted us. *"I ran after you. You were too quick... So I thought I'd just have to wait and talk to you at work. I decided I'd somehow tell you without gettin' us in trouble. Use some sort of cryptic message that only you would work out, like what we talked about when we were together or something."*

"Oh," was all I managed to say. My chest tightened. I felt really stupid now for running off, but I had to get out of there. *"I'm sorry. I felt so bad, I mean, telling you all that... I felt like such a bitch... And I thought that whatever you had to say would just make me feel worse about what I'd done to you, so I just ran."* I sighed deeply, which hurt my ribs. *"When I had a chance to think later, I decided that I'd tell you everything at work, no matter what the consequences were. And when I got there and you were in such a good mood, I didn't know what to think..."* I trailed off. I didn't know what else to say.

"Now you know why... But it was hard because I couldn't just come out and say I knew who you were."

Relief flooded through me. *"I... thought maybe you'd found someone else."*

It took some self-control not to cry after that last sentence, but it did feel good to talk to him and get the facts straight.

What am I doing? Talking about all this when his life is in danger! Get with it, girl.

I knew I had to focus. He still needed to get out of there.

"How'd you find out who I was?" he asked.

"They mentioned your full name in the news report," I told him. *"And then they showed a full-screen picture. I was blown away... I had no idea."* I need to focus! *"We need to get you out of there, though."*

"I bet you were... I didn't think you knew, or even suspected... It must of been a shock."

"Yes, it was..." Stop it! You need to get him out of there! Focus! He needs to tell me more information.

I forced myself to focus on what needed to be done to get him out and safe. I took a deep breath and winced at the pain.

"Umm... okay... First things first. We need to get you out of there safe and sound. Report. Where are your injuries?"

As he described them, goose bumps spread over me and the hairs on the back of my neck stood on end. His injuries matched exactly what I was feeling with the phantom pains. I'd sort of known I was right about it, but for him to actually confirm it...

Daniel's injuries were bad. He was sure he had broken bones in his shoulder and leg. Maybe the arm as well. And he'd lost consciousness a few times, too. That must have been the times when I couldn't feel the pain.

Considering the circumstances, his injuries could've been a lot worse. There would be several tonnes of earth and rock around him. To be alive and have escaped more serious injuries... he was extremely lucky.

I forced myself to remain calm and professional. *"Okay. Report your current situation."*

Daniel told me he was trapped where he'd fallen, lying on his back. The Mech-suit was trapped under some large boulders and he was pinned down. He'd tried to shift them, but although the Mech-suit was capable of lifting heavy weights, it was no match for the load on him and its left arm wasn't functioning at all. The suit had done a pretty good job of saving his life, however.

I sucked in a breath when he said that.

The suit still had power, but the Com was damaged, so he hadn't been able to call for help or tell them where he was. It had reported that his satellite equipment was also damaged, so they probably couldn't pinpoint his location accurately, if at all.

I told him they were aware of his last coordinates just before the collapse. He'd been standing in the same place for a fair while, so the readings should be accurate. I confirmed that they couldn't locate any of the other Diggers by satellite tracking either. I also told him about Nazan and the names of some of the missing Diggers that I could remember. He groaned.

"They're all good friends," he told me.

"Yeah, I thought so." My heart sank. I tried to imagine what he was

feeling.

I felt a sudden stabbing pain in my left leg and we both cried out in pain at the same time. He must've tried to move.

"What is it? What's wrong? Is it your ribs?" I could hear the concern in his voice.

"You're trapped underground with severe injuries and could've died and you're asking me if I'm okay? Are you nuts?"

I thought he would probably believe me at this point if I told him the truth. After all, I was talking to him through telepathy... What did I have to lose?

"My ribs are still painful, but there's something else I have to tell you. I know this sounds weird," I hesitated for a few moments, *"but I can feel your pain."*

CHAPTER 43
Stop Wasting My Time

What? How?"

I squirmed. *"I don't know, but when the tunnel collapsed, I felt an explosion of pain in all the same places you've been hurt. It even knocked me to the floor. I thought the ceiling had collapsed on me or something, but when I looked, there was nothing there. I've even passed out a few times because of the pain."*

"That's just— How can it be possible? I don't even know how we can be talking like this either. It's just... I don't know..."

I sighed. *"Yeah, I know... I have no idea... but I'm glad it's happening — I mean the talking to you part — not the pain part."*

"Me too... Especially if you can help them find me quicker. Otherwise, I think I'll soon be a dead man."

My heart clenched. *"Don't say that! They're gonna find you."*

"But it's true."

"We need to concentrate on getting you out of there," I said firmly. I needed to push any thoughts like that out of my mind.

"I've managed to slowly shift myself around so that the Mech-suit's no longer pushing hard against me," he told me. *"I knew that crush injuries would be the death of me, or at the very least, I would be in deep trouble..."*

I cringed, but he was right.

"Yes. You would be," I agreed. I shuddered at where those thoughts led me, then pushed them away fiercely.

I couldn't just sit here. I needed to do more than talk to him. I needed to get help to him somehow.

"Jav... Daniel, I need to try and contact The Company to tell them

you're still alive and what your injuries are. Can you hang on down there while I try it?" It was weird calling him Daniel. To me, he'd always been Javolo. But then, it wasn't Javolo's voice I was hearing in my head...

Aagh! I'm gonna need some counselling after this, I thought to myself.

I was glad he couldn't hear every thought in my mind. Only the ones I kind of pushed toward him. It was bizarre.

"Yeah," he answered.

"The problem is, they'll probably think I'm crazy. How could I possibly know that information? And I can't tell them how I know. They'll lock me up."

"Or have you tested for Talent," he said. *"It has to be strong if you can reach all the way down to the planet from up there."*

He was right. I hadn't thought of it that way. Surely they'd believe me.

And for me to be able to reach him at such a distance? That must be good. I had no idea how this worked or how far the average Talent could stretch their ability.

I felt his pain increase when he moved. My heartbeat sped up. I didn't want to leave him, but I felt I had no choice.

"I don't know if I'll be able to do this again — connect to you like this, but I have to call them. I have to at least try."

"I know... Okay, go. I'll be alright," he assured me.

Suddenly, I didn't want to do it. *"But what if I can't do this again? What if this is a one-off deal?"* The thought that this might be the last time I ever spoke to him hit me hard and the tears streamed down my cheeks.

"It's okay, Cal. If you can't do it again, that's alright." My heart melted a little hearing him call me Cal. *"If you can help them find me before it's too late, then it wouldn't worry me if we can never do this again. But you got to go and talk to them. You got to try. Before time runs out."*

My heart twisted at the thought. I knew I had to go. *Right now.* Enough time had been wasted. *"I know... I just don't want to leave you, knowing I might not be able to talk to you again..."* Maybe not ever...

He needed to get medical attention. Now. I just hoped my delay didn't lead to his death. I'd never forgive myself if something happened to him because of me...

He moaned as the pain increased. *"I know... But you need to go now. Do your job as my Nav Operator. Get going. I'll talk to you soon."*

I felt selfish for wanting to stay with him. *"Okay... Sorry. I need to get my head into gear and move it. I'll try to connect or link to you again somehow... or whatever this is, okay? But, I need to tell you. I... I love you."*

"You do?" He sounded surprised. Then his voice in my head sounded more playful. *"Of course you do. You told me."*

Oh, yeah. I did. *"But—"*

"Hey. Stop talking like this is the end. This is not goodbye. This is just 'I'll catch you later,' okay?"

I suppressed a sob. *"Okay."*

"And it's alright. No need to apologise for anything. I'll talk to you soon. I'll see you soon, when this is all over... Bye."

"Bye."

I opened my eyes and felt his mind disappear. The connection was gone.

Oh, man. I hope I've done the right thing.

I raised my head, which caused a wave of lightheadedness. I sat a while longer and took some slow, deep breaths so it would pass.

Tears threatened to fall. Had I made the right decision? Would I be able to do this again? I didn't know, but I had to try to get help. And quickly. I would make them listen... somehow.

As I slowly got to my feet, a flood of exhaustion washed over me and the world went black.

———— ⋆·☆·⋆ ————

When I regained consciousness and my mind was able to focus enough so that I could remember what was going on, I dragged myself — very slowly — on my hands and knees till I reached the Vid. It was still on, reporting on the progress of the rescue.

They'd managed to get Nazan out and were in the process of transporting him to the station. He was barely conscious and was in danger of losing his legs through crush injuries. They hadn't reached Daniel or any of the others yet. The room was spinning and my limbs were like lead. It must take a lot of energy to communicate like that using your mind. Or something... I was clueless when it came to the Talented and their abilities.

I needed to contact Katoa, but I didn't want to speak to Sonrisa; he'd find out I wasn't in the Infirmary. After calling the Operations Unit, I asked for the man I despised: Mr Janga. His long face appeared on the screen and I hurriedly told him I knew Daniel's location.

"Of course you do," he told me. "It was on the screen when the tunnel collapsed."

"Yes, but he is alive and in need of urgent medical attention."

He sighed heavily, annoyance in his tone and on his face. "*If* he is alive, he would most certainly need urgent medical attention."

How can I get you to listen? "He *is* alive. I know it. And he's injured. He has several broken bones in his left arm, leg and shoulder—"

"How do you know that? How could you know that?" he asked.

Because I am some kind of psychic...? Yeah, that'll work... "I... umm. I just know it. I can't tell you how."

Now that sounded stupid. But what could I tell him? I wasn't even sure what had happened to allow me to talk to Javolo — Daniel. How could I be normal my whole life, then suddenly be able to use telepathy?

"You can't possibly know. Now stop wasting my time." I heard him press a few buttons. "I can see here that you were replaced by Shara Kastelan after you failed to follow procedures, which could have easily meant the death of your Digger." I cringed at the reminder because it was true. "I suggest you stay home till we can make a full inquiry into your behaviour."

"But—"

He terminated the call. I knew I'd be in big trouble, but for Janga to say it just made it more real. My head hurt.

I couldn't deal with the threat of an inquiry right now. I had to find someone to listen to me. Every second counted.

Why are my hands hurting?

I opened my hands and saw that I had deep marks in my palms from my fingernails. I flattened my palms against my thighs to try to stop myself from causing any more damage.

I couldn't give up now. I would have to go to work. My mind was racing, trying to think of what I could do.

I walked as fast as the pain would allow and grabbed a taxi. The phantom pain was debilitating. Reaching into my bag, I took two painkillers and popped them into my mouth. I hoped it was time for me to have another dose without overdoing it. My ribs had been getting gradually worse again as I walked. I sat in the taxi wishing the medication could rid me of the other pains as well...

My mind was working hard. I didn't know how, but I would have to get someone to listen to me. Somehow...

When I finally arrived, I had no more luck than I'd had on the phone. I tried to speak to several people and even told them I could talk to Daniel using telepathy. I was scoffed at and ordered to go home, and they insisted that I make an appointment with the counsellor first.

No way! I thought to myself. *I'm not crazy! ... Am I?*

The thought that maybe I'd lost my mind planted its seeds in my brain. When I thought about all the things that had happened to me, I wondered if it was even real. What if it was all in my head? What if I hadn't spoken to Daniel at all? What if those things hadn't really moved on their own? I couldn't deal with that. It must have been real. It had to be.

My head throbbed just thinking about it. I had to sit down somewh ere...

I wandered around aimlessly, listening in to conversations to try to find out what was happening. They hadn't reached any more of the men yet and Nazan was in the ER. I hoped they could save his legs...

My mind whirled. What if I was crazy? Maybe I should've stayed in the Infirmary. Maybe they could help me. Maybe I had a concussion and it was making me hallucinate...

No. I couldn't be imagining all of it. The pains down my side proved it... didn't they?

It was obvious no one was going to help me, so I decided to try to talk to Daniel again. Somehow. The least I could do was give him an update on the progress of the rescue effort and tell him that they weren't listening to me. I hoped I could connect with him again, but I wasn't sure what I actually did to establish contact with his mind in the first place.

But still, I had to try.

Plus, I had to hear his voice in my mind again. It gave me comfort. And he probably needed some comfort right now too.

I found a comfortable bench seat in the corner of the staff cafeteria and curled up on it. Lying on my left side was painful, but I knew I wouldn't be doing any damage because there was nothing physically wrong with me.

Thankfully, there was no one else in here.

Now what do I do?

I noticed the pain on my left was starting to fade a little. Was Daniel losing consciousness? Was he...? I couldn't finish that question... I'd have to hurry.

Relax... I told myself as I closed my eyes. *Breathe deeply... Now, what did I do before? I closed my eyes and wished really hard that he could hear me...*

I breathed slowly, deeply... *"Daniel? Javolo? Can you hear me?"*

Nothing.

I felt myself getting anxious — time was ticking by — but I knew I couldn't expect to get it right the first time.

I was too tense. I rolled my shoulders — carefully — and tried to relax my arms, then my legs.

Try again... relax... breathe... "Daniel? Daniel? I need you to hear me... They won't believe me, but I tried..."

Silence. I fought back the tears. I couldn't cry now.

"Daniel? Please answer! Please hear me!" Tears welled up in my eyes. *"I need you to hear me again..."*

Maybe it wasn't working because he was unconscious. The pain was gone now. I would need to wait till the pain returned. But what could I do in the meantime? There wasn't really anything I could do.

Maybe I could use the time to relax enough to be able to link with him again. I concentrated on my breathing and tried some relaxation techniques.

The pain returned full strength, making me lose my concentration. I took a few deep breaths, causing pain to my ribs, and took a few slower breaths. I needed to relax all over again...

Relax... breathe... in... out...

The pain returning meant he was still with me and conscious again, but it made it much more difficult to focus.

"Daniel? Please answer... I need to connect again... I need to tell you that it didn't work... I couldn't get them to listen... Oh, I can't do this... I don't know what to do... I need you... I love you!"

I felt a strange feeling of travelling through the darkness again. *"Daniel?"*

"Lennina?"

My heart skipped a beat. I'd done it! *"Yes! I didn't think I was going to be able to do it again... How are you? I mean, I know how much pain you're in, but how are you coping?"*

"I'm okay... considering... I think... I think I passed out again... I'm not sure... What happened? Did you get anywhere?"

He sounded weaker. I could feel panic creeping up my spine. I couldn't panic now. That wouldn't help him.

"No, of course not," I told him. *"They wouldn't listen to anything I said... They thought I was lying about being able to contact you. They told me to make an appointment with the counsellor before I went home."*

"That's the last thing I wanted. But... if they play back our last conversation, I will be seeing a lot of him too."

I thought about our last conversation over the Com. Javolo — Daniel — had seen a Ghost. He would be in so much trouble, I couldn't even imagine what was going to happen to him. They'd think he was loony for sure.

The Ghost had tried to communicate with him just before the tunnel collapse. It caused me pain to remember the final minutes before everything went wrong and then what had happened to me straight afterwards. Besides the physical pain, I felt so much pain in my heart thinking I'd lost my best friend forever. Tears formed in my eyes.

A thought came to me. The Ghost was frantically waving at him and trying to get Daniel to follow him. *"Hey, I think that Ghost was trying to warn you."*

"You think?"

"*Yes. He must have known the roof was going to cave in. Maybe he could sense it somehow.*"

"*Amazing... I didn't know what it was doing. I thought maybe it was being hostile at first.*"

I thought about that for a while. It did seem that way when it knocked him over.

I wondered if anyone else from Katoa had actually tried to communicate with the Ghost.

What Daniel said next stopped me in my tracks.

"*Uh oh...*"

There was a sinking feeling in the pit of my stomach as all sorts of scenarios played in my head. "*What? What is it?*"

"*The suit is telling me I have an air leak.*"

CHAPTER 44

You Have to Believe Me

Adrenalin rushed through me. *"No!"*

Tears flowed freely down my cheeks, my grief overwhelming me. I tried to stop, but my body wouldn't listen. An air leak was a death sentence. If Rescue didn't find him *very* soon, he would be dead before they got there.

No, no, no, no, no! I started to sob uncontrollably. I couldn't stop myself.

"Hey, it's okay," he said. *"Don't cry. They'll find me."*

I couldn't answer. I kept thinking of what would happen and that I couldn't do anything about it. An image of Daniel's lifeless body lying in a half-crushed Mech-suit in the darkness popped into my mind. I couldn't bear it. I couldn't help him. All I could do was talk to him until he ran out of air. I wanted to scream.

No, no, no!

Daniel's presence vanished from my mind. I'd lost contact with him, which only made me cry more. I curled myself up into a ball and cried harder.

I knew now it was only a matter of time before I could lose him forever and there was nothing I could do about it. How could I help him now? I had to try. Had to do something.

I jumped as someone put a hand on my arm and when my eyes flew open, Malvolio was right in front of me. I gave a small yelp and jerked away from him, causing the pain to become unbearable.

"Lennina. What's wrong? Why are you sleeping in the cafeteria? Why are you crying?"

Panic clawed at my insides at the sight of him. "What are you doing here?"

"Don't answer a question with a question. Why are you in here?"

I wanted to get up and run, but I couldn't just yet. I needed the pain to recede at least a little and my head to stop spinning.

This was the first time I'd seen Malvolio since *that night*.

"I was kicked off my workstation for being too slow. But why are you here? I would have thought they wouldn't let any non-employees in at a time like this."

"Never mind about that. I wanted to know if you were okay."

Then I remembered the air leak and my chest tightened. I needed to tell someone about Daniel. I needed to make them listen.

"I need to go," I told him. "It's urgent. I need to tell them my Digger's suit has an air leak. I need to get out of here!"

I sat up slowly, even though everything in me was screaming at me to run.

"How could you know that? You said you were asked to leave your workstation."

"I can't really tell you how, but I know it and I need to go."

I put both feet on the floor, ready to run. He wore a smug expression, which puzzled me.

He put his hands on my upper arms. "You can't leave. I need to speak to you."

I pulled free of his grasp. "No. You don't understand. He'll die if they don't get to him in time!"

I had to go. *Now*. I leapt up out of my seat, determined to get help, only to crash to the floor again as a haze of blackness engulfed me.

———— ⋆·☆·⋆ ————

When consciousness reached me, the pain returned with it. Now there were pains in my knees, my right elbow and the right side of my head from where I'd hit the floor. I'd forgotten that I experienced such immense exhaustion after linking with Daniel before. I cursed myself, but really, how was I supposed to know?

My surroundings looked familiar, though I couldn't be sure whether I was in the same room as before. They all looked the same. I had to get out of here. Again.

I checked my arms. No cannulas. Grabbing my bag and shoes from under the bed, I slowly made my way to the door without fainting and opened it. I was surprised to see Anterres in the Infirmary and ice ran through my veins as I saw her face full of tears.

"Anterres! What happened?"

"It's Nazan. He's... he's dead!"

She started to sob and I put my arms around her. "But how? I heard they found him and were getting him out."

"They did. The Coms came back online and I was talking to him. He was fine."

I opened my mouth to ask what had happened, but nothing came out. There were tears on my cheeks.

She shuddered. "It was the crush injury. His blood was poisoned. They gave him all the right medications. They did everything right. But not long after they removed the rocks..." She couldn't finish.

She didn't have to. Her shoulders shook as she sobbed.

Things suddenly became more urgent. If they didn't get to Daniel... I squeezed my eyes shut. *He can't die. He can't...*

"Nadesha, I have to go. I'm sorry. I have to tell them that Daniel's — Javolo's — suit has an air leak. They have to get to him urgently. He's gonna—" I swallowed. I couldn't say it.

She pulled back and looked at my face. "How do you know that?"

"Um, it's a long story, but I do. And I have to tell Sonrisa."

I pulled away from her and apologised again. I hurried down the corridor. Somehow, I had to make them listen.

I tried to decide whether to sneak back to Operations again or just talk to the first person I found. I decided to find the nearest person and make them listen.

The corridors were quiet but it didn't take me long to find a man dressed in a nurse's uniform heading my way.

"Excuse me," I called.

He stopped walking. "Can I help you?"

"Is there someone around here I can talk to?"

"You can talk to me."

"I mean, someone in charge, like a doctor or supervisor."

"What seems to be the problem?"

"I'm a Nav Operator with Katoa—"

"What are you doing here? Shouldn't you be at your post?"

"If you'd let me explain, I was replaced and wasn't feeling well. I ended up in here because I fainted. I have to let someone know that my Digger has an air leak."

"What?"

"My Digger was in the tunnels when they collapsed and now he has a breach in his Mech-suit."

"How do you know that if you haven't been at your post?"

I resisted the urge to roll my eyes. I didn't want to have to explain this to everyone I met. "I don't have time to explain. I just do. It's an emergency—"

"Of course it's an emergency. We're all on alert waiting for the next patient to arrive."

"That's not what I meant. I mean they have to get to him sooner or he'll die."

He was getting annoyed. "They're working as fast as they can. Do you think they're just playing around down there?"

"No, of course not. You don't understand. It's now more urgent to get to him. His name is Daniel Javolo."

"I think you're just wasting my time, miss. There's not any way that you could know this extra information."

I sighed, which hurt my ribs. "Look. I don't know how I did it, but I spoke with Daniel using telepathy."

His eyebrows went up. "You're kidding me, right? Telepathy. Now I *know* you're wasting my time. What's your name? I need to report this."

Instead of answering, I turned and rushed down the corridor before he could grab me and insist I see a counsellor.

"Hey! Come back here!"

I ignored him and kept going. He would probably call security so I had to hurry.

As I turned a corner, I called out to a woman with curly red hair who looked like she might be a doctor.

"Yes?"

I stopped in front of her. "I need to get some information to Nav Operations. It's urgent."

"What is the information?"

"My Digger, Daniel Javolo, is trapped underground on the planet and his Mech-suit has an air leak."

"Who are you? How do you know this?"

Here we go again.

"I'm Lennina Callista. I'm a Nav. Daniel Javolo is my Digger. You need to tell Mr Sonrisa that Javolo is going to run out of air. You have to believe me. You have to listen."

"What are you doing here? Why aren't you at your station?"

"I was replaced. I'm not well. I fainted and I guess Malvolio must have brought me here."

"So how could you possibly know your Digger has an air leak?"

She didn't believe me.

"I've been able to talk to him with some kind of telepathy. I don't know how. I've never been able to do it before."

Her expression changed. "Telepathy?"

She was going to think I needed to see the counsellor.

"Yes. I don't know how I did it. But that doesn't matter. He's running out of air–"

"Come with me to my office," she said.

"Okay. Are you going to call Sonrisa?"

"Yes. We'll do that." She started walking down the hallway and gestured for me to follow her. "Tell me how you initiated the contact with your Digger."

I frowned. After what I'd told her, she was focusing on that? "I don't really know how I did it. I already told you that. I just really wanted to let him know the search teams were getting closer."

She was taller than me with long, slender legs, and I had to walk fast to keep pace with her. She pulled a small device out of her pocket and pressed a button on it before putting it back. Before I could think too much about what it was, we'd arrived at her office and she unlocked it with a thumbprint and a retina scan and ushered me in.

I sat down in the chair she offered and she took the comfy chair behind the big desk. I expected her to place a call on the Vid on her desk, but she sat staring at me like I was a long-lost family member.

A few moments passed and she kept staring. "Um, aren't you going to call Sonrisa?"

"Oh, yes," she said.

It looked like I'd pulled her out of a trance. She commanded the Vid to call and sat there staring at me some more.

When it connected, Sonrisa looked flustered and his normally-neat hair was sticking up in places. "Doctor Rowen? What can I do for you? Do you have news of the others?"

"Hello, Mr Sonrisa. I have one of your Nav Operators here with me. Her name is... What's your name again, Honey?"

Honey? "Lennina Callista."

"Lennina Callista. She says she has information from her Digger. She thinks he has an air leak in his suit and wants you to double your efforts before it's too late for him."

"An air leak? How could she know that? She was replaced hours ago. She has no access to Operations."

"She claims to be telepathic. Do you know anything about this?"

"She did not declare any Talent when she applied for the job. Is she undocumented?"

She turned to me. "Are you?"

"I told you I didn't know I could do any of this until today."

"So, is that a yes?"

"I guess so, but I didn't know. It's not like I deliberately lied to The Company."

Her eyes narrowed. "We'll see."

My fists clenched. "I'm telling you, I didn't know."

"Yes, well, like I said, we'll see."

Sonrisa cleared his throat. "So, am I meant to take this claim seriously?"

I looked at the screen. "Of course! I'm telling you the truth. I've spoken to him. I can even tell you where his injuries are. All down his left side. He managed to shift out from under the part of the suit that was pushing against him so he won't have crush injuries to worry about.

He has broken bones and is in a lot of pain and would probably have been okay till someone found him, but now the suit's reporting an air leak. You have to get there or he'll die like Nazan!"

My voice cracked on the last few words.

"How do you know about Nazan?"

"I saw Anterres in the hall."

He chuckled. "I thought you were going to tell me you read her mind."

"This isn't funny! Her Digger is dead! And I'm trying to save mine! Stop sitting there laughing and do something!"

He sobered. "Don't speak to me like that."

"I don't care how I speak to you. I quit this morning, remember? You can't fire me for being disrespectful. Just get them to get to Daniel sooner so he'll have a chance to survive."

I buried my face in my hands. How could I make them see?

He cleared his throat again. "I'll see what I can do. Doctor Rowen, was there anything else you wanted?"

"No. That's all."

They said their goodbyes and disconnected.

There was a knock at the door and Dr Rowen called for whoever it was to enter. I looked up and gasped as Malvolio walked in.

CHAPTER 45

Why Didn't You Tell Me You Were Telepathic?

There wasn't enough air in the room. What was he doing here?

His eyes locked onto mine and the grey seemed to darken. "You wanted to see me, Doctor?" he said, not breaking eye contact.

"Yes, Mr Dermid. I've been talking to, uh, this Nav Operator and she claims to have some telepathic ability."

His eyes widened, but then I saw the smugness return. "She does?"

What has he got to do with any of this? "What are you doing here?" I asked. I turned to the doctor. "Why did you call him here?"

"Mr Dermid has a vested interest in anyone on the station showing signs of any form of Talent."

I sucked in a breath. "What? Why?"

"Don't ask one-word questions, Lennina."

I clenched my fists. "Don't tell me how to speak!"

He lifted his chin. "I'm only trying to help you. I've always been trying to help you. You know that."

"I don't want your help. What are you doing here?"

His eyebrows drew together. "You've had that question answered already. I need to know when someone shows signs of Talent. We need to have you tested immediately and your abilities graded."

There was a spark in his eye, like this was exciting for him. It made me feel ill.

"I don't need to be tested and graded right now. I'm here to get help for Daniel."

His eyes darkened. "Who is Daniel?"

"My Digger. Javolo."

"I thought you said you didn't know his first name."

"I didn't say that. I said he might not remember mine. Why are we talking about this? I just want someone to listen to me and step up the rescue effort before he runs out of air."

Dr Rowen jumped in with, "And you've achieved that. I called Mr Sonrisa for you."

I looked back at her. "Yes, you did. Thank you."

I didn't know what else I could do, but Malvolio being here had thrown me. Why was he involved with any Talents on the station? It didn't make sense. He managed a company that made Mech-suits and other mechanical vehicles. What was I missing here?

Malvolio made himself comfortable in the chair next to mine and I instinctively shrunk away from him. "Lennina. Why didn't you tell me you were telepathic?"

I didn't want to answer him, but I wanted him to know I hadn't been lying to him the whole time we'd been together. "I didn't know. I've never been able to do it before now."

"I'm not sure what to say to that. It's a bit late for you to be suddenly showing signs. People usually show signs during puberty."

"Well, I don't know what to tell you. I don't know anything about Talent or when I'm supposed to be showing signs of it. I only know it's never happened before."

"We need to have you tested."

I looked from him to Dr Rowen. They were both staring intently at me. "What? You mean now?"

"Yes."

"But why now?"

Dr Rowen stood. "Telepathy can be used against people in the form of mind-reading. You need to be trained in how to control it and the proper conduct for those with Talent. Also, it is extremely important that anyone showing signs of Talent be tested and observed in case they possess other Talents that could be potentially dangerous."

I gasped. "Dangerous? How?"

She frowned. "You do know what some Talents can do with their power?"

"Yes." I had to think. What could they do? "Oh. You mean like moving things with their minds?"

"Yes. It can be very destructive if wielded by an untrained Talent. We need to protect you from yourself and others from you."

My chest tightened. I hadn't thought of any of that.

The doctor stepped toward the door. "Let's get you settled in a safe room until we can organise the tests."

That sounded a lot like a prison cell. "Does the room have a bed?"

She looked confused. "Yes. Why?"

"I'm tired."

"Okay. You can rest until we're ready for you."

"Lead the way."

I had no intention of sleeping.

I tried not to think too much about Daniel and what would happen if they didn't find him in time, but all I could think of was that he was going to die slowly. In the dark. Alone. I nearly fell to my knees at the thought.

The fact that Nazan was dead made it so much worse.

We finally made it to the safe room.

Dr Rowen used her thumbprint to open the door and swept her arm toward the room. I looked in and saw a bed and some chairs in there, a complicated-looking machine with wires everywhere over in one corner, and not much else.

She ushered me in. Malvolio was making me nervous. I didn't want him in the room with me. I didn't want him near me right now. Or ever.

"How long do I have to wait?"

"Maybe an hour. We're still on alert."

My first instinct was to protest, but had to remind myself that I wanted a long wait time. "Okay. I'll stay in here on one condition."

"And what's that?"

"That Malvolio doesn't come in here at any point, or hang around outside the door. I don't ever want to be alone with him."

Malvolio stepped forward. "Lennina—"

"No. I don't want anything more to do with you. I don't even understand why you're here." I turned to the doctor. "Do I have your word?"

"Why are you so hostile towards Mr Dermid?"

"Because he assaulted me and broke my ribs!"

Her eyebrows shot up and she looked at Malvolio.

"I did not!"

"Don't deny it." I spat. "There are records with the Medical Facility and the Enforcers." I looked at Dr Rowen. "Can you keep him away from me or not?"

She looked from him and back to me. "Okay. If that's what you wish."

I walked further into the room and she closed the door. I heard it lock. The only positive thing about that was that Malvolio was on the other side of the locked door.

Oh, and maybe I wouldn't be disturbed while I contacted Daniel.

I crawled under the covers and lay carefully on my side and found it was easier to contact him this time. It didn't make sense when I was so worked up and upset, but I wasn't going to complain.

"What happened?" Daniel asked me when we had re-established the connection. *"You just disappeared."*

I squirmed a bit. *"I... kinda lost control of the connection after you said... after you said that..."* I took a breath.

"It's okay. I probably would have lost it too..."

"When I opened my eyes, Malvolio was there. He wouldn't listen to me when I told him about the air leak. Then I tried to get up to tell someone who would listen and blacked out. It must drain all my energy or something doing this. I've blacked out both times afterwards... I woke up in the Infirmary."

"So, what did they do? Did they believe you this time?" There was so much hope in his voice.

My heart twisted in my chest. *"There was no one in the room when I woke up. But then I saw Anterres. She..."* I took a deep breath. *"Nazan didn't make it."*

"What?"

"His legs were crushed. Once they moved the rocks..."

"Aw, no. Not Nazan! He was going home in a few weeks. His contract was almost up. He has a wife... a kid..."

My eyes were already closed, but I squeezed them tighter. *"I don't know what to say."* What could I say? *"I found a doctor and she called Sonrisa to tell him about the leak, but she seemed more interested in the fact that I've shown signs of Talent than helping you."*

"What? Why would she do that?"

"She says that undocumented Talents can be dangerous. She thinks I might start developing telekinetic powers and become destructive."

"I guess she has a point, but you wouldn't hurt anyone."

"She seems to think so. So I'm in a room waiting for someone to come and test me for Talent somehow. I only agreed to come in here so I could try to contact you again. I'm glad it worked. It seems to be getting easier to do."

"That's good. I mean the part about it getting easier."

"The weirdest thing was that she called Malvolio."

"What? Why?"

"Apparently, he has a 'vested interest' in anyone displaying signs of Talent on the station. Whatever that means."

"That's... I don't know what to make of that."

"Yeah. So, all we can do is wait and hope they took me seriously."

While we waited, thinking he would most likely run out of air before help arrived, tears ran down my cheeks.

"I've been doing a lot of thinking lately," I told him, *"about Malvolio, work, you and everything — even before I met you."*

"Yeah?"

"Yeah. And I could see that even with all the things Malvolio and I did on the station, and the times I spent out and about with all his friends, the only time I was truly happy was when I was at my Nav Station talking to you." I tried to hold back the flood of tears threatening to overwhelm me.

"You know," he said, *"I have to say those were my happiest times, too. We couldn't say too much over the Com, but when I think about it, we said a lot. It was what kept me goin'..."*

My heart warmed. *"Yeah. And I know we got into trouble a lot for talking, but it was worth it."*

"And they couldn't complain — we out-mined everyone else most days."

I sighed. *"We did. But now they can stick it, because I quit today — even before the collapse. And right now, we can say whatever we want. No one's listening — no one could possibly be listening."*

Daniel was quiet for a few seconds, like he was trying to think of what he could say now that our conversation wasn't being monitored.

I thought of what we'd talked about the most in our more recent conversations, which made me think of Malvolio. *"You know, I talked about Malvolio too much. I hope I didn't bore you to death."*

"No, you could never do that."

I smiled. *"I hope I didn't upset you too much then."*

"No. It's all good."

My smile faded as I thought of Malvolio and all the horrible things he'd done. *"I realise now that my relationship with him was really doomed a long time ago. I just didn't see it."*

"Really?"

Tell him... *"Yes. And..."* It might have been my last chance to tell him how I felt, so I pushed myself. *"And I want to tell you that... I realise now that I've been in love with you for a long time and didn't even know it."*

He was quiet for a moment. *"I know."*

CHAPTER 46

It Was You

"You know?"

He chuckled. *"Yeah... you did tell me."*

Duh. Twice even. How could I forget...

"But I didn't tell you how long I've felt this way and not realised it. Only that I did. I didn't know what to think or feel after Malvolio... manipulated me. He... I don't really know what he did to me... but I haven't been the same since. It was like he took my heart away and put it in a box somewhere. I was like an empty shell and didn't realise it... But when I came to work each day, I had so much fun talking to you. It was probably the only thing keeping me sane.

"Maybe you brought my heart back out of the box for a few hours each day... I really enjoyed talking to you, you know, and I didn't care when they gave me lectures about how we're not supposed to socialise. I was dangerously close to losing my job — more than once. And one of my supervisors told me he was recommending reassignment. The only bad thing about that would be that I probably never would have found you outside of work, especially when I'd forgotten your first name... I'm sorry. I'm raving on..."

"No, it's okay. Please continue to rave."

I felt self-conscious. I tended to ramble when I was nervous. And telling someone how you felt about them is never easy. I couldn't help wondering if he felt the same about me... In the silence that followed, Daniel gave another little chuckle.

My heart sank a little to think that he was laughing at me. *"What are you laughing at?"*

"The strangeness of the situation. It's just so odd."

Strange wasn't the word. Or odd. *"Which part of this whole bizarre mess of a situation are you talking about?"*

"Well, basically, you fell for me twice, right?"

I felt a little flutter in my chest. *"Yeah."*

"Well, I fell for you twice, too."

The flutter suddenly felt like a whole swarm of butterflies were dancing around in my rib cage... My head swam.

It was amazing; you wouldn't even read about it in a book or see it in a movie. How could we have done that?

"I was already in love with my best friend, who, of course, I wasn't allowed to be in love with and who was taken anyway... Then I met you and couldn't help myself. I was drawn to you. It felt like a betrayal to Callista, but I knew I couldn't be with her. I had strong feelings for you both, but then you mentioned Malvolio and everything clicked into place. Then you dropped the bomb that you were in love with your Digger, and I was blown away.

"So, I thought that once I somehow told you who I was, maybe by mentioning something that happened at the restaurant or something, you'd know who I was without our audience catching on... And we would just have to keep our feelings a secret and work something out... I'd already gotten away with sneaking into the Navs' Section more than once, so maybe we could have pulled it off... But then I saw the Ghost... and then the tunnel collapsed..."

He was talking slower and sounded weaker. There wasn't enough air for him to breathe normally.

I was losing him. This couldn't be happening. He couldn't just die. There had to be something I could do. I felt so helpless.

I could somehow feel him growing weaker. Could feel the tears forming again in my closed eyes.

This can't be happening...

"Suit is telling me... I'm almost... out of air." He was struggling for coherent thoughts in his mind. I could hear it. I could feel it. They weren't going to make it to him. Surely they were getting close...

I could feel the panic rising. *"Can you hear anything? Any sounds that might mean they're near you?"*

There was silence while he listened and it seemed to stretch on forever.

"No," he finally said. *"Nothin'... Well, at least... I won't die alone..."*

"NO! Don't say that!" I knew it was going to happen, knew I couldn't stop it, but I didn't want him to talk like that.

He sighed heavily. *"Lennina. I need to... to say goodbye... before it's too late... and I can't talk anymore... I feel really weak... I can't breathe properly..."*

Oh... no... "No!" How could I stop him from thinking like that? How could I save him? My heart was breaking... I wanted to scream...

"I love you..." he told me. *"I've loved you... for such a long time... and... and... the woman I saw... that night... that I said was... the most beautiful woman... I had... ever... seen... it was you..."*

"Oh, Daniel..."

That statement just hit me — went right for the heart. And I melted. And cried harder. I couldn't believe what I'd heard. Surely it wasn't true. I remembered how he'd described her and more tears came flooding down my cheeks.

"She has long dark hair and bright blue eyes that seem to flash at you when she smiles..." It was so... Poetic? Romantic? Yes. It sounded *so* romantic. Such a beautiful way to describe someone. But he'd used those words to describe me. It warmed my breaking heart.

He'd also said she had "the most perfect bod." I didn't think I had a 'perfect' body, but that was what he'd said from his first impression...

I'd loved his poetic description of my eyes... He'd been talking about me and neither of us knew it... It was too weird...

I smiled through the tears. So that's what he thought when he saw me... That I was beautiful... That was unexpected. I wasn't ugly, I knew that, but I wouldn't have described myself as beautiful. Maybe he was just saying it so I would feel better or something. But that couldn't be right. At the time, he didn't even know it was me...

Then I thought about when I'd met him. I was practically drooling over him. He was gorgeous... and I couldn't stop staring at him... and he kept staring at me...

My thoughts returned to the present. I needed to do something, and fast. But what?

"You're not going to die!" I told him. *"You* can't*! Not* now*! I need you to just... just hang on... they'll be there soon... I just* know *they will!"*

I wondered if he could hear the lie in my voice.

There was a pause. My heart was thumping inside my chest, trying to get out through my throat. What was I going to do? Then I realised he hadn't spoken for a while. Was he okay? I started to worry that he had lost consciousness, or worse, and the panic shot through me.

"All along... All this time... It was always you..." It was like a whisper in my mind. He was barely there. Just a small thread...

I clung to the thread.

"No... more... air... it says... it's... empty..."

"NO! Oh, crap. Hang in there! Don't die on me! I love *you! Daniel! DANIEL!"*

CHAPTER 47

Allador

There was only silence. It felt like my heart had stopped beating. I waited. And the tears wouldn't stop.

"Daniel?" I whispered across our connection.

I waited for him to take his final breath. I cried some more. I didn't think I had any tears left, but they came.

I was determined not to let go till I was sure he was really gone...

Then something slammed into the side of my face so hard that I saw stars.

There was a foggy blackness in front of my eyes after the stars faded, but I stayed conscious. The right side of my face throbbed. I couldn't feel Daniel's presence anymore.

"Look, she's coming out of the trance now..."

"What?" I squeaked. My brain was fuzzy.

"Hey, you alright, Miss Callista? Miss Callista? Can you hear me?"

A man's ugly face came into focus, then Malvolio's face flashed before me. All the horror of that night came crashing in. I recoiled and my head hit the headboard. My breath came in short bursts and my heart thudded loudly in my chest.

"D-don't touch me!" I screamed. The ripping feeling in my side only added to the emotional pain. My mind was reeling. It wasn't Malvolio, but it was like it was happening all over again. I couldn't deal with it right now. I felt like I was coming apart.

He'd hit me hard enough that it would probably leave a bruise, which was way more force than was necessary.

He frowned at me. "You wouldn' wake up. You went into some sort of trance, and nothin' we did or said helped... I had to do somethin'."

"You didn't have to hit me!" Anger boiled inside me. There wasn't enough air in the room. "Just get out!"

I needed to get the connection back. I needed to know what was happening to Daniel.

"You were cryin' out and stuff and we couldn' wake you..." he told me again. "And you screamed. The doctors are concerned, Miss. Were you dreamin'?"

We?

I looked behind him and recognised Dr Rowen. "I'm okay. I don't need any help. Just leave me alone."

Dr Rowen spoke up this time. "You are *not* okay. We came to run the tests and found you in this state."

The man holding me started to drag me to a sitting position.

"No! Let me go! You don't understand. He could be dead. You broke the connection and now I don't know if he's—" I tried to pull out of his grasp and the room spun out of control.

Despite my protests, he was too strong for me. As soon as I was sitting up, my head felt heavy and my vision clouded. I knew what was coming next.

"Sorry, Miss. Can' do dat," he said.

My head lolled to the side as I was enveloped in blackness again.

—— ⋆·☆·⋆ ——

I opened my eyes. I'd collapsed again. I groaned. Was this going to happen every time I used telepathy? It wasn't a very practical ability if this was the result. Or maybe there was something wrong with me. I'd have to ask if it was normal.

My heart crumbled into tiny pieces as I thought of Daniel. Unless by some miracle they'd found him just after I'd been slapped, he'd be long gone. I couldn't bear to think it.

He'd said he couldn't hear any noises. No sounds of digging. Tears ran from the corners of my eyes and into my hair on either side of my face.

A blinding light forced me to cover my eyes. *What?* I shielded my eyes and found that there was a figure made of light hovering in front of me.

The Ghost. It had to be. Right in front of me. How did it get up here on the station?

Colours swirled within its body. It was beautiful.

The Ghost's mind felt like it was inside my head somehow and it showed me a series of images of Daniel in his Mech-suit, standing in an open area underground. Then the roof collapsed. I gasped and squirmed in the bed. It was difficult to watch and I was reminded of the incredible pain that had struck me. It was almost too much to bear.

Then I saw the Ghost lift the boulders off him using telekinesis. He was in a mess, but Rescue would be able to get him out of the suit without too much digging.

But was he alive?

Something changed. Something clicked in my mind. Suddenly all the things the Ghost was trying to communicate to me were as clear as if he'd said them in Basic Terran. But how? Had he worked out how to speak Basic?

It didn't matter. What mattered was telling him that Daniel needed to get out of there right now. He needed urgent medical attention if he was still alive. As I started to tell the Ghost, it disappeared.

I was temporarily blinded as my eyes adjusted to the dim lighting in the room.

The name Allador popped into my head. The Ghost's name was Allador.

I lay there for a while staring at the ceiling with my mind reeling.

Dr Rowen entered the room, her springy hair bouncing as she walked. I hadn't even heard the door. She checked the chart on the end of my bed before she spoke and asked about why I was crying out and sobbing, and why they couldn't wake me, which made my eyes sting with unshed tears.

I sat up. "I need to know what happened to my Digger. He ran out of air. Did they find him? Is he okay? Is he alive?"

My voice cracked on the last word and my chest felt tight. He had to be alive. I couldn't deal with losing him.

"You were communicating with him?"

Two tears made their way down my cheeks. "Yes. I told you he had an air leak. The suit said it was empty. The air had run out."

Her eyes widened slightly but her face didn't change. "He has been found and is being prepped for the ER right now."

A sob escaped me and I closed my eyes. He'd somehow made it. I tried hard to appear calm on the outside while my insides were churning. "How did he survive?"

"Rescue found him before he ran out of oxygen."

I sighed. "I was talking to him when that guy hit me."

My voice hardened on the last few words. My face had only just healed after Malvolio's assault.

She didn't comment.

I was relieved that Daniel was finally getting the medical attention he needed, but he wasn't out of trouble yet. He would have a long recovery ahead of him. It made my broken ribs look trivial in comparison.

I wanted to ask more questions about him, but I was only his Nav and wasn't supposed to care as much as I did.

"Right," she said, "Let's get started."

I looked around, wondering how we were going to get started, when the door swished open and Malvolio walked in, followed by a short man I'd never met.

My heart leapt into my throat. "Why are you here?"

He smiled. "Observing."

The other man, who was dwarfed by the other two, gave me a friendly smile. "Hello, Miss Callista. I'm Doctor Kharim. I will be conducting some tests today to gauge your abilities."

I swallowed. "Okay, but how can you test my mind?"

"If you have any telekinetic abilities, we can obviously see what you can do. But to get a better picture of what's going on up here," he pointed to my head, "we need to hook you up to an electroencephalograph to measure your brain activity while using your abilities." He gestured to the machine in the corner.

"I don't think that's going to work," I told him.

"Why not? It's standard procedure."

"Well, I don't know how I'm even doing it. I've never shown any signs of having any abilities until today."

He frowned. "That's okay, dear. You're a late bloomer. I've been told that you have been in contact with your Digger through telepathy?"

"Yes."

"We'll get you to contact him again and test you."

"Okay. I don't know if I can do it again, though."

"Just relax and try."

I had my doubts, but I nodded anyway.

He headed to the EEG in the corner. "We'll get you set up with this first, then we'll get started."

I kept stealing glances at Malvolio while the doctor put the wiring harness on my head. He made me nervous and I wished I could get him to leave.

Maybe I could.

"I can't be in the same room as Malvolio," I said. "I have an RO out against him."

Dr Rowen looked from me to Malvolio with a frown. "Why?"

"I told you. He assaulted me and broke my ribs."

"Those things are irrelevant in this situation," she said. "Doctor Kharim and I are here and this is a professional setting. Nothing will happen to you."

"I want him to leave."

"That isn't going to happen. This goes far beyond your petty squabbles. He is part of this whether you like it or not."

My heartbeat sped up. "Broken bones are not *petty!*"

Malvolio stepped forward. "Lennina, darling. I don't know why you're being so hostile. We're here to help you."

"*Don't* call me darling. I'm not your darling."

Dr Kharim turned from the machine and cleared his throat. "Okay, you may begin."

"What?"

"Contact your Digger."

My mind faltered. How was I supposed to do it on cue with them staring at me?

"I can't just do it on demand."

"Just relax and pretend we're not here."

I sighed. Carefully. "Easy for you to say," I muttered.

I took a deep breath and closed my eyes. This was much harder than

I thought.

Relax. Breathe.

I tried to concentrate and ignore them. I needed to pretend I was alone, like he said.

After a series of relaxation attempts, I called out to Daniel. I reached out to see if I could feel his presence, but there was nothing.

I called again with no response.

Then it hit me. I couldn't feel his pain. Which meant that he wasn't conscious. He would probably be in the ER by now. He was under anaesthetic. There was no way he was going to hear me.

Duh.

My eyes flew open.

Dr Rowen leaned forward. "Did you contact him?"

"No."

"Why not? What happened?"

"You said he's in the ER, right?"

"Yes."

She still hadn't got it. "So he's under a general anaesthetic."

Realisation dawned. It was comical seeing the look on her face when she discovered her blunder. There was even a slight blush. I pressed my lips together and tried not to smile.

She turned to Dr Kharim. "We need to postpone the testing until her Digger is awake."

He'd turned a shade of red — which was hard to see with his brown skin — and started to shut down the machine. He took the wiring harness from my head.

Before they left, Dr Rowen said, "Don't worry about a thing. We'll get this sorted out for you. You'll know your Rating soon enough and be able to make plans for the future. We will be back later—" she looked at her watch, "—make that tomorrow — to retest you. In the meantime, I'll make sure dinner is served to you."

Once the door swished behind them, I waited about ten minutes before heading for the door myself. To my surprise, it opened. That was their first mistake. Now I needed it to stay that way because once Daniel was awake, I was going to find him.

So many questions raced through my mind as I waited to see Daniel.

Was he going to recover fully? Would he be able to use his shoulder and left arm properly? Would he be able to operate a Mech-suit again? Would he even want to?

If it was me, I wouldn't want to go back underground again. Ever.

Images from when I was trapped in that hole ran through my mind, making me shudder. The sides of the hole seemed to push in on me. Ants crawled along one wall and some weird beetles walked over my feet. It almost felt like I was back there. I shuddered again and shoved them from my mind.

I needed to be thinking about the here and now. And I would have to wait to find out about Daniel.

I must have dozed a little after I'd eaten dinner. Time was hard to judge. As I lay there listening for any sounds of people nearby, pain started to niggle at my shoulder, then crept down my arm. After a few more minutes, parts of my left leg were aching, but it was dull. It sucked that Daniel was in pain again, but I felt a tingle of excitement because it meant he was awake and that I hadn't lost whatever connection I had to him.

It was still unnerving that I could feel pain that belonged to someone else, but it made me feel closer to him somehow.

I wanted to connect with him, but if I did, I wouldn't be able to go to him. I'd end up passing out again instead. I needed to actually see him this time. The need to see him was so strong. I felt a pull toward him somehow, like a giant invisible magnet was pulling at my soul.

I crept out of bed. The lights in the hallway were dim, so I assumed it was late at night.

The door swished open. I had no idea where Recovery was, so I picked a direction and followed the signs in the corridors until I reached it. I moved silently down the hallway, wondering how I was going to sneak past the nurses' station, but found Daniel before I'd reached it. The room had a large observation window and a digital display next to the door showed his name.

Once the door slid open, my breath caught. Daniel was lying shirtless on a hospital bed with the side rails up. His eyes were closed and his chest rose and fell slowly. Tears stung my eyes. To see him like that was heartbreaking.

He had wires stuck to his chest. There was a bag of fluid with a line running into his right hand and bandages around his head and left shoulder. His left leg and left arm were bandaged and had plaster backboards. He was covered in cuts and bruises. The monitors next to the bed spewed out information as the lights flashed.

I'd known what his injuries were, but seeing him made it real. I couldn't break down now. I had to get it together.

The beeping that signalled his heartbeat increased slightly. I wondered if he was aware of what was going on around him. He must have been conscious on some level if I could feel his pain. It would've been nice if he knew I was here.

I wanted to go to the bed and touch him but wasn't sure if I should. I didn't want to hurt him. My legs moved on their own and I approached slowly. I reached out a hand, but dropped it at the last second.

I thought about how we could link our minds together. Where did the ability come from? All I did was wish I could contact him, and then I actually did it. And it wasn't just Daniel, I'd communicated with Allador too. An alien that was made up of pure energy and light.

I pictured his bright form in my mind. Pure energy...

A bright light pierced the darkened room and I had to shield my eyes again. It was too bright to be the lights on the ceiling. I slowly opened them as Allador approached me. He'd done it again. He'd found me.

He inclined his head. *"Greetings, Lennina."*

CHAPTER 48

Hey, You

I smiled nervously. *"Hello, Allador."*

My heart was in my throat, but I knew he wouldn't hurt me. I wondered how he'd managed to travel all the way from the planet to the space station.

He studied me for a while. *"I am concerned, Lennina. You are in pain, but your injury is on the other side of your body."*

I wasn't sure how to explain it to him. I realised that the phantom pains had increased. Daniel must have needed more painkillers; the pain was steadily rising.

I wasn't sure if I could see a frown on Allador's face, but I could sense it.

"Your companion was hurt badly, but you..." He leaned over me and placed his hand on my forehead, which surprised me, but I kept still. His hand was warm. He stayed like that for a few moments, then looked at me questioningly. *"It is not your pain."*

I pointed at the bed. *"No. It's Daniel's pain."*

"How?"

"I don't know. We're linked somehow. It's not normal for humans."

I thought about how much pain I'd felt when it first happened and knew that Daniel had felt it just as much, only he had the injuries and the fear of dying thrown in. A tear ran down my cheek. It would've been terrifying.

I felt a tinge of panic as I thought of what would happen if someone walked in and saw Allador in here, but I tried to stay calm.

"Do not worry, Lennina. I will set things right. I will heal him."

I gasped.

He floated over to Daniel and placed one hand on Daniel's shoulder and the other on his leg.

"I was preparing to heal him when your people found him."

My heart raced and I remembered the images he'd shown me before. *"You were down there when he ran out of air?"*

"Yes. He was alive when I found him and badly injured. I wanted to help him."

"How can you heal him?"

"It is easy to do now that I have scanned you both and sensed the inner workings of your carbon-based bodies."

The fact that Daniel could've been healed sooner made me want to cry.

So he wasn't just checking why I was experiencing so much pain, he was checking my biology. Weird.

So Daniel could have avoided all that pain, and even the surgery, if the humans hadn't interfered... or if they'd found him a bit later...

And I could've avoided all the pain too...

I couldn't take my eyes off Daniel. A colourful glow had spread across his body from Allador's hands and was concentrated in the injured areas.

Tears ran down my cheeks. This was hard to take. The memory of him fading away and me waiting for his last breath caused an ache to spread across my chest.

I kept watching, and the thought hit me that this was Javolo, my best friend in the universe. More tears slid down my cheeks. Everything I felt for him poured out to him from my heart and made a lump form in my throat. But then this was also Daniel. My brain couldn't connect the two people together. It refused to put Daniel and Javolo together into one identity...

I could feel a warmth seeping into my body as the pain receded. The relief as the internal injuries were healed. The bones knitting back together. It didn't hurt, but it creeped me out.

The cannula and external stitches were pushed out of his skin. They were no longer needed. All the cuts turned pink before healing altogether, and the bruises disappeared, leaving his skin looking smooth and healthy.

Please, just let him finish, I pleaded to no one, thinking that someone could walk in at any minute and prevent Allador from healing him completely.

As the phantom pain faded away to nothing, it seemed that someone had heard me and given Allador the necessary time to finish the job. Relief washed over me and I let it overwhelm me. It wasn't just that the pain had left me. It was knowing Daniel was okay. I couldn't believe it. One minute he was in pain, recovering from surgery with broken bones and stitches and tubes everywhere, the next, he was fully healed and as healthy as ever.

I looked back to his face and realised he was fully awake. I gasped. He was staring straight at me.

He smiled. "Hey, you."

I choked back a sob, but then smiled through my tears. "Hey."

Allador moved back a little and Daniel looked up at him. "Thank you."

Allador inclined his head. *"It is an honour."*

The door opened and a nurse stopped in the doorway, staring at Allador. I knew our luck couldn't last.

"Help! I need help in here!" she screamed. "Intruder alert! Get away from him! Leave him alone!"

CHAPTER 49

I'm His Nav Operator

"It's okay," I said, and she skittered sideways. I hadn't meant to scare her. "He's not hurting him. He won't hurt you."

She looked from me to Allador, then at Daniel, who was now sitting up and glowing. She pulled a device from her pocket and pressed a button. "Security!"

"It's okay. We're okay. Don't be scared. He's from Kronos. He's a friend."

It was no use. She ran from the room calling for help.

I turned to Allador. "Maybe you should go. She won't listen to me."

"I cannot. I have depleted a large amount of energy."

I hadn't thought about that. His light was dimmer than before. It would have taken a huge amount of energy to heal Daniel's injuries. I needed to think. What could we do? Maybe he could hide. I looked around the room, but there was only a small cupboard in one corner. He wouldn't fit inside.

"I don't know what to do. You're too bright. We can't hide you."

Allador moved over to the corner near the cupboard.

Daniel looked down at his body in amazement, moving his arms and legs and feeling his shoulder through the bandages. The glow was fading. The machines were beeping wildly as some of the wires had detached themselves from his chest.

Security guards ran in with their stunners drawn and ordered Allador to back away from Daniel. He couldn't back away any further. The nurse threw a couple of things at him, which went right through him and hit the wall.

I told them to stop. I tried to explain that he hadn't hurt us and that he'd healed Daniel. It didn't matter what I said; they paid no attention to me at all.

Allador kept backing up until he'd gone right through the wall. The security guards stood there with their mouths hanging open.

One of them turned to the other three. "Go into the next room and see where it went. I'll stay here with these two."

They left and the guard started asking questions. "What was that thing?"

Daniel pulled the remaining wires from his chest as the nurse cringed. "A Ghost from down on the planet. He healed me. Tell your men not to hurt him."

The guard didn't look convinced. "How do I know you're telling me the truth?"

The nurse stepped forward and had a closer look at Daniel. "He is telling the truth. About the healing anyway. He's just had surgery after being involved in the tunnel collapse." The guard's eyes widened. "He had multiple fractures and was recovering from surgery."

The guard finally closed his mouth and turned to me. "So. What's your story? What are you doing in here in the middle of the night?"

"I had to see if Daniel was alright."

Daniel looked at me and I smiled.

"But who are you?"

"I'm Lennina Callista. I'm his Nav Operator."

He was still frowning at me. "How did you get in here?"

"I walked from where they were keeping me for testing."

His eyebrows rose. "Testing? Testing for what?"

"Talent."

His eyes were wide again. He looked me over more carefully, as if he'd be able to see my Talent if he looked close enough. "You shouldn't be here."

"I know, but I needed—"

"To see if he was okay. I get it. What am I supposed to do with you now?"

I cringed, anticipating a negative reaction. "Let me speak to Daniel?"

"Seriously?"

I ignored the fact that he still held a stunner and walked over to Daniel's bed. "Are you okay?"

He reached up and cupped my cheek with one hand. "Yes. I'm *better* than okay. I feel great."

I leaned into his hand and placed one of mine over it.

"Alright, break it up. You're gonna have to go back to your room now, Miss."

I looked into Daniel's eyes and smiled. As I turned away reluctantly, his hand slid from my face and the guard stepped closer to us, his stunner held higher to prove he meant business.

I was still smiling. "Okay."

He seemed surprised that I didn't protest.

The other guards returned and reported that they couldn't find Allador. It was a relief that he wasn't harmed.

Dr Kharim entered and the questions started again. I took advantage of their inattention and stayed with Daniel until Dr Kharim asked me to move aside so he could examine him.

His eyes were wide and his excitement palpable when he announced that Daniel's injuries were completely gone. He called the nurse over to help him remove the bandages and the guard took me by the arm and manoeuvred me out of the room. I protested and tried to say goodbye to Daniel, but he wasn't having any of it.

The walk back to my room was silent and this time, the door was locked behind me.

I crawled into bed with a smile on my face. Daniel was healed.

After I'd been given some breakfast, Dr Rowen barrelled into the room. "What were you doing in Recovery in the middle of the night?"

Yeah, good morning to you too. "I wanted to see if my Digger was okay."

"I gave you a report on his condition yesterday."

"I know, but I wanted to see him for myself."

Her eyes narrowed. "What is the status of your relationship with your Digger?"

"What? Are you serious? We're just friends."

"Not from what I've been told."

My stomach dropped. Malvolio had probably told her his version of what he thought was going on. "You mean Malvolio?"

Her face was stone.

"Malvolio was a jealous boyfriend. He thought I was cheating on him and picked my Digger because we get along really well and talk and joke while we work. How could it be anything more when we're not allowed to meet each other?"

I couldn't believe this was coming up again.

"That's not consistent with the report from Security last night."

Oops. How could I explain that?

"That was just him thanking me... for my concern. That's all. We haven't broken any rules."

"That remains to be seen."

The door swished open and Malvolio walked in, followed by Dr Kharim. My chest tightened.

Dr Kharim smiled at me. "Morning. Let's get started, shall we? Your Digger is awake now."

I tried not to show my fear of Malvolio. I couldn't stand being in the same room as him after what he'd done to me. Apparently, the fact that I never wanted to see him again was unimportant, and now I'd have to put up with him until this testing for Talent stuff was over with. That sucked.

His smile was as fake as it was yesterday.

My stomach twisted into knots. How was I going to communicate with Daniel while they all stared at me?

"I don't know if this will work," I told them.

Dr Kharim smiled again. "You'll be okay. Just relax."

I glared at Malvolio. "I can't do this with Malvolio in the room."

Dr Kharim's smile faltered. "Why not?"

"He's not supposed to be near me. I told you. I have an RO against him. He's breaching it by being here."

Dr Rowen sighed heavily. "I told you that he stays. It's not negotiable."

"But he's breaking the law!"

Malvolio narrowed his eyes. "Lennina. Stop being childish. This is important work we're doing here."

"You need to be tested for your own good," Dr Rowen added.

It was my turn to sigh. How could I make them listen? "He better not be sticking around for my training."

"I will be wherever I need to be, Lennina. This work is necessary. You don't have any authority here."

CHAPTER 50
I Didn't Think I'd Ever See You Again

I looked at the floor. Now what could I do? My options were limited.

Dr Kharim set up the EEG and put the wiring harness on my head again.

My stomach felt like I'd swallowed a brick. "Can I lie down?"

"Sure." Once he'd rearranged some of the wires, Dr Kharim stepped back. "All set. Whenever you're ready."

I looked at their expectant faces. How could I relax? This wasn't going to work.

Dr Kharim was the only one smiling, so I concentrated on that. I closed my eyes to block them out.

It took a long time for me to relax just a little. I had to ignore the fact that they were in the room.

"Daniel?"

Nothing.

"Daniel? Can you hear me?"

Still nothing.

It took a few more tries and a few more rounds of me doing some relaxation techniques before I got a response.

"Lennina? How are you?"

"I'm okay. How are you?"

"Never been better. I still can't believe he healed me completely."

"Neither can I." I sighed. *"The doctors have me hooked up to an EEG to test my telepathic ability."*

"They have me hooked up too."

"Really? I guess that makes sense." They could see if he had any abilities at the same time. *"They say I can't get out of here until I'm*

tested. They can't have 'potentially dangerous' Talents running around untested and ungraded."

"That's what they told me too. I guess that sounds fair. We need to keep the universe safe from you."

"Hey!"

"Just kidding."

I frowned. "I don't know how long we're supposed to talk for."

"As long as we want, I guess. They didn't say."

I took a deep breath. "What happened out there when the suit was empty? Some guy slapped me across the face and I lost contact." I squeezed my eyes shut. "I thought you were dead."

"The air ran out completely and I could hardly breathe. But I didn't pass out. There was air coming in and I thought I was a dead man. Only it didn't kill me."

"How? That stuff's deadly."

"Well, that's just it. The air on Kronos is not toxic."

"What?"

"It's thin, so you still need a mask, but there's oxygen."

We'd been told during our training that the atmosphere was so toxic that we wouldn't last five minutes without a mask. If Daniel had breathed air from outside his suit and survived, what did that mean?

"They've been lying to us?"

"Yes. To everyone. As I was struggling to breathe the small amount coming into the suit, a piece fell from the rock somewhere above me and busted a hole in the front shielding on the Mech-suit. I thought I would be a goner once I got a proper lungful, but when the atmosphere rushed in, it was the air I needed."

It was unbelievable. According to Katoa, he should be dead.

"They told me Rescue found you before you ran out."

"Of course they did. They don't want anyone to know."

"And that's why we need to tell everyone."

"Exactly." I could almost see his grin.

I remembered something that I needed to tell him.

"I think we might in for some trouble. Malvolio has told them we were having an affair."

"What? Seriously?"

"Yeah. Remember I told you that he thought I was cheating on him?"

"Yes. How could I forget?"

"Well, he was accusing me of sleeping with you, even though we'd never met."

"That's crazy."

"I know. But even if I can convince them that it's not true, the guard last night reported when you touched my face."

"Oh. Sorry. I couldn't help myself. I didn't think I'd ever see you again when I was down there, you know?"

My eyes stung. *"I didn't think I'd ever see you again either. I'm so glad you made it."*

I was brought back to the room with the doctors and Malvolio when someone shook my arms and pain shot through my side. I opened my eyes to find Malvolio shaking me and the memory of that night hit me.

I jerked away from him. "Don't touch me!"

My heart thundered in my chest and my breathing became shallow. The urge to run from him was strong and it felt like someone was digging knives into my ribs.

Dr Rowen said something I couldn't quite hear and he let me go.

I turned to her. "I told you to keep him away from me! Get him out of here! I don't want him here. I don't want him to touch me. I'm supposed to keep still because of the broken ribs *he* gave me, not be shaken around like a rag doll! Now I need a painkiller."

Malvolio stepped toward me again. "You never had a problem with me touching you before."

CHAPTER 51

Everyone Has a Right to Know

I clenched my fists. "That was before you punched me in the face and kicked me in the ribs!"

Dr Rowen called someone on her personal Com to ask for painkillers to be brought in.

Dr Kharim removed the wiring harness and told me he'd need to study the results.

"How long will that take?"

"Oh, a few hours. I will speak to you again afterwards."

He pressed a few buttons and gestured to the others to follow him out of the room.

Dr Rowen looked back over her shoulder. "Your painkillers will arrive shortly."

———— ⋆·☆·⋆ ————

After doing a whole lot of nothing, having lunch, and talking to Daniel some more, I discovered that I didn't black out if I didn't sit or stand up too soon after using my Talent.

The door swished open and Dr Rowen bounced in. "Good afternoon, Miss Callista. How are you feeling?"

I'd be better if I wasn't locked up in here. "I'm okay. The pain from my ribs is back, though."

"We can give you something more for that. Don't you worry. So." She took in a deep breath and smiled. "I'm here to inform you of your results."

I sat up a little straighter. "Yes?"

She straightened her collar. "They weren't quite as clear as we'd expected."

I frowned. "What does that mean?"

She gave me another fake smile. "It means we need to keep you here a bit longer."

My heart sank a little. That sounded kind of convenient. "How long? Can't I go home and come back in for the tests?"

The smile disappeared. "Home?"

"Yes. Back to my home here on the station. After I sort everything out and you don't need me to answer any more questions, then I'll be going home to Azaeli."

She grimaced and cleared her throat. "Yes, well, before you can do that, there will be two gentlemen from Katoa in to see you tomorrow morning to question you as part of their investigation into the tunnel collapse."

"Oh. Okay." I expected as much, but I didn't think I'd need to be here in the Infirmary for that. "So, after that, can I go? I'm feeling a lot better and don't need to be in here for broken ribs."

That stern expression I hated so much was back. "Not so fast."

What now? "What do you mean?"

"We need to run some tests and run a check on your blood and DNA—"

"Blood and DNA? What for?"

"You and Daniel Javolo have both displayed at least one Recognised Talent that you claim you were previously unaware of. We need to test you to find out your T-Rating and see if any other abilities have manifested and blood work and DNA testing are part of our studies."

"T-Rating?"

"Yes. Talent Rating. That's what we call it when we give you your Rating. We determine the strength of your ability — or abilities — and give you a rating out of ten; one being the highest and ten being the lowest. This rating allows others to see how useful you may be as a potential employee."

My mouth dropped open. "Employee? I've never considered that as an option."

"Oh, yes. Many opportunities could open up for you now. But first, we need to determine what you are."

What I am.

That sounded horrible. Like I wasn't even human anymore.

"Then am I free to go?"

The smile was back. "Of course."

Why didn't I believe her?

"How long will all of this take?"

"That depends on how cooperative you are and how many Talents you actually have. These things take time."

I closed my eyes and took a deep breath.

Give me strength.

All I had to do was wait it out. I could do that. Then I could see Daniel, and I'd soon be heading home to Mum and Adamo.

— ⋅☆⋅ —

Somewhere in my dreams, someone was calling me. I couldn't see who it was. I'd been running from Malvolio and flinched each time I heard my name. But it wasn't Malvolio's voice I could hear.

"Lennina."

I rolled over and pain shot through my right side, so I quickly rolled onto my back. Why was I in pain?

"Lennina?"

A few things hit me at once. My ribs were broken. I was still in the Infirmary. It was Daniel's voice I could hear.

"Daniel?"

"Hey you," he said.

"Hey."

"Are you okay?"

"Yeah. I was asleep."

"Oh, sorry."

Realisation dawned. *"Hey, you can do it too."*

"Yeah. Cool, huh?"

"Yes! This is great! I'm glad I'm not the only one. But it means they will be running tests on you too."

"They're gonna do that anyway, even if I don't show any signs of having any Talent, so don't worry about it."

I rubbed my eyes. *"It looks like they're not going to let us see each other for a while, but we can bypass their crap and still talk."*

"Without anyone listening in."

I couldn't think of anything to say. What was wrong with me? We had a chance to say whatever we wanted, and my brain decided to go blank.

It might have had something to do with the fact that I'd just woken up.

"They came to see me tonight after dinner," he said.

The lights were dim in the room and there was no clock. I had no idea what time it was.

"So, what did they say?" I asked him.

"There's going to be a full investigation into our behaviour, our relationship, the collapse, our telepathic abilities, and the Ghosts. I don't think they're happy about Allador's visit."

I frowned. *"I don't care what they think. He healed you."*

"They don't seem happy about that either."

"What? You'd think they would be excited that you'd made contact with a new alien species and that they are sentient and have the ability to heal." And I was so thankful for that.

"I don't think they want the public to know. They'll probably make us sign something so we can't tell anyone."

"Seriously? Everyone has a right to know. They have a right to know about the air too. We need to get the word out."

"We'll have to wait and see what their plans for us are. We're only employees; they can't keep us here. We've breached our contracts and you've quit anyway. Once you're feeling better, you should be able to sign yourself out. They're running tests on me for now for Talent and my sudden lack of injuries, but once that's done, I'm outta here."

"Do you think we might need legal representation?"

"I hope not. I'll call my uncle if we do. He'll know how to handle them."

I felt a bit better knowing that. It was always good to have someone in the family or a good friend who understood the law.

"What are your plans for when we get out of here?" he asked.

I want to kiss you again. "Ultimately, I want to sort out my stuff here and go home to Azaeli. But I really want to see you first once we're out of here. What about you?"

"I want to eventually go home too. And I definitely want to see you.

I'm quitting too. If I'm not employed by The Company anymore, I'll have to move out of the Diggers' Section, which is fine with me."

"Okay, well, I still have my hotel room. We could go there once we're out. I don't think I told you that I only booked the hotel for a week to get away from Malvolio. He wouldn't leave me alone and I thought he might have been following me."

"Is that who you thought you saw that day?"

"Yes. I still don't know if it was him." I didn't want to think about him anymore. *"So, we can spend some time together and work out what we're gonna do after all this is over."*

"That sounds like a great idea."

I didn't know what would happen between us, but I had to admit that I no longer wanted to stick to my promise of no more relationships. Daniel made me feel alive. I wanted to feel that way forever. My love for him ran deep, like he was part of my soul.

But something inside me had changed after thinking Daniel was dead. Almost like something had broken. It made me realise how much he truly meant to me. I didn't know what I would've done if I'd lost him.

Something told me that if I did see where things went with Daniel, it wouldn't end up being the dumpster fire that my relationship with Malvolio had become.

There *were* men out there in the universe that were worth taking a chance on.

Could things work out between us? I wasn't sure. I had already given Daniel my heart. We would have to take things slow and see where it took us.

Meanwhile, I planned to tell anyone who would listen that there was breathable air and sentient life on Kronos.

—— ★·☆·★ ——
THE END
—— ★·☆·★ ——

This is the end of this story, but not the end of this book. Keep reading for some extra goodies:

A bonus scene
An excerpt from the second and final book in the *Lightning Touch Series*, ***POWER OF LIGHTNING***
An offer of a free book
Acknowledgements
A list of other books by Susan McKenzie
About the author

Did you enjoy this book?
Help the next reader to enjoy it too.
Reviews are such a fantastic way for people to express the way a book made them feel. A way to share it with the world.
Indie authors don't have the huge budgets that the big New York publishers have, but we have something more powerful. We have loyal readers like you.
It would be so awesome if you could share what you thought of this book by leaving a review on the site where you purchased it.
Thank you so much.
Sue

Keep reading for a bonus scene from Daniel's point-of-view

BONUS SCENE
The Restaurant from Daniel's point-of-view

After I carefully helped Lennina out of the taxi, we went inside the restaurant. I was worried about her. It seemed like she was going to faint at any moment. She wasn't as pale as she'd been the other day, the day we'd met, but she still wasn't good.

I kept thinking about that woman we'd seen on the way here. She'd assumed Lennina and I were an item, and despite the fact she'd said it in such a nasty way, I'd felt a spark inside me at the thought of being Lennina's boyfriend. Yeah, we'd just met, but there was something about her. I couldn't explain it. I couldn't keep my eyes off her, and she kept looking into my eyes with — I don't know how to describe it. I couldn't place it. Like she was looking into my soul.

Ever since I first saw her, I hadn't been able to get her out of my head. Not the other day when she'd tripped over my bags and nearly broken her arm; I'd seen her before that. It was the first time I'd dared to try out the fake thumbprint Sharwok had organised for me. He said it would allow me to sneak over to the other part of the station and see how the rest of them lived before my contract was up and I could go back home.

Going over there to the other side of the station was just to satisfy my curiosity, but that's when I'd seen her. She was the most beautiful girl I'd ever seen in my life. She had long black hair and these dazzling blue eyes. She'd smiled at something the dude with her had said and it lit up her whole face. There was a certain rare beauty in her that seemed to radiate from within. I'd only seen her for a few seconds, but that was enough.

I'd even told my work partner, Callista, about her. I couldn't help myself. I wanted to tell the world. Cal had teased me about it, as usual, but it didn't stop me.

I knew I had to see her again. I had no idea what I'd say to her, if given the chance, but I'd still do it. But, of course, there was a problem. She was with a guy, which probably meant he was more than likely her boyfriend. Or more than that. Just my luck. Every girl I was interested in was taken.

And Callista was someone I was more than interested in. I'd been madly in love with her for months and she had no clue. I couldn't tell her. It was against the rules. There was no way in the universe I was gonna ruin her career by telling her how I felt about her over the Com. At this stage, I didn't give a damn about *my* job, but I couldn't do it to her. And, of course, she'd been going out with this douchey older guy for about a month and from the sounds of it, he was full of himself. It didn't help that he was the MIC of Galaxy Mech. How could I compete with that? He could give her the universe, and I had a crappy shit-kicker job as a Digger. The lowest of the low on the station.

Only, Cal didn't seem to see me that way. It was one of the things I loved about her.

I snapped out of my thoughts. I had to concentrate on the here and now. The Ambrosia was dimly lit and there was a pretty big crowd. The smell of whatever they were cooking in there made my mouth water. Didn't matter that we'd just eaten. I could go another round.

I noticed Lennina looking around nervously, then she seemed to relax a bit. This ex of hers must be a real dick. He'd already given her a black eye, so I couldn't blame her for being edgy.

The only vacant table was in a darkened corner with a bench seat on one side. The other chairs had been stolen by some people nearby, so it meant we'd have to sit side-by-side. I was down with that, but Lennina looked at me and told me not to get any ideas. But that made me think of ideas. I couldn't help the grin that spread across my face. I saw a small smile tug at the corner of her lips. What was she thinking?

When we sat down, I made sure I didn't touch her. Not that I didn't want to, but with the freaky lightning thing we had going on, I didn't want to hurt her. It always seemed to hurt her more than it hurt me, which was weird. It didn't really hurt that much, and the buzz it caused was kind of thrilling and calming at the same time, but if it didn't feel that way for her, I didn't want to be causing her pain.

I still couldn't believe I was sitting here with her. It was like something out of a dream or HoloMovie. She was so gorgeous and genuine and honest and so... vulnerable. She seemed like she was only just holding it together. The bust up with the bastard that liked to hit women must have been worse than what she'd told me. I wanted to protect her and hold her in my arms and tell her that everything would be alright. And I wanted to punch the dick right in the face and then some.

We sat there for a while, not saying anything, just looking out the big windows that looked out onto a small courtyard. There was some real grass, flowers and a small fountain with statues in it. It was nice, but I still found it strange having parks and stuff on a space station.

"I was going a bit stir-crazy at the hotel and just needed someone to talk to," she blurted out. She started tapping her fingers on the side of her leg nervously.

"I'm already crazy, so we should get along just fine," I told her, and couldn't help chuckling.

That made her smile, which warmed my heart. I was glad I was able to make her happy.

I turned and looked her right in the eye. "But seriously, I will be here for you whenever you need me. *Any* time you need someone to talk to, I'm here."

I wanted her to know I was serious.

But then I thought, *You idiot! You're not even supposed to be here. How are you going to be there for her?*

Tears welled in those beautiful blue eyes. "Thank you."

A lone tear escaped and slid down her cheek. I smiled as I watched the tear make its way right down to the underside of her jaw. I couldn't help myself, I reached out a hand and wiped the tear away with my thumb, sending little sparks of electricity through my fingers and up my arm; giving me a little thrill, but making her gasp. My hand stayed there for a moment, then I pulled it away. I didn't want to hurt her and felt selfish that I'd left my hand there so I could feel the buzzing just that little bit longer.

Lennina gave me a small smile and turned back toward the window. My heart dropped. Maybe she didn't like the feeling. Maybe I shouldn't be touching her. But she didn't try to move away from me, and she started to talk about the fountain and how beautiful it looked. How peaceful it made her feel.

I kept stealing glances at her. She was beautiful. I wanted to look at her, not the fountain.

"The guy I work with," she said, totally changing the subject, "we have to work closely together as a team and he's so easy-going, so easy to talk to. There's never any stress, except the everyday stresses that come from our work. I can talk to him about anything, and can have a dig at him or joke with him."

Yeah. I knew exactly what she meant. That's the kind of relationship I had with Cal. "I have someone at work like that, too."

The job had just been a mundane mining job till Cal came along. My third Rotation didn't start out with Callista as my Nav Operator, though. The girl I'd had first, Lonara Dezaki, had gotten a promotion, which was rare for a Nav, but hey, I wasn't complaining. It was nice to see someone at the low end of The Company make it out of the shit-kicker class.

I wondered what they would do with me while I didn't have a partner. I was worried they'd give me some desk job till they found someone, but the next time I turned up for work, I already had a new Nav.

Callista had just lost her Digger — a guy named Rogan — who'd lost his shit in the tunnels. And that was the best thing that had ever happened to me.

Until now. Meeting Lennina was amazing.

"He never loses it like my ex always does," she continued, almost making me jump. "Even when the pressures at work get too much, you know... he could always keep his cool, even sometimes when I couldn't... Always the level-headed one..." She sighed. "I don't understand it. Where did I go wrong? Why did I have to pick such a self-centred, egotistical pig for a partner?"

I turned to her, determined to let her know what people like him were really like. "Hey, it's not your fault. Don't blame yourself."

"I can't help it. I feel like such an idiot. He was really nice at first, you know? He was always a gentleman when we went out, paid for everything, and bought me gifts — even when I told him not to. I don't care about money. It's not important."

She didn't care about that stuff? I smiled. "No, it's not."

"It is nice, though. An added bonus..." She twirled a piece of her straight dark hair around one of her fingers. I didn't think she was even aware she was doing it. "He *was* nice to me... Then things changed. I'm not sure when, but I didn't notice at first. I thought maybe he was just stressed at work or something... I don't know..."

I tried to give her a reassuring smile. "These guys are experts at what they do. Master manipulators. They have everyone fooled. You weren't to know."

That immediately made me think of my friend, Yolonda. She'd been through hell before she'd gotten out of that relationship.

Lennina's eyebrows drew together. "I'm usually a really good judge of character, you know, but he really had me thinking he was a *genuinely* nice guy..."

She looked so beautiful when her cheeks flushed pink. She shouldn't have felt embarrassed about falling for his bullshit.

I nodded. "It happens. They are manipulative and domineering. And it's always good people who suffer..." *Like Yolonda. And like you.*

Her eyebrows went up. "You sound like you're talking from experience."

I couldn't help the wince. "I've seen them in action. A good friend of mine was so taken in by him that she even went as far as marrying him... They're divorced now..."

"Oh..." She shuddered. Then she turned back to the fountain.

I thought of Yolonda and what could've happened to Lennina if she hadn't gotten away from him. "Getting out before it was too late was the best thing — the only thing — you could've done. My friend wasn't so lucky. Her husband gave her a severe beating and broke her arm in several places and shattered her cheekbone before she left him." My heart still clenched thinking about it. At least she hadn't ended up dead.

"Oh, that's... horrible." She kept her attention on the fountain. "Can you see that bird?" she asked as she pointed toward the window.

I turned and saw a Fantail perched on top of one of the statue's heads. "Yes. Looks like a Fantail. Must have been imported from Earth."

Her face brightened with a big smile. It was good to see her smiling again.

Suddenly, she was up out of her seat. "Let's go outside." I made a move to join her, but as soon as she stood, she let out a yelp and as she sunk back down again, my elbow connected with her side and she almost screamed.

My stomach dropped. "Sorry!" I'd hurt her again. But that little nudge shouldn't have hurt *that* much. "What's wrong?" I put my hand on her arm, wanting to help, but not sure what to do, but then the jolt from whatever weird freaky thing we had between us made her jump. *Shit!* "Sorry!"

I'd hurt her again. *Fuck!*

I couldn't do anything right. And she looked really pale again. She closed her eyes and took some slow, deep breaths. Was she going to faint? Right here in the restaurant? Bloody hell. I was useless.

"Lennina! Are you okay?" My voice shook a little.

Her eyes flew open and she looked terrified. Was she terrified of me?

But then she dropped a bomb on me. "I... ah... I have three broken ribs..."

My heart rate doubled. I was going to kill him. "WHAT? As well as the black eye? Did it happen since I saw you last?"

She didn't answer. Then it all fell into place. She was so sick the other day. I knew there had to be more to it than the black eye and the twisted ankle. "Or do you mean... I can't believe it! Why didn't you tell me?"

Her face paled even more. "I... I didn't know you..." she stammered. "It's... private... humiliating... It's not something you tell a complete stranger..."

Oh, I'm such a tool. "I guess... But I could have helped... done something more... if I had've known..." I raked my fingers through my hair, wishing I could do something to help. Then it hit me. "*Shit.* I caused you to trip and you had broken ribs!"

She blinked up at me. "Don't... Don't do that to yourself. You didn't know. And you did more than enough to help me. And thank you for that. But I didn't want to have to answer a whole bunch of questions, you know..."

My vision blurred. I'd been such an idiot. "But I caused you to fall. You must have been in agony..."

"You weren't to know..." she said. She looked around, which made me glance around at the people around us. A lot of them were staring. I did my best to ignore them.

I ran my hand through my hair again and grimaced. "But that doesn't change the fact that it caused you so much pain..."

She looked out the window again and told me her ex had thought she'd been cheating, which sounded like Yolonda's ex. Lennina told me he'd slapped her, punched her in the face, and then, once she was down on the floor, had kicked her in the ribs. My hands clenched into fists and I wanted to punch something. I wanted to find out who this arsehole was, but I couldn't help noticing she hadn't mentioned his name. Or any other names. Well, I hadn't told her much about me either, so I wasn't going to push it. She'd tell me if she wanted to. Maybe once we got to know each other better. And yeah, I wanted to get to know her better.

I looked across and saw that the tears had returned and were streaming down her cheeks and some of the anger seeped out of me. I couldn't just sit here and watch her cry. I reached out and put my arm around her, causing the sparks to fly as she sucked in a breath.

Fuck! I can't even touch her!

I was about to pull my arm away, but then she started sobbing. I put my other arm around her and to my surprise, she turned into me and leaned her head against my chest.

"Hey. It's okay. Let it all out. I'm here for you. Always."

I held her close while she sobbed uncontrollably. I wasn't sure what to do, but I couldn't let her go. The buzzing spread right through my body and made me feel amazing. I just hoped it wasn't hurting her too much.

A guy a couple of tables over caught my attention. "Hey. Is she alright?"

I made up some bullshit about her having some bad news and that she'd be okay. That seemed to reassure him and he turned back to the man he was sitting with. I noticed they were holding hands.

My heart pounded. I felt so bad for her. She must have been hurting, and all that crying would feel like being stabbed in the side.

After she'd settled down and stopped crying, she pulled back enough to look into my eyes. The sadness in her eyes almost undid me.

I swallowed. "Feeling better?"

She nodded. I wanted to get lost in those wells of blue forever.

"I can't believe he did this to you." My voice came out as a hoarse whisper. "How could he hurt you like that? I could never do that. Could never hurt you. I want to protect you from him. I know we've only just met, but I... I can't help it. Can't explain it. I feel I need to just... help... any way I can."

My vision blurred again with unshed tears. She put her head back on my chest and gave me a squeeze, so I gave her a careful squeeze back. It took an amazing amount of willpower for me not to cry. Yeah, all my mates would say I was a wuss, but I couldn't help but feel for her. And the need to protect her from the douche that had hurt her was overwhelming. I hardly knew her, but that didn't seem to matter. I felt like I'd known her for a lifetime — as weird as that was.

Lennina sucked in a deep breath, slowly — probably so it wouldn't hurt her ribs so much. I couldn't help taking in a deep breath too. She smelled of flowers and shampoo. I could breathe that scent every day for the rest of my life.

What was I thinking? I hardly knew the girl.

I didn't care. I'd protect her, no matter what. I held her a little tighter. I meant it. I would do whatever it took. I wished I lived on this part of the station so I could protect her properly.

I thought I should probably let her go now that she'd calmed down. I didn't want her to get the wrong idea. I didn't want her to be afraid of me, too. I'd never hurt her. As I thought about that and enjoyed the buzz, I noticed she was holding me tighter. Okay. I wasn't going to let her go if she actually wanted me to hold her.

But why did she want me to hold her? Was she scared? Insecure? Or did she feel the same as I did? I knew how I was feeling. It was so much the same way I felt for Cal. But that didn't seem right. It felt like I was betraying Cal. But I couldn't be with Cal. She was in love with that stupid Malvolio dude.

Lennina slowly moved so she could see out the window to the fountain again. I had to squash my disappointment and told myself to stop being stupid. I adjusted my hold on her so that I still had an arm around her. I wasn't going to let her go unless she told me to or gave me a sign that she wanted me to back off. The buzz wasn't as intense now, but it still felt good flowing through my body. Right down to my toes.

Lennina told me about the problems she was having with the Enforcers. They didn't seem to be doing much about her ex because he was some big wig on the station. That got my blood boiling again.

"His status shouldn't make any difference. He assaulted you. He has to pay the price like anyone else."

She was silent for a while, then she turned to me and I couldn't look away. She was so beautiful. She didn't deserve to be treated that way. If she was my girl, I'd treat her right. She'd never have to worry about me punching her in the face, that's for sure.

I wanted so much to show her how much I cared. I leaned closer to her and she sighed. Actually sighed. Then she blushed. So sexy. My heart leapt into my throat. Maybe she did feel the same. I searched her eyes and she looked down to my lips. I wondered what she was thinking.

I leaned forward some more. I could feel her breath on my mouth. I wanted to kiss her so badly. I looked at her lips. Were they as soft as they looked?

There were so many questions in her eyes. She looked back up at me and I couldn't help myself. I moved a little closer.

"But... they won't... He's..."

I cut her off when I leaned my forehead against hers. The buzzing ran through my brain. Weird. "Shhh... Don't talk about that now..."

I touched my nose against hers and she stopped breathing. Then she closed her eyes. My whole body felt alive, and it had little to do with the buzzing. She made my body feel so amazing. And my heart. She made it feel like it was twice its natural size.

She opened her mouth to speak, but I stopped her. "Shhh. Breathe."

She took some breaths and I relaxed a bit. She kept her eyes closed for a while and I sat there looking at her. I wanted to kiss her. I needed to kiss her. I needed to make her feel good. After what she'd been through...

I couldn't keep thinking about it. I'd back out if I started over-thinking things. I just went for it, hoping she wouldn't slap me for it.

I pressed my lips to hers and lightning shot right through my whole body. Amazing.

It was such a light kiss, but it packed a wallop. She gasped, but didn't jump out of her seat. I peeked and she still had her eyes closed. So I took another chance and kissed her again.

I took it slow at first, but once she started to respond, I felt like I couldn't get enough. The kiss became urgent. I couldn't help it. Something in the back of my mind was telling me to slow down, to take it easy, but I felt like she was something I needed as much as I needed air. And I couldn't believe she let me kiss her. It seemed like she wanted this as much as I did. I deepened the kiss and the buzzing intensified.

Everything else faded. Nothing else mattered. All the tension. All the worries. Gone. It was just her.

She slid a hand into the hair on the back of my neck, pulling me closer. I growled low in the back of my throat like a bloody animal and kissed her hungrily. I couldn't stop myself. She was driving me wild.

But then I remembered where we were. We had to stop. I had to slow things down. I reluctantly pulled away. She sat with her eyes closed for a few seconds, taking a few deep breaths, then opened them. She must've been affected just as much as I'd been. I had a hard time getting my head around it.

I searched her face. Her eyes. Was she okay with this? Was it too much? We were practically strangers and I'd kissed her the second time we'd met. Not just kissed her, but had a make-out session in the middle of a crowded restaurant. I must be crazy. She probably thought I was some kind of creeper or something. Once the shock of the kiss wore off, would she tell me to take a hike?

I was still breathing heavy and I noticed she was shaking. Was she scared of me?

Crap. What had I done?

Her eyes got that glassy look. She was going to cry again. I didn't want to be the cause of more tears. And even though her eyes were red from all the crying, they were still so amazingly pretty.

"Your eyes are so blue," I breathed.

She probably thought I was an idiot. I *was* an idiot. She'd just broken up with an abusive partner. She didn't even really know me. The last thing she needed was another guy coming on to her.

My face felt suddenly cold. "I'm so sorry. I shouldn't have done that. I don't know what came over me."

Lennina went pale.

I felt the need to explain more. "After— I mean— You must think I'm— Ugh, I'm not explaining this very well." I paused, trying to get my brain and my mouth to work together. "After what he did to you, the last thing you'd want is me... Please don't get the wrong idea. I don't want to upset you. I just... I couldn't help it..." I trailed off. My eyes pleaded with her to understand that I didn't want to hurt her.

Something that looked like relief swept across her pretty features. "It's okay," she said. "You haven't done anything wrong."

Then she leaned forward and planted one on me and my insides melted. Her lips lingered on mine and I wrapped my arms around her again. I couldn't believe it. I kissed her again and I dared to lick her lips with my tongue. I was shocked when her lips parted and I felt her shudder as I pushed my tongue into her mouth and I thought my body would combust right there. She pulled me closer, like she couldn't get enough. She was going to make me lose my mind.

We kissed for a while like that and it drove me crazy. I thought I was going to lose it and start running my hands all over her body right there in public, but I still had my wits about me enough to stop myself. I wasn't worried about the people looking, I was worried it would be too much for her. I couldn't even imagine what she'd been through with her ex.

I pulled away before I lost all control and she gasped. Her pupils were big and I couldn't help staring into her eyes while we caught our breath. There were a lot of people staring at us and Lennina's face flushed bright red when she noticed them. She closed her eyes and buried her face into my neck. I tried to look out the windows and ignore the stares, my cheeks heating.

She stayed like that for such a long time, I started to worry about her. I probably shouldn't have been doing this. Was I just taking advantage of her after what had happened with her ex? Rebound relationships weren't a good idea at the best of times, but she'd had her ribs broken. She was really vulnerable right now. I shouldn't have kissed her. I should've kept it platonic.

Fuck! What was I doing? What if this ruined everything for us later on, once she got her head together?

I seriously needed to calm down. It was too late; I'd already kissed her. I'd have to sort all of that out when the time came. Right now, I'd give her the comfort she needed.

She hadn't moved. She must've needed a hug to make her feel like someone cared. It was easy to feel alone out here in the middle of space, holed up in a big tin can with a bunch of strangers.

They'd been a bunch of strangers to me at first, but I'd made some good friends here. Some good mates. That made me think of Callista. She was only a friend to me, as far as she was concerned anyway. To me, she was much more than that.

We'd talk for hours while I wondered around in those dark and lonely tunnels, and the tunnels didn't seem so lonely anymore. With her static-y, off-frequency voice coming through the Com, I felt like I could do anything. There were two main reasons why we collected more Amakio than any other team. One was because I knew that if we fell behind, they'd assign my arse to a new partner, but the other was because while I was using the rock-breaker to dig up the mineral, I couldn't talk to her. So I always did the job as quickly as I could so we could start up our conversation where we'd left off.

Crazy, I know, but I couldn't get enough of her easy-going nature and great sense of humour.

We were so close to losing each other as partners — I'd been threatened by my supervisors so many times — but I didn't think she realised how close. I had to do something about that. We only had like a month to go, but I couldn't lose her before then.

I wished I could tell her how I felt. I wished I could organise to meet her outside of work. Maybe once I'd finished my contract, but that was seven months away, and besides, she was taken. She seemed to be really happy with that douche, although lately I'd noticed something had changed.

And that last day of work. She wasn't just sick. There was something else going on. Something bad. Something that made Cal forget what she was doing. She *never* messed up like that, and had only had one sick day since we'd started working together.

My heart felt heavy thinking about what could've caused her to mess up and leave work early. Maybe something had happened to her mum or her brother. My chest tightened. I hoped it wasn't that. She loved them so much.

And I loved her so much.

As I sat there listening to Lennina's steady breathing, I felt weird, like being in her arms was somehow betraying Callista. But that was just craziness. Cal had a boyfriend. She wasn't mine. I couldn't be with her. Company rules wouldn't allow it anyway, even if she was single. There were no stupid rules stopping me from seeing Lennina... except the fact that I was on the wrong side of the space station.

Shit. I was an idiot.

My heartbeat was racing out of control. What was I supposed to do now? I'd fallen for one woman, and now I had strong feelings for a second one, both on the wrong side of the station. Both of them forbidden. How could I let this happen? I was in some serious trouble.

I thought about how each one made me feel. It was different with Cal, because we didn't have anything physical between us, but we had months of friendly banter and corny jokes. Lennina, well, we hardly knew each other, and the physical side of things was strange and amazing at the same time. The weird buzzing and jolts of electricity were some really weird shit.

Without even thinking about it, I leaned forward and kissed her on the top of her head. I didn't even know why I'd done it. I was really messed up and couldn't stop all the things from racing through my mind.

What did I feel for Lennina? Was it just that she needed my help and comfort? Was I just being protective? Or maybe it was just a physical thing? If that was the case, I shouldn't have been sitting here with her.

She looked up and I wondered what she was thinking. I shouldn't have kissed her on her head. I shouldn't have kissed her at all. I was such a tool.

But she didn't move away. It was weird that once we looked into each other's eyes, we couldn't seem to look away. I thought it was just me at first, but she wouldn't look away either. There was something there. Like there was this invisible connection between us. And the lightning seemed to solidify that.

I knew it the moment something changed. I could see it in her eyes. Oh, no. It was something bad. Something really bad. I braced myself.

Her eyes widened and started to fill with tears.

"Lennina? What is it? What's wrong?"

She moved back. "I... I've got to go... I've just realised something... I have some serious thinking to do." She started to pull away from me.

No. This couldn't be happening. Was it something I'd done? *Of course* it was something I'd done. I was an idiot for kissing her.

I didn't want her to go. "What? What do you mean? Did I do something wrong?"

There was a strange look on her face. I looked down at my hand on her arm and gasped. *Fuck!* What was I doing? After everything she'd been through, the last thing she needed was for me to be manhandling her like that. I let go quickly and the buzzing faded away. I missed it already. "Sorry."

She looked back up into my eyes and determination filled them. I cringed, waiting for whatever she was about to say. "I... I like you... a lot. But like, more than just friends."

I blinked and my eyes widened. That was so not what I was expecting. A smile crept onto my face. I couldn't help it. "What's so bad about that?"

Her eyes got a little wider, and then she stammered out her next words. "I... I think that... I just realised... that... I'm in love with... someone else... I think I have been for a while... a long while... I... just didn't know it..."

No.

Tears streamed down her cheeks.

Don't tell me she's realised she really does love the arsehole that gave her the broken ribs and the black eye? Is she insane?

"What are you saying?" I asked her. "Who are you talking about? You mean your ex?"

She looked horrified. "NO! Not him! *No way!* Malvolio is the biggest jerk in the universe—"

Wait — *what?* "Malvolio? Did you say Ma—"

"It will never be him! Not after what he did..." She shuddered.

If her ex was Malvolio, then that meant—

No. It couldn't be!

All the pieces of the puzzle fell into place. Lennina was *Callista?*

She looked really shook up. I reached out and touched her arm and the buzz raced through me. She didn't jump or pull away.

I couldn't believe it. This was *Cal*. They were the same person.

Lennina stared at me with a weird expression on her face. She was Cal? I couldn't help the smile that was spreading across my face. She was *Cal*. The woman I'd been crazy over for months. My heart pounded so hard I thought it was going to burst through my chest.

"No," she continued. "It's the guy I work with. I've known him for like four months and I didn't realise I loved him till just now." My eyes widened. She loved... *me?* "Which is crazy because I've never met him because he's a Digger..."

She *loved* me. My brain stuttered to a stop. It was having trouble trying to process what she was saying. "What?"

She shifted in her seat, looking really uncomfortable. "I don't know why I didn't tell you I'm a Nav Operator—"

"*What?*"

"I didn't know what to tell you... I didn't know you... Anyway, I have to go. I have to think... Sort my head out..." She moved away from me and I sat there like a moron. "Please understand... I have to tell him I love him... even though I'm not allowed to." She pushed a hand through her hair and I still couldn't move. "I'm sorry, but I do — but... I think I'm... I can't! Not both of you! I've got to get outta here!"

She shifted further away and avoided touching me. She was leaving. I had to do something. I had to tell her. "Lennina, I..."

Her eyes were so full of tears. It must have been tearing her up inside. My heart went out to her. I needed to tell her who I was. My vision blurred. I blinked away the tears. I needed to tell her. "Lennina, please, listen to me. I need to talk to you... Tell you—"

"No! I have to go..."

I tried again, but she cut me off. "No. Don't. I'm sorry. I'm *really* sorry. I have to go... Don't look at me like that... I *have* to. I need to think..." She looked away from me. I had to make her see. "I have to go!"

Then she got up and stumbled through all the tables and I jumped up to follow her. To hear her say she loved me like that, not knowing who I was, did funny things to my heart. I never thought I'd hear her say that. I never thought I had a chance with her. Ever.

I had to stop her. "Wait!" She kept going. From the way she was kinda limping, she must have been in a lot of pain. "Lennina! Wait! I have to tell you something! *Wait!*"

She was out the door, and my brain was in slow-mo. I started after her, calling her name. I even called out Cal, thinking that might stop her.

She ducked into a shop. I had to get to her. I couldn't tell her who I was because I wasn't supposed to be here. Everyone was staring. Listening. If someone here worked for The Company, I'd be in deep shit.

My eyes darted around, but she wasn't in there. I spotted a back entrance, so I headed through it and looked around. I couldn't see her anywhere. I looked in all of the shops I passed, but there was no sign of her. I called her name over and over, but it was no use. I'd lost her.

I looked in all the shops in the area with no luck. She moved pretty quickly for someone with broken ribs.

Disappointment flooded through me, dampening all the elation I'd felt at finding out who she was. I had to shove it aside because I needed to focus. I could tell her tomorrow. I had to hope she showed up to work tomorrow. Then I'd have to work out how to tell her without getting her fired. I didn't care about my job anymore. I had to tell her.

Maybe I'd just quit my job after this and move to the other part of the station. Then I could see her without breaking any rules. That's if she ever wanted to see me again. This was so messed up. She might walk away from all of it, and I couldn't really blame her if she did.

I still couldn't wrap my head around it. Then it hit me. I knew Malvolio was a douche, but he'd *hit* her. He'd hit *Cal. My* Cal. My best friend. The girl I loved.

THAT FUCKING BASTARD!

I wanted to kill him. White hot rage surged through my body. I could hardly focus on where I was going.

Tears welled up in my eyes and ran down my cheeks as I walked back to the spot where I could cross back into the Diggers' Section. Tears for her. She was such a good person, deep down, where it counted. She was honest and funny and easy-going. How could he do that to her? How could he actually kick her while she was lying on the floor? My stomach churned. That was a deliberate and callous act. It took a special kind of twisted, screwed-up fuckwit to do something like that. And to a *girl?*

I had to try to get a grip. My head was starting to pound. I had to think about something else.

I still couldn't believe it. No wonder she hadn't been at work. I wanted to punch something. Or rather, some*one*.

And I couldn't wait to get to work tomorrow.

———— ⋆·☆·⋆ ————

Keep reading for an excerpt from the second and final book in the *Lightning Touch Series*, ***POWER OF LIGHTNING***

———— ⋆·☆·⋆ ————

Excerpt: Power of Lightning (Lightning Touch Book 2)

Chapter 1

I swiped my finger across the screen to access the next question.

How long have you known about your Talent?

I frowned. I'd only managed to use my Talent to initiate a telepathic conversation for the first time a couple of days ago, so I typed in my answer.

Our records indicate that you did not declare a Recognised Talent when you applied for the position of Navigational Computer Operator with Katoa Intergalactic Mining and Exploration. Can you tell us why you did not declare your abilities?

I didn't know I had any psychic abilities when I'd started working for the biggest mining company in the Known Universe five months ago.

"This is stupid," I said to no one.

The answer to the previous question kind of negated this one. How many more questions like this would I have to answer? This was getting ridiculous. The investigators from Katoa that were going to question me about the events surrounding the tunnel collapse down on the planet, Kronos, were probably going to ask me the same questions anyway.

I sighed and felt a twinge of pain from my broken ribs. I needed some more painkillers.

After a few more stupid questions, I wanted to throw the Palm-pad across the room.

A bright light had me shielding my eyes as my heartbeat picked up. Once my eyes adjusted, I could make out the rough shape of a man made of coloured light floating before me.

I smiled.

"Allador!"

I was so relieved to see my alien friend, but worried that someone could walk in and cause a panic.

Allador inclined his head and answered me telepathically. *"Greetings, Lennina. It is good to see you."*

I wasn't sure what to say. "What are you doing up here on the station?"

"I wanted to heal you."

I sat with my mouth hanging open. He would risk being seen so he could heal my broken ribs?

"If that is acceptable to you?"

"Oh, um, yes... Thank you."

He moved forward slowly and reached out his hand. Once it made contact with my right side, a warmth stretched out across my entire body. Closing my eyes, I relaxed and breathed a sigh of relief.

I trusted Allador after I'd seen him heal my work partner, Daniel Javolo, who'd had multiple injuries after the tunnel he was working in down on the planet had collapsed.

I felt one rib knit back together and it made me queasy. I'd felt the same thing when Allador had healed Daniel, through our weird connection that caused me to feel Daniel's pain, but this was different. This time I knew it was my bones.

The door swished open and a nurse walked in wheeling a cart. She screamed and Allador backed away from me.

"It's okay!" I told her. "He's not hurting me. He won't hurt you."

Her big brown eyes were wide and she was shaking. "What is that thing?"

How could I stop her from freaking out and calling security? "It's an alien from Kronos. His name is Allador."

"Wh-what's it doing here?"

"He was healing me."

She looked at me. "What?"

"He was healing my broken ribs." *And you interrupted.*

Allador fluttered around in the corner. *"I will return."*

Before I could say anything, he vanished.

"Where did it go?"

I crossed my arms. "He left because you were freaking out. He didn't get to finish healing me."

"Oh."

"Why are you here?"

"Oh, I came to give you a blood test. They said they told you about it."

I sighed. Might as well get it over with. "Yeah. So, where do you want me to sit?"

"Just on the edge of the bed. I'll position the cart to suit."

"Okay."

I sat and tried not to look as she took five vials of blood from my arm. That seemed like an excessive amount.

"Why so many vials?"

"Oh, there are so many things we need to test, and each one requires a different treatment of the sample."

"Oh." What else could I say to that? It wasn't like I could demand that she put it back.

After fiddling around with the vials and asking me to check my name and date of birth on the labels, she packed up her equipment and left me with a wish that I have a nice day. Considering who I'd be talking to next, I highly doubted it.

Sure enough, I didn't have to wait long for the two investigators to be ushered in to see me.

Dr Rowen said she'd leave us to it and left with a fake smile on her face, and the two well-dressed men stepped further into the room. They too, had fake smiles and I gave them one in return. I had nothing to smile about.

They introduced themselves as Mr Deunan and Mr Kessik, saying that I needn't worry as they just wanted to ask me some questions about what had happened on the day of the tunnel collapse. It was their job to interview everyone involved and try to piece together what had taken place and why, and blah, blah, blah.

I relaxed a little. They hadn't mentioned anything about a possible breach of regulations or any relationship with Daniel.

I knew I was still in a lot of trouble, though. Sonrisa had already blasted me for my slow reactions after it all happened, so I expected them to be asking about that too.

I waited and tried not to fidget. The first questions were pretty standard. How long had I worked for The Company and where was I from and so on. Then they asked about my first Digger, Arkena Rogan, which made me wonder why. Why would they ask about that? Did they think I had something to do with him seeing a "Ghost" in the tunnels and being taken off active duty to go to counselling?

And what did that have to do with the tunnel collapse?

Nothing.

The simple answer was: nothing. I took a deep breath. Maybe they were trying to intimidate me. It was possible. Or make it seem like I couldn't do my job properly. Both of my Diggers had "gone crazy," which is Katoa's explanation when anyone claims they've seen bright lights or a Ghost down on the planet. The Ghosts were real, though. They were Allador's people — a race of beings made out of light and energy.

The official word was that the planet was uninhabited. The Company couldn't let the people know that there was sentient life on the planet we were mining, because then they would have to get the inhabitants' permission to be able to continue mining.

I decided not to let them intimidate me. I had other, bigger things to worry about. I tried to answer the questions as best I could.

Then they finally decided to ask me about the events leading up to the collapse.

"Everything had been normal and the morning went ahead as usual," I said.

My mind kept wandering back to when I wanted to talk to Daniel and tell him how I felt about him, so I had to make sure I didn't say anything that would give any of that away. I just stuck to the facts surrounding the other events.

"Daniel had dumped a load of Amakio back at the shuttle and had finished digging out the next vein when he saw a bright light." There was no point in denying the Ghost sighting. It was all recorded.

When they looked at me questioningly, I sighed. "You would have heard what happened by listening to our recorded conversation."

"Never mind that," Kessik said calmly. "We want to hear your version of events."

I sighed again. "The recording *is* my version of events."

"Now, Miss Callista, there's no need for the sarcasm. Just tell us what happened."

I groaned. "That wasn't sarcasm..."

He exhaled heavily through his nose. "Just tell us what happened," he repeated.

I told them what I could remember, but as for the four minutes and twenty seven seconds before I made the first call, I didn't know what had happened to me. "I found myself on the floor, staring up at the ceiling. So I think that means I must have blacked out somehow." They didn't look convinced. "I've had several blackouts since then."

They simply nodded and Kessik typed something on his Palm-pad.

There was no hope of coming out of this unscathed, so I tried to be as truthful as possible. I'd have to leave some things out about Daniel and I.

They kept asking more and more questions and it reminded me of Malvolio when he was convinced I was already seeing Daniel and wouldn't even listen to me. It was upsetting to think about him. Those wounds were still raw. I'd forgotten about him for a while, even with the pain in my ribs to remind me every time I moved. I'd been so focused on Daniel. The memories flashed before me and the tears threatened to start. The pain in my chest flared and I couldn't think straight.

I tried to focus on the current situation, with no success.

"Why didn't you report to your supervisor right away that your Digger was in trouble?"

I tried to hold back my rising frustration. "I told you. I fainted. Play back the recording and you'll probably hear me fall to the floor. And you could probably hear me get back up again after the four minutes and whatever seconds..."

Kessik turned toward me. "Do you know the correct procedures to be followed in an emergency situation?"

I stared at him incredulously. "Yes, of course I do!"

He cocked a bushy eyebrow. "You seem to have had trouble carrying them out. Can you tell me why that is?"

"I told you..." I'd had enough. He was another Malvolio. I wanted them to go away and leave me alone. "Look, I'm not feeling—"

"What is the status of your relationship with Daniel Javolo?" Deunan interjected.

—— ★·☆·· ——

POWER OF LIGHTNING *(Lightning Touch Book 2)* is available right now. Click **here** to grab your copy!

YOUR FREE BOOK IS WAITING

The novelette

THE ALIEN

is free for a limited time. You just need to tell me where
to send it

When Lilliana crash-lands her spaceship on a Primitive
planet, she'll have to rely on help from an attractive
local to survive.

**Use the QR Code to follow the link, then enter your name and
email address to get your free book delivered to your inbox**

Or type this link into your browser: https://www.sub-
scribepage.com/thealien

ACKNOWLEDGEMENTS

Up until recently, I've always worked alone when writing. Sure, I've had the support of family and friends, but now I have a group of authors that understand what it's like and help me along my journey. I'd like to thank them personally. They are the 10K Readers + SPF – Sydney Meet Up group. I don't know where I'd be without you all.

I've also gathered a small group of beta readers and I'm so thankful for their help.

And of course, I'd like to thank all of the members of the Sydney Shadows Club who have supported me. I am honoured to be a member of the club.

To my family and friends, a big thank you. Love you all.

Lastly, to Pete, for sharing your life with me. I love you.

BOOKS BY SUSAN MCKENZIE

THE JADORI SERIES (ONGOING SERIES):

Fire and Magic is being released in a serialized format (1 chapter per week) on reamstories.com right now!

——— ⋆·☆·⋆ ———

THE TAMISAN SERIES (COMPLETED SERIES):

Tamisan

Enigma

——— ⋆·☆·⋆ ———

A Tamisan Novella – Shakiran: Larissa's Story

THE LIGHTNING TOUCH SERIES (COMPLETED SERIES):

Touch of Lightning

Power of Lightning

——— ⋆·☆·⋆ ———

Just remember, a completed series means you can binge read the whole series now.

——— ⋆·☆·⋆ ———

About the Author

Susan McKenzie is an Australian author who loves creating worlds of fantasy and science fiction with fascinating characters and slow-burn low-spice romance.

Her books are full of interesting and relatable characters who use their psychic abilities or magical powers to fight their way out of trouble.

She loves stories that hit you in the feels.

She's not a typical author coffee addict - but chocolate? Now that's a different story. When she's not writing, she loves to paint, draw, sing, and play the guitar.

Get in touch with Sue.
ReamStories subscription:
https://reamstories.com/susanmckenzie
Amazon author page:
https://www.amazon.com/author/susancarter
Visit Sue's website:
http://susanmckenzieauthor.com
Follow Sue on Facebook:
https://www.facebook.com/SueMcKenzieAuthor